· IT'S A ...

Dear Little Black Dress Reader,

Thanks for picking up this Little Black Dress book, one of the great new titles from our series of fun, page-turning romance novels. Lucky you — you're about to have a fantastic romantic read that we know you won't be able to put down!

Why don't you make your Little Black Dress experience even better by logging on to

www.littleblackdressbooks.com

where you can:

- ♥ Enter our **monthly competitions** to win **gorgeous** prizes
- ♥ Get **hot-off-the-press** news about our latest titles
- ♥ Read **exclusive** preview chapters both from your **favourite** authors and from brilliant new writing talent
- ♥ Buy **up-and-coming** books online
- ♥ Sign up for an essential slice of romance via our **fortnightly email** newsletter

We love nothing more than to curl up and indulge in an addictive romance, and so we're delighted to welcome you into the Little Black Dress club!

With love from,

The *little black dress* team

Five interesting things about Lucy Broadbent:

1. Unlike the heroine of my novel, who moved to LA from Britain in order to marry for money, I moved there thirteen years ago in order to work for it – as a journalist.

2. I've lunched with more celebrities than most agents (though I doubt they'd remember me), and on more than one occasion I've been the last to get the interview before the star died. Really, it was nothing I said.

3. In my pre-Hollywood days, I was travel editor of *Hello!* magazine – and once (because I'm too fond of chocolate to be able to do it again) climbed Mount Kilimanjaro.

4. My life's ambition is to fit into the clothes hanging in my wardrobe.

5. I live in West Hollywood and wake every morning with three men in my bed – my husband, who's meant to be there – and our two boys, who are not.

What's Love Got to Do With It

Lucy Broadbent

First published in 2008
by LITTLE BLACK DRESS
An imprint of HEADLINE PUBLISHING GROUP

A LITTLE BLACK DRESS paperback

2

ISBN 978 0 7553 4522 9

Typeset in Transit511BT by Avon DataSet Ltd,
Bidford-on-Avon, Warwickshire

Printed and bound in Great Britain by Clays Ltd, St Ives plc

Headline's policy is to use papers that are natural, renewable and
recyclable products and made from wood grown in sustainable forests.
The logging and manufacturing processes are expected to conform to the
environmental regulations of the country of origin.

HEADLINE PUBLISHING GROUP
An Hachette Livre UK Company
338 Euston Road
London NW1 3BH

www.littleblackdressbooks.com
www.headline.co.uk
www.hachettelivre.co.uk

In homage to William Makepeace Thackery,
whose social commentary of nineteenth-century
Britain would not be out of place in
twenty-first-century Los Angeles.

Acknowledgements

Special thanks to Suzanne Herrington for her blind faith, Ginie Sayles for her kind support, Karolina Sutton and Catherine Cobain for taking a chance with a first-time author and their clever guidance, Sara Porter for her patience, Tom and Jack for being such good boys, my parents for their life-long encouragement, and David Norland, whose originality is always inspiring and who not only made me persevere but really and truly answers the question *What's Love Got to Do With It?*

'A woman with fair opportunities and without a positive hump may marry whom she likes.'
William Makepeace Thackeray

I don't know what inspired me to say it, really. Except that cracking jokes in times of extreme terror is what the Brits always do. 'Think I'll catch the next one,' says the Brit who's just avoided death at the bus stop during the July bombings. A Brit will be looking at death head on, and still find time to crack a joke. It's what we do. It's what British soldiers do as they go into battle. It's what my mother did in a rare moment of clarity as the nurses prepared her for surgery for a brain aneurism, not long before she died. 'If you wouldn't mind putting a brain with a memory back in, I'd be so grateful,' she'd quipped. 'That would be such a useful addition.'

Anyway, I now know that American immigration officials, and in particular those at Los Angeles International Airport, are several punchlines short of a joke book. And no matter how terrifying that immigration hall is – especially if you haven't got a visa and you're promising that you're here for a holiday and not to work – this is not the place for badinage. All I said was turn to page sixty-three of my passport for my full criminal history. I didn't expect the silly old duffer to start looking for it. My passport doesn't even have a page sixty-three. I was just bored of staring at the follicularly challenged patch at the top of the official's head as he laboured over my forms. And I really thought I'd get those lips, spread so thinly beneath the moustache that they looked like a couple of worms, to break into some kind of smile. A smirk. A grimace. Anything that might suggest a human within. Unfortunately, this official turns out to be robot man himself, who marches me to his supervisor, also clearly made of so much metal you'd have thought she'd have been rusting in certain parts, into a special office full of other robots, whom I then had to convince of no criminal past.

Two hours later, though, I'm through and finally on an American sidewalk outside Arrivals. The heat hits me – I'd call it more a recipe for roast pork than weather. But I breathe it in – exhaust fumes, pollution and all. Finally I'm here, and hailing a yellow Checker Cab like I've been doing it all my life. Unfortunately, you don't hail cabs outside the airport in LA. You have to wait in line for one. Someone told me eventually, after twenty or more had passed me by.

Los Angeles is not a beautiful city. From the air it's spectacular in terms of its size. It's like a giant exposed electronic circuit board with miles and miles of gridded streets that go on for ever, broken only by some great looming hills shaped like a sleeping drunk with a huge beer belly in the middle of it all. But spectacular is not the same as beautiful. It is a well-known fact that the city sprawls for over 2,500 square miles, criss-crossed by thousands of miles of freeway. Rather like a twenty-stone woman, it's hard to have those kinds of gargantuan statistics and still look like a cover model. From a yellow Checker Cab window, the city didn't look much prettier either. We drove past rows of suburban bungalows, concrete mini-malls, and buildings that looked like they ought to be the back of something grand and stylish except they weren't – the bland, boring boxes were as good as it got. And giant billboards advertising cars that could make you a social success, but leave you a financial cripple, and underwear promising to make you thin, but crippled in other ways.

The sun sets, making everything pink, but not pretty. Nothing could soften the concrete. It doesn't matter – I'm not here for the view. In fact, a sidewalk covered in garbage cans, litter and homeless people is perfect. You see, I've carried something with me all the way from Surrey that I particularly want to find a special place for. Somewhere really grubby and especially squalid – some traffic lights outside a McDonald's is perfect. Inside my bag, I have a Bible. It's a cheap one, with a picture of Jesus with his disciples at the Last Supper on the cover. It was a parting gift from the convent and had been thrust into my hands as I got on the train at Guildford. Inside, the head had written, 'Remember that you never walk alone. The Lord always walks with you.' I throw it out of the window and the Bible bounces into the gutter, pages flapping helplessly, where someone has generously left a puddle of vomit. It feels fabulously good. More comforting than chocolate, better than sex, better even than a night at the movies. Now I can move on. A new me, a new life. Oh, and I suppose a new lipstick because I realise too late that I must have thrown the old one out with the Bible by mistake.

By the time I reach Beverly Hills, it's nearly dark. The house is up in the hills – much classier than the streets below. There are leafy trees and fancy gates hiding gazillion-dollar mansions. The taxi driver points at one of them and tells me Britney Spears lives there.

'Zees is the trailer-trash section,' he says, guffawing through a thick Russian accent. 'You been here before?'

I tell him no sharply, because I can't be bothered to make conversation, not to mention I'm feeling ever so slightly car sick. There are a lot of bends in these tiny winding lanes. The taxi pulls up at number 1043. There are some elaborate iron gates, through which I can see a drive leading up past bushes and lawns to the house. The house looks Spanish, and is covered in purple bougainvillaea. I get out here – I could use the fresh air – and tip the driver a dollar. He looks at me as if I'd just murdered his grandchildren.

'Sorry, mate, it's all I've got,' I tell him. He slams my door shut and the car squeals off, sending up a cloud of dust. I press the buzzer on the intercom.

'Who is it?' asks a male voice.

'It's Isabella Spires. Your new nanny,' I reply, sounding as posh as the Queen.

The gate buzzes open.

Americans like British nannies. I don't know why. My theory is they like us in the same way they like designer-named clothes. If you pay more for it, and it comes with a fancy name, then it's got to be better. It goes with having the Mercedes SUV, the Prada bag, the Jimmy

Choo heels. They also think that the accent is something to trust. You can be robbing them blind, but if you're British you're someone to take care of their car keys, their wallet, their private sex tapes, their gun collection, their children, their trust fund, their dog. All the big Hollywood stars want British nannies. If you're British, you're down to earth and full of common sense – or at least they think you are, and compared to the kind of people you find in the hills – the Hollywood hills, that is – we are.

I saw the ad for a British nanny in *The Lady* back in England. I'd thought it might be some kind of juicy porn magazine when I'd picked it up in the corridor outside the Mother Superior's office – perhaps it was something she'd confiscated. I was waiting for at least an hour so I had plenty of time to peruse the pages. The ad was in the back, among the classifieds for holiday rentals and hair restoration treatments. *The Lady*, it turns out, isn't saucy at all. It's all about royalty and what to wear to Ascot. The ad asked specifically for a British nanny who wouldn't mind living in California. Wouldn't mind? I couldn't get on the phone fast enough. It was a British telephone number, but a broad Texan accent answered.

'Hi,' it cooed. 'You're interested in the jaaab? Grrreat . . .'

The female owner of the voice rolled her r's so much, she sounded like the tiger in the Frosties TV commercial. I could hear her inhaling deeply on a cigarette.

'How soon can you get here, honey?'

Candice Shawe was that keen to meet me. She was in England, staying at The Dorchester. The suite had reeked of perfume – sweet, and so pungent I'll swear I saw the plants on the balcony heaving over to one side. My mother would have said it smelt like a tart's boudoir. But then she'd have called Candice a tart. She didn't like Americans – and she hated women who were flashy with their jewellery and overlavish with their make-up. 'That woman looks like a bloody Christmas tree,' I could hear her saying inside my head.

In fact, Candice Shawe was perfectly all right. She was all smiles and dental perfection – a sort of Sharon Stone lookalike, if you know what I mean. Mid-thirties probably, trying to look twenties. Lots of blond highlights woven through a tousled bob, plucked eyebrows and the taut look of plastic surgery. You could tell she was from Hollywood just by the way she was groomed. Even back then I could see it. You see, Hollywood Woman is different from other women. She looks like she's just thrown everything on and doesn't give a damn. That's the fashion. She might have three closets of designer clothes, but she always dresses down in a uniform of torn jeans, T-shirts and flip-flops, so on first impressions it's easy to mistake her for the cleaning lady.

Fortunately, the cleaning ladies at The Dorchester are better dressed than this, so there was no mistake. But you've got to look closely at Hollywood Woman to really distinguish her. Because beneath the T-shirt the arm muscles are toned – sculpted so carefully, you know there's serious effort at the gym behind them. Look at the toenails – Hollywood Woman would no more go out without a pedicure than go naked. Check the hairdo – the highlights on that just-got-out-of-bed look are expensive. And of course there's the plastic surgery.

Subtle, but you know it's there because why else would plastic surgeons in Hollywood warn pregnant mothers to avoid Botox before birth, telling them that they've found that expressionless mothers lead to expressionless babies?

So there we were – expressionless Candice with her French-manicured toes and me, all chirpy chat and enthusiasm, stuffed into the navy-blue polyester Marks & Spencer suit I'd saved for months to buy. She seemed relaxed as we sipped tea, brought up on a trolley by room service, and she told me about her husband, their three children and their iddy-biddy ten-bedroom mansion. I liked that she was so casual. Her accent slurred and slurried along like a lazy river. And she puffed away on Marlboro Lights, jangling the gold bracelets on her wrist and flashing the whopping great diamond rings she'd crammed on to her fingers. She asked about my family, and I told her, leaving out the fact that they were all dead. Also my experience with kids, leaving out that I didn't have any. And she seemed happy. Didn't even ask for references.

I didn't really think I'd get away with it. But there was something between us that clicked, some strange connection that I couldn't really put my finger on. Anyway, perhaps she was feeling generous. Perhaps she liked the way I talked about routine and dis-cipline in children's lives – I'd picked that line up off some programme on the telly. And come on, how hard can looking after kids be? But she said she liked to trust her instincts when it came to hiring staff and she liked me.

*

It's dark by the time I climb the long flight of stairs up to the house, hauling my suitcase behind me. There's a wonderful smell of flowers everywhere – jasmine, I learn later, which only lets off its scent after dark. The stairs open out on to a terracotta patio with a lit-up, turquoise swimming pool alongside. There's a stone fountain in the corner, fancy garden umbrellas, loungers, potted plants, flowering bushes, and a view to warrant some expletives not suitable for children. But no one to meet me.

I call 'Hello' through some open French doors leading into the house. Mrs Shawe had promised she'd be back here before me to meet me herself. Inside the French doors is a living room which must have been nearly three times the size of the dormitory I'd shared back at the convent. There's a giant unlit fireplace, some dark paintings I can't really see, more sofas than a hotel lobby and not much light, except from down a corridor where I can hear the laughter of a TV show.

I call again. Nothing. So I wander in and I'm about halfway down the corridor when I meet one of the servants. I assume he must be a servant because his jeans are ripped, the T-shirt has something nasty down the front, and the hair – what little there is – is all over the place. Remember, I was new to Hollywood.

'How do you do? I'm Isabella. I'm here to meet Mr and Mrs Shawe.' I tell him I've left my bag outside. 'You don't mind fetching it in for me, do you?' I say grandly because I'd like them to think I'm used to servants.

'And I'm Stephen,' he says, smirking. 'Stephen Shawe. But call me Stephen. How ya doing?' And he shakes my hand heartily.

Okay. Find me a rock and I'll crawl under it.

'I'll get your bag in, don't you worry,' he reassures me. 'Cute accent, by the way.'

It seems like an odd place to be making introductions – not to mention cramped. Stephen is practically the width of the corridor. About five foot nothing, and rotund as a Christmas bauble. It doesn't look like he's ever been handsome, and now he's in his fifties I don't suppose he ever will. Think Danny DeVito and you've got him in a nutshell. Hollywood Man clearly doesn't have to put in hours at the gym to keep up appearances like Hollywood Woman. Stephen seems momentarily unsure of himself. I'm not sure whether he's going to lead me back to where he's just come from, or if I should turn round to get the bag. So for a while we both stand there like a couple of stunned mullet. I clearly wasn't what he'd expected.

'My wife usually deals with the domestic stuff,' he says, by way of explanation. And then adds almost as an afterthought, 'I guess I thought you'd be older.'

'I can do a walking stick, but you have to pay extra for that,' I joke. 'Besides, inside every older woman is a younger woman, just wondering what the hell happened.'

He laughs. Best impersonation of a donkey I've ever heard.

I ask where Mrs Shawe is. And the smile vanishes faster than a streetwalker on parole. I can't work out if he's embarrassed or angry, but a dark expression spreads over his face. Mrs Shawe is not in, he tells me.

'She doesn't live here any more,' he growls.

I say, 'Oh' in a matter-of-fact, never mind, she must

have just nipped out to the shops sort of way, because I wouldn't want him to think I was about to pry into his drama. But there must have been one – I met her only last week.

He leads me eventually to a small room, to meet the kids. In a house this big, with a living room the size of an aircraft hangar, it strikes me as weird that they should all cram themselves into the smallest room to watch telly. But what do I know?

There are three of them. Craig is surprisingly tall. Who knew eight year olds could be so big? A mass of freckles spreads across his nose, a pair of piercing blue eyes peek out beneath a blond fringe that needs cutting and there's a defiant jaw. He looks like he's going to be handsome. He's hunched up in a bean bag on the floor, arms folded across his body, determined not to take his eyes off the TV. Marcie is six. Long mousy hair scooped into two pigtails, blue eyes that sparkle with mischief and a cheeky smile revealing big gaps where her front teeth should be. 'Look, I lost a tooth,' she tells me excitedly. 'The tooth fairy left me ten dollars.' She delves into the pocket of her dress to show me a ten-dollar bill, and I tell her to keep it safe. Logan is two. A platinum blond, with soft cherubic curls, ivory skin and hands that I discover are sticky as he presents me with a toy truck.

'Craig, could you take your eyes off the TV and say hi to Jessica please,' Stephen growls at his eldest.

Without moving his eyes from *Who Wants To Be A Millionaire?*, he mutters, 'Hi.'

'Actually, it's Isabella,' I say. 'But you can call me Bella. Everyone does.'

'Bella, then,' Stephen says gruffly and wanders into the kitchen. The toddler follows him, so I sit down on the sofa next to Marcie.

'So what are you watching?' I say.

'Sssh,' says Marcie. 'This is the exciting bit.'

Stephen returns with a beer for himself and collapses into an armchair. 'How was your flight?' he asks.

Actually, it was exciting and terrifying all at the same time. I'd loved every minute, staring out of the window, looking at the clouds and promising myself a future. But it was the first flight I had ever taken in my whole life. Not that I am going to let Stephen know that. The sky is a great place for ambition, I'd discovered. You can look at the limitless horizons and there you are on top of the world, queen of the heap, mistress of all you survey, and the world is yours to conquer.

'It was fine,' I tell Stephen. But he's not listening anyway. He's been sucked into the telly too. So now I'm on the other side of the world, in someone else's living room, watching the screen with another family who can't be bothered to talk to me. Fortunately, if there's one thing I'm good at after years of foster homes, it's this. Only difference – I'm being paid for it now. Ha, ha, ha.

No one uses the word orphan any more. Not to your face anyway. They talk about orphans in Africa, or Kurdistan, or other faraway places. Or in the distant past, like in Charles Dickens' novels and *Anne of Green Gables*. But not in modern day Britain. In Britain, you're a disadvantaged child or a child in public care, or a child suitable for fostering or adoption. It's like the big white elephant in the living room – too awkward to call what it is.

I'd have preferred to have been orphaned when I was younger – maybe when I was five. It's never a good time to be orphaned, but that would have been better. Old enough to remember something of Mum and Dad, but young enough for the memories to be hazy. The trouble with being orphaned at thirteen is its vividness. It's too much like looking back on a soap opera. There aren't enough blurred lines. Psychologists say that children who lose parents when they're toddlers or infants feel a sense of absence rather than loss. Because they never really knew their mum and dad, they don't have that same sense of being torn away from them. Adolescents, on the other hand, have the worst time because it's such an intense time of change in their lives, and to have no parent to guide them through it means chaos. I know all this because over the years I've had more bereavement counselling than most kids have had school holidays.

Our life wasn't really like a soap opera. Too normal for that. Too middle class. Our house was in the suburbs of Surrey. Three bedrooms, curtains at the windows, tidy hedges, that sort of thing. I had bunk beds in my room, in case I had friends to stay, and orange curtains with flowers on them. There were bookshelves all over the house, all covered in books and CDs. Mum loved opera and there wasn't a book about opera that she didn't own. She'd wanted to be an opera singer once – and might have been one, except she'd fallen in love with Dad while she was at music college and abandoned her dreams when they got married. She became pregnant with me shortly after. All that remained of her career after I was born was a grand piano in our living room, where she'd trill and warble over the keys.

My mother was very beautiful. Of course all little girls think their mothers are beautiful. But mine really was. I have a couple of photos of her and I sometimes look at her now and still wonder how anyone could be so flawless. Her face was mapped out in perfect angles: high cheekbones, a refined nose, a gracious jawline. Her eyes were big, brown and deep set, and she had the kind of smile that I remember disarmed people. Her mum had died when she was very young – cancer, I think. I can't really remember. She used to tell me stories about my family all the time, but I never listened – seemed boring then but now I wish I'd paid attention.

My parents loved the arts and creativity. 'There's nothing more important,' Dad would say, on his way to our garage, which had been converted into a studio where he used to paint. He'd be in there for hours, poring over his oils and brushes, stretching canvases over frames. I don't think he ever sold a single painting. Not that he tried very hard. He occasionally had them hanging in a couple of cafés for a while, but they didn't really stand out. He painted more for himself than for anyone ... and for me. It was always what I got for Christmas – another painting from Dad that I had to look chuffed about. My bedroom walls were covered in wobbly sea views and overly colourful pastoral scenes.

I remember bursting into tears one Christmas because I'd pinned all my hopes on a talking doll that I'd seen advertised on the telly. I'd been convinced that's what Mum and Dad would give me. Instead I got a blank canvas, personally stretched across a wooden frame by Dad, a set of oil paints in a neat wooden box with a handle, a tube of real hair paint brushes, and a little easel and collapsible stool that folded away into next to nothing, and could be carried over the shoulder.

'But I wanted the talking doll,' I'd howled, almost knocking the Christmas tree over in my haste to storm up to my bedroom. I can still remember the disappointment.

'But darling, you'd be bored with that doll in an instant,' my father had said soothingly to me in my bedroom, as he tried to coax me down. 'And look, you've already got a doll, which you never play with.'

'That's because she doesn't talk,' I'd pointed out.

'But painting is so much fun,' he'd carried on. 'I

thought you'd like your own paints, and we can go on painting expeditions together. I thought we could sit out in the fields together and paint views. Wouldn't that be nice? Just you and me?'

I'd conceded that it would be. I loved nothing more than spending time with Dad, no matter what we did.

'And can we take a picnic?' I'd asked, forgetting about the doll.

'Of course we can, sweetheart. We'll have our own creative day out.'

I never felt I missed out by not having a brother or sister. I don't even know if Mum and Dad wanted to have more children. I often wonder if they did. I was good at amusing myself. Our garden had a paved path where I'd ride my bike up and down, up and down, past flower beds filled with roses. Mum loved gardening and taught me the names of all the flowers. And I used to make endless fairy houses out of leaves underneath the laurel bushes at the bottom of the garden. It was a marvellous way to make money, because almost every time I ever made one, I'd find a coin there the next morning. There were stories and picnics, trips to the toyshop, art exhibitions and zoos. Dad was always home before I got tucked up in bed at night, and every day I'd go to a private school with a purple uniform and grey felt hat.

Mum was in the bath when it happened. Her brain went pop. That's how she described it anyway when I saw her in the hospital. She was having a nice hot bath, cup of tea balanced by the plugs like it always was, *Daily Telegraph* lined up carefully on the bath mat. Dad's at work, I'm at school. And something goes 'ping' inside her head. So she gets out of the bath, because she thinks that's sensible, and lies down on the bath mat and the *Daily Telegraph*. After a few minutes she starts to worry that if she's going to faint or pass out, someone might find her naked, so she gets up, puts on her dressing gown, hops into bed and phones her friend Sheila who lives next door.

'Sheila, my brain's just gone pop. What do you think it could mean?' she asks, as casual as if she were asking how long to bake a Victoria sponge.

'Oh, I don't know. Hang on, I'll ask Bernard,' says Sheila, equally casual, like she's about to look up the answer in one of her recipe books.

She shouts out of the window to Bernard, who's pruning his roses in the garden. 'Lily says her brain's just gone pop. Do you think it's anything to worry about?'

As it happens, Bernard is a dentist taking the morning off. And as it happens, he thinks it is. 'Sounds like an aneurism,' he says straight away. 'Better call an ambulance.' So they do. But they're not worried, because it was only a little pop, and neither of them knows what an aneurism is. And anyway, it can't be too awful because the ambulance takes ages to arrive. Plenty of time to pack a make-up bag. Mum never went anywhere without her make-up bag and a Max Factor lipstick. And some spare nighties. And what about some of those duty-free ciggies? Do they let you smoke in hospital? Better pack them anyway.

By the time I get to the hospital, she's incoherent. She's talking about measuring the cat, dancing with teacups, climbing the fridge. Dad had come to get me from school and brought me straight to the ward at the Royal Surrey Hospital.

An aneurism is when there is a weakness in an artery leading into your brain and its wall bursts open. That was the pop she heard. Then the blood seeps everywhere except to the place where it ought to go in your brain, and within a few hours you're sailing in and out of sanity. The surgery is straightforward enough – the surgeon simply plugs up the hole. If it's successful, you carry on as normal. If it's not, you're either dead or a vegetable for the rest of your life. The problem is, it's major brain surgery – and that's serious.

They moved Mum to a different hospital in Oxford once they'd diagnosed the problem, where we were told they had the best brain surgeons in the world. While we waited for the operation, she issued orders. There were quite a few moments where she was the mum I knew in between the spells of gibberish – always funny. It was like there wasn't anything wrong with her at all. 'You're not to leave me a vegetable,' she whispered to my dad in one of those moments. 'I don't want to be a vegetable. This can leave you a cabbage, you know? I don't want be a cabbage for the rest of my life.' Then she smiled and added as a humorous afterthought, demonstrating just how scared she must have been: 'A string bean wouldn't be so bad. At least string beans are thin.'

The surgeons had clearly filled her in on every detail. 'I've got important things to tell you,' she told my dad. 'My jewellery is hidden in the pockets of my dressing gown, the one in the cupboard in the spare room. It's all for Isabella. Don't go and throw the damn dressing gown out with all the jewels still in there, will you?' She winked at me. 'And the prescription for Isabella's cortisone cream needs renewing in case any of her rashes come back. The washing machine repair man is coming next Monday. Some time between eleven and three. You've got to be there to let him in. And you'd better cancel the bridge social. Tell them I'll be right as rain for the meeting next month. There're pork chops in the fridge for supper.' She stopped to think of what else was on her list.

We told her she was going to be fine. That she was going to be back home in time to let the washing machine man in herself. And I really thought she would be.

I nearly die when Stephen shows me round the house
the next day. I think, 'What am I getting myself into?
What am I doing?' I mean, the house is the size of
Guildford station. It's a maze, with door after door
leading off this giant hall where there's a chandelier so
major that I shouldn't think even Buckingham Palace
could match it. The kitchen is enormous – hell, there
must be five-star restaurants with smaller ones. The
bedrooms – all ten of them – each have a dressing room
attached that would count as a living room anywhere
else. And the garden goes on for ever with tennis courts,
jacuzzis and even a three-bedroom guest house.
Honestly, it's all I can do not to fall over my jaw.

Mrs Shawe had hired an interior decorator, Stephen
tells me as we sail past sofas that no one ever seemed to
sit on and chintzy curtains everywhere. The family
had moved into the Beverly Hills Hotel for three
months while it was all being done. He's not sure why
the house had had to be redecorated – he thinks maybe
Candice had been bored. Says he's a family man. Loves
his kids. And as well as the three he has with Candice,
there's a grown-up son from a previous marriage, called
Jamie.

'I have three wives,' he says so matter-of-factly that I think I must have looked shocked. 'It's just that I sleep with only one of them. Your job is to look after my children like you're their mother. Pearl's job is to run the home.'

I'm just wondering if he's forgotten that the wife with sleeping duties doesn't appear to be around any more when he leads me through his office – vast, with one entire wall covered with trophies and awards, and noticeably void of paper – into a smaller room where there's plenty and Pearl is making lunch reservations into a headset telephone. Pearl is his personal assistant at home. He's got another at his office in town.

'Hi,' she says, looking up from papers on her desk. 'Welcome to the States. Mrs Shawe said you'd show up this week. How's your room?'

My room is luxury such as I've never experienced. It has a four-poster bed which last night had swallowed me up in a sea of feather duvets and pillows, a carpet so thick my feet had sunk into the shag-like sand, a balcony overlooking palm trees, my own computer, TV, sofa and bathroom. It was everything I'd imagine the finest suite in a five-star hotel would be.

'It's fine,' I say, trying to sound like I sleep in rooms like that all the time.

Pearl smiles – the kind that says she knows I don't, but she's not going to let on. She has an air of efficiency about her, almond-shaped eyes that look me over carefully and a mouth that's the most perfect cupid bow. Her hair is dark, cut short into a neat bob, with a long fringe that hides her eyebrows. She dresses very hip – none of your starchy secretarial gear. Leather moccasin boots, bare tanned and shapely legs, miniskirt and a taut, sleeveless T-shirt that I'll bet didn't come from Woolworths. I guess that she's just a bit older than me – early twenties maybe – and very pretty, in a Mia Farrow, Winona Ryder sort of way.

Everyone in real life looks like a movie star if you look closely enough. Ever tried it? It's true. There's always a famous face that looks a little bit like everyone you know. Only thing is, you've got to have seen enough movies to know all the stars. I like the movies. Love them. Even the bad ones, even the ones with Kevin Costner drowning in a sea of bad lines in *Waterworld*, even Elizabeth Berkley drowning in a sea of bad taste and sequins in *Showgirls*, even the Little Mermaid drowning in sap. Bad lines don't bother me. Just as long as I'm transported away from being hunched up on someone else's sofa in someone else's house in front of their crappy telly. Ever since Mum died, I've watched movies. That's what I do. You could say it's my area of expertise. But just because I like the movies doesn't mean I want to be in them – all that paparazzi attention and overexposure. Frankly, there are easier ways of getting rich.

Stephen leaves me in Pearl's office to have my duties explained to me and we both watch him waddle away. My duties, it seems, aren't going to leave me much time to kick back in my gorgeous room. I have to get all the kids up in the morning, transport the older ones to school, the younger one to playgroup, oversee naptimes, mealtimes, homework, playdates, bathtime and bed. Craig has to be taken to soccer practice, piano lessons and a child psychologist. Marcie has ballet practice, singing lessons and a lot of friends. And Logan needs to be watched constantly – he has an oral fixation, Pearl warns me. Everything goes in his mouth: old cigarette stubs, bits of Lego, berries from the garden.

'I will be able to be paid in cash?' I say to Pearl, once she's rattled off her list in her soft, rolling Californian accent. I'm a bit nervous about asking. But Candice hadn't been able to organise me a visa in time. She promised she would if things worked out. Until then, I was here on holiday, working illegally.

'Sure, no problem,' Pearl says, without even asking why. Then, after considering for a few seconds, she looks kindly at me and adds: 'Need an advance?'

'An advance?'

'Yeah, dummy, something to tide you over till pay day.' She's smiling, and while I'm still wondering what the catch is, she's reaching for a petty cash box from a drawer in her desk. She hands me three crisp hundred-dollar bills.

'Can't be easy when you've just arrived from overseas,' she says gently, slamming the box shut again.

I like this girl.

'Well, so far it's been just fine,' I say, and stick the bills down the front of my bra. 'Thanks.'

Then she hands me a mobile phone and the keys to a car that she tells me is going to be mine. I try hard to not look like I've just won the pools.

'It's a blue BMW SUV,' she says, watching my face with what I can see is growing curiosity. 'It's parked in the garage.'

'An SUV,' I repeat, as casual as possible. 'Right.'

'It stands for sports utility vehicle.' She's smirking.

'Ah.'

I can see she's enjoying this. She has the look of a benign headmistress giving out school trophies.

'You can drive, can't you?' she asks.

'I can,' I say with quiet personal triumph. But never having owned a car, I haven't had much practice. I'm not letting her know that, though. 'Yeah, I used to do a lot of driving back in Guildford. I was in and out of town all the time. Used to drive a Vauxhall Cavalier.' It was the first car name that came into my head.

'What's that?' she asks. 'Don't think we have those here.'

'Oh, it's very fancy. Very high end.'

'Cool,' she says and smiles that smile again, which I suspect means she doesn't believe me, but she's not going to call me on it. She begins riffling through some papers on her desk.

'So, do you live here too?' I ask eventually. Seems like Pearl might be good to make a friend of.

She laughs. 'What, in this hornets' nest? With that monster?' She points in the direction of Stephen's office. 'I live a few blocks down the road. I'd go crazy if I lived here.' She laughs again. It's a laugh that doesn't betray any malice. I'm about to ask her why when she finds the papers she's looking for. 'Come on, we've got a lot of paperwork to get though here,' she says, resuming an efficient air.

Among it all is a confidentiality agreement, promising I will never divulge details of the family's private life to the press. All the staff at the house have to sign one – five gardeners, one housekeeper, three cleaners, a maintenance man, a window cleaner, Pearl and yours truly. Turns out Stephen is an agent – runs the biggest talent agency in town.

Craig is in hysterics when I take up my duties in the afternoon. There's been a temporary nanny in during the day while I find my feet, a Hispanic lady who rolls her eyes to the ceiling and waves her hands flamboy-antly in a 'What can you do?' kind of gesture as she departs. This could be harder than I thought.

We're all in what I'd have called a nursery, but they call their den. It's like a living room for the kids, with their own flat-screen telly on the wall, a computer, and books and toys everywhere, and each of them has their own room leading off it. Marcie has Craig's Bionicle, a one-eyed robot-like creature that wields death-dealing plastic discs in one claw, which Craig had built himself from a kit. Marcie has dressed it in a pink feather boa and lined it up alongside her dolls for a tea party. Craig, of course, has dozens of these things on the shelves in his bedroom, but objects to the less-than-masculine touch his sister has given to this one. And the abuse is terrifying. The word tantrum doesn't do justice to the behaviour we're witnessing. Marcie, however, is used to it and carries on pouring tea like the Queen ignoring a bomb going off somewhere in the palace.

I ask Marcie to give it back to him. She won't. Craig hurls a book at her. It misses but hits the Cinderella Princess doll in the eye. Now there are tears from Marcie. Then out of the corner of my eye I catch sight of the two year old, who has climbed on to a desk and is trying to reach a toy car balanced on a pile of books on a shelf. I race over just as the books cascade on his head, knocking him to the floor. More tears. I'm feeling like Julie Andrews in *The Sound of Music*, but without the songs, good humour or, frankly, the expertise, when in walks Stephen.

'Glad you've got things under control,' he says to me when everyone's calm and we've both worked like demons to soothe tears and tantrums. But he doesn't look cross.

'Piece of cake,' I say. 'Such quiet and easy children.'

Note to self: Buy some childcare books.

When the kids are finally in bed, I find Pearl in the vast hallway with its overhead chandelier and flower arrangement that must have taken a small tropical jungle to grow. She's searching through her bag for car keys.

'You look tired. Going home?' I say cheerily.

'Yeah, finally,' she sighs.

'Want a wind-down drink?'

I didn't think she'd go for it. I imagined she'd have better things to do than hang out with me. But she says she's at a loose end this evening and leaps at the offer. And I'm pleased. I need a guide to the Shawes, to LA, and to life in this new universe. Pearl could be useful – not to mention being easily the friendliest face I've found here yet. She says there is a hotel bar not far away. Maria, the housekeeper, will keep an eye out for the kids. 'Better change,' she warns me, eyeing up the black knee-length skirt, sensible shoes and rather grubby white shirt I'm wearing. I race to slip on jeans, heels and a clean shirt, tuck one of those crisp green banknotes into my pocket, and then we climb into her open-top jeep and head off into the warm night air. It's glorious.

Sunset Boulevard is buzzing. Nightclubs and restaurants are spewing out crowds and loud music. There are bright lights everywhere, billboards the size of skyrises and, even at 10 p.m., traffic jams. The whole town feels like one big party. The pavements are packed with revellers, and the cars send out deep thumping beats. Pearl's good company – she points out the café where *Annie Hall* was filmed, the hotel where John Belushi died, and the nightclub that Johnny Depp once owned, and we decide that even though he's getting on a bit he's still the sexiest man on screen. We pass the Sunset Tower where *The Player* was filmed, and the Beverly Hills Hotel where Elizabeth Taylor always used to stay. Suddenly all the movies I've ever watched are coming to life. Pearl seems to watch a lot of movies too. I tell her how much I love them and instantly we're comparing notes.

'All time favourite film?' I ask her.

She doesn't hesitate. '*Doctor Zhivago*.'

'The David Lean version?'

'Of course.'

'Panned by the critics, but won several Oscars in 1965,' I tell her. She seems impressed. 'What others?'

'*The English Patient* . . .'

'Directed by Anthony Minghella. Won nine Oscars in 1996, including Best Picture. Ralph Fiennes as Count Ladislaus de Almásy. I love Ralph Fiennes, don't you?' She nods. 'What else?'

'*The African Queen*.'

'Humphrey Bogart's only Oscar.'

'*An Affair to Remember*.'

'Bit of a romantic, aren't you?'

'Bit of a movie guide, aren't you?'

We laugh together. By the time we pull up outside a stark white hotel, where a crowd is spilling off the pavement, we're reciting Al Pacino lines and promising ourselves a trip to the cinema.

Pearl doesn't even bother to park her car. Just pulls up, hands the keys over to a Hispanic type who comes dashing out to greet her and waltzes off without a second thought. I do my best to look like I do this all the time and follow. It's extraordinary. She doesn't bother to join the queue of people waiting to get in either. Just marches straight up to the bouncers guarding a velvet rope. Doesn't say hi. I don't think she even smiles. The rope simply opens up for us. It's like being a deity walking on water – we just stroll right on in.

Some fancy bar this is. And some fancy clientele. All of them look like they've just scraped themselves off the pages of *Vogue*, the women baring serious amounts of flesh and belly button jewellery and the men, barrel-loads of attitude. Pearl orders us Martinis at the bar and we go out on to a deck, where there's a sub-lit pool, a view of the city below and large double beds on which to lounge. It's a scene. Everyone's checking out everyone else. Even the waitresses are beautiful, dressed in bikini tops and sarongs. There's techno music pounding and a huge crowd by the bar. Pearl steers me to a lounger beneath an outdoor heater.

'That's a good thing you've got going with the bouncers,' I say, gawping at the crowd, absorbing it all. 'Can anyone do that or is it some special perfume you wear?'

Pearl just shrugs her shoulders. The waitress brings the drinks, and I absent-mindedly clink my glass against hers, unable to tear my eyes away from the show going on around me.

'Hold on there. You gotta look me in the eye when you clink glasses with me,' she tells me sternly. I turn to see her grinning. 'Don't you know it's seven years' bad sex if you don't look each other in the eye?'

We laugh. But now I'm wondering what I'm meant to do with the olive that's floating in my drink, pierced by a small plastic sword. A half of lager seems so much simpler.

'Anyone you fancy?' I say, as I see her scanning the crowd, like she's looking for someone. She doesn't answer. 'Me, I'd go for the bloke in the suit at the end of the bar.'

I've got her this time. She lets out a whoop of laughter. 'He's the hotel manager. He's there to get you a table in the restaurant. You can't fall for him. Don't you know anything?'

'Me? I don't even know what to do with this,' I say, pointing at the olive. 'Back home we eat our vegetables with the Sunday roast, not in our drinks.'

She chuckles. A bloke comes over, whom Pearl kisses in a brush-off kind of way, like he's a nuisance. Then she introduces him to me.

'Isabella Spires this is Adam Sisskind. Adam Sisskind this is Isabella Spires. Isabella's working at the Shawes'.'

Adam's short, looks a bit like Tom Cruise with glasses. He's a man who is almost handsome, but just misses the mark. His eyes are just a wee bit too close together; his chin isn't quite prominent enough. I've found out since that he also smokes a lot and stutters sometimes. But you can tell straight away he's keen on Pearl. He's got that mushy kind of look about him, and won't take his eyes off her. But he's wasting his time. Pearl's gaze is still all over the bar. Adam says there's a party at someone's place, why don't we all go? But Pearl tells him not tonight.

The hardest thing about being a Brit landing in California and not knowing anything is it's tricky to size someone up. The way people dress really doesn't tell you much. I always thought a suit spelt money, not restaurant manager. In LA, Pearl tells me, the only men who wear suits are limo drivers and hotel managers.

The way Americans speak doesn't help either. Of course they have accents, but they're difficult to distinguish if you're new to the place, and they don't really tell you much about them anyway – except maybe if they're from Texas, where they all sound like cowboys, or New York, where they all sound like Robert De Niro in *Taxi Driver*. In Britain, of course, it's different. You only have to open your mouth there to peg yourself into a social niche. If you speak mockney then you're loaded and pretending to be just one of the lads. If you speak posh then you're middle class and trying too hard. If you speak plumber, then you're working class and have a chip on your shoulder about it. In America you can have a whole conversation with someone and have no idea whether they grew up in a mansion or a pig farm. Without asking them, of course, which is the simple solution and saves a whole load of groping in the dark.

The Martinis kick in and I'm talking up a storm because I'm always entertaining when I've had a few. Or at least I think I am. Adam is telling me all the cultural sights I ought to see, like the Getty Museum – he says everyone overlooks the culture that LA has to offer. Pearl's telling me not to waste my time, all I need to know is the way to the nearest cinema and shopping centre, and I'm just telling them how pleased I am to be here when something turns Pearl's face from mirth to misery faster than you can say 'I'll have another one'.

'Piece of shit,' she mutters to herself, and, cool as anything, walks over to a tall, debonair sort at the bar who's just walked in. Now this is a man who'd stand out regardless of which side of the Atlantic you live. Blimey, he'd stand out anywhere. He's tall, he's good looking and he knows it. An aquiline nose, a mouth that smirks like Elvis's, eyes that invite primeval lust, and an attitude that's spelling out sex appeal in the biggest capital letters I've ever seen. There are women crawling all over him.

'Oh, dear,' Adam warns, as we watch the sideshow. 'He told Pearl he was away on location.'

'Who is he?' I ask.

He's Pearl's boyfriend. According to the critics in the *Hollywood Reporter*, Brett Ellis is a star in the ascendant. Pearl's been dating him for over a year, given him more help than he deserves, Adam says. He was nothing but another wannabe when he met Pearl. She introduced him to Stephen Shawe, who recommended him to directors, producers, and got him the right roles. Meantime, Pearl got him into the parties that mattered, even helped him out when he was broke. But he's an unrepentant philanderer and everyone in town knows it. Except Pearl, of course.

'When you're Hollywood royalty like Pearl is, you can have anyone you want,' Adam sighs wistfully. 'But she won't give him up. It's like she's blind. It's a joke. And she's such a sweet, kind person. And he's ... he's ...'

Over at the bar, I can see exactly what he is. The body languages says it all. He's a self-made man who's in love with his creator. Pearl's arguing with him. He's trying to placate her. She's angry and eventually storms off. He simply shrugs his shoulders, says something that makes those around him laugh, and lets the other girls creep back into his arms.

We chase after Pearl, but her jeep is speeding off down Sunset by the time we make it out of the hotel lobby. Abandoned again. It's the story of my life. Now I've lost my lift back to the house, and I've spent most of my money at the bar.

'Couldn't give me a ride home?' I ask Adam, who I notice is looking somewhat bereft. I offer him the sweetest smile I can muster given that my face is now numbed by alcohol.

'Sh-sh-sure,' he stutters.

Turns out his car is a Golf just like my dad's used to be. Except they call them Rabbits here.

4

Owing to a big mouth and disdain for authority, not to mention lack of interest, there's not an awful lot that I remember of early school life. But I do remember one of the lines from a school play I ended up in. According to Oscar Wilde, losing one parent is a misfortune, to lose both is carelessness. I like the lack of sentimentalism, because I'm not sentimental about mislaying mine. I hate soft-boiled concern. Dad died less than a year after Mum. He killed himself. Took himself off in his Golf and crashed it into a wall doing ninety. Can you believe that? I still have trouble believing it myself.

Our lives had spiralled into a big old mess after Mum died. Clean clothes, a stocked fridge and a tidy house became distant memories. So did our painting trips and days out at the zoo. But it didn't come close to the confusion that hit after Dad snuffed it. Turned out the national debt was nothing to the arrears he'd racked up. Dad used to run a silk-screen printing business. It wasn't huge, but he employed a staff of fifteen or so, and he had his plant on the outskirts of Guildford, where he'd churn out printed T-shirts and so on. He'd done it for years and although it hadn't made him rich, the work was constant. Kept us and the company car going. But the competition is tough in that world. Clients had become scarcer, and there was new technology out there that Dad hadn't understood. Suddenly he was remortgaging the house to keep the business going, and when Mum died he had as much fight left in him as an unstuffed teddy. He raided his pension fund to pay his staff, sold his shares – all those nice middle-class fallbacks that my mother had put neatly in place, he plundered. Thanks, Dad. Then, when he had nowhere else to turn, he took the car for a less than joyous joy ride. I guess the future had looked that bleak.

As it turned out, Mum's jewellery wasn't worth anything, and Dad's life insurance policy was peanuts because he'd stopped paying into it, so when my only aunt heard that no fat trust fund came with me she told the social services she couldn't help. Said she couldn't afford to keep me – not with three children already.

I was the only child at the foster home with a plummy accent and purple school uniform.

Thanks again, Dad.

The sun pours into my room the next morning, waking me up to the theatrical presentation of a Californian sunrise with little pink clouds dissipating into a powder-blue sky. Mornings don't get more outrageously beautiful than this. Outside my window, two squirrels are chasing each other up a waving palm tree, birds are singing and Disney would be hard-pressed to create a day with as much zippety-doo-dah potential. Except that my head is thumping. Blimey, those Martinis must have had a kick to them.

It was only when I'd fallen inelegantly on to my arse from Adam's car the night before and had to punch in the security code three times in order to open the wrought-iron gates guarding the Shawes' estate that I realised how much I'd drunk. No wonder that hundred-dollar bill had disappeared.

By the time I'm dressed and in the kids' rooms to begin my early morning duties, Logan is halfway over the bars of his cot with a look of dogged determination. I catch him just as he's about to fall several feet to the floor. Marcie wears an expression of pained self-righteousness because she has had to get dressed all by herself this morning and Craig is hiding under his bedcovers. He's refusing to come out. I try the gentle approach. 'Come on, Craig. It's a gorgeous day out there, and you've got soccer after school today.'

'I hate soccer.'

'I thought you loved it. It's going to be great.'

'No, it isn't.'

'Of course it's going to be great. Shall we have your favourite breakfast this morning? Can you tell me what your favourite breakfast is?'

'Shit,' he tells me.

'Oh, dear. That doesn't sound very nice. Hey, can you tell me about some of these Bionicles you've got here?' I pick up one of them from beside his bed. 'What's this one?'

'Leave me alone,' he whines.

'Oh, it can't be that bad.'

'Leave me alone.'

I pause. Think hard. 'Okay. You want to behave like a brat, then I'll treat you like one. You've got to the count of ten to get your scrawny arse out of this bed or I'm calling your father.'

No trouble. He's out of there like a shot. Next hurdle: breakfast. Marcie wants Coco Pops. No, she wants waffles. No, she wants toast. She settles for porridge, or oatmeal as she calls it. Craig doesn't want anything. 'Come on, you must have something. What do you like to eat?' He throws his head and arms down on the table and bellows like someone in the grip of demonic possession. He won't stop. He wants his mum. The baby, meanwhile, having wiped enough raspberry jam over his face and hair to look like an extra from *The Chainsaw Massacre*, has picked up his entire bowl of

Coco Pops, topped up particularly generously with milk because what do I know about children, and hurled it at me.

I wasn't looking that good in the first place. I hadn't had time to put on any new make-up and last night's mascara was still lingering in rings beneath my eyes. My breath probably smelt like I'd drunk from the lavatory. My hair was stoically refusing to lie flat, giving me that punk rock breakthrough look that was fashionable aeons ago. And now there's chocolate milk dripping down my T-shirt, making the bra beneath excessively visible, and Coco Pops are popping off my chest like fleas. It's precisely at this point that a tall, fiendishly handsome, but somewhat dishevelled guy wanders into the kitchen.

'Hi, I'm Jamie,' he says, and something tells me he expects me to know who he is. The cogs in my brain whirr and grind a while, then I remember. He's Stephen's eldest son from his first marriage.

'I'm Bella,' I say, and in an effort to tidy up run a hand across my hair but instead smudge jam across my forehead. Then I shake his hand and the jam spreads into his palm. He looks down at it with a wry smile. 'So sorry,' I say and hand him a tea towel that somehow is also covered in jam. Fortunately he thinks this is funny, so Marcie begins to laugh too.

'Wow, buddy. That wasn't you I heard crying, was it?' he asks Craig, who's now stopped sobbing. 'Some girl broken your heart, has she? Give me her number. I'll sort her out.' Craig manages a smile. 'It wasn't this beautiful young lady here?' Jamie asks, and nods in my direction as he helps himself to a cup of coffee. 'She looks like she could be a heartbreaker ... although probably wearing Logan's breakfast puts her at a disadvantage.'

'Actually, Coco Pops are really in this season,' I say. 'It's what everyone is wearing on the catwalk.'

'Is that so? And jelly make-up too. It must be the way they're doing it in Europe these days.'

He's wearing a T-shirt that reads *Scarface* across his chest, but his face is anything but. Heavens, his mother must have been something. They don't make men like this in Guildford. He must be at least a foot taller than his father. Dark curly hair, which falls in a big mop over a high forehead, a dark shadow of stubble on his chin, and, dominating his whole face, a broad, easy grin. He's the picture of masculine good looks – but in spite of all the testosterone there's something gentle about him. His demeanour is kind, his big brown eyes gleam with sensitivity and the kids love him. Craig clings on to him like a life raft and Marcie tells him one of the longest and most protracted stories possible, from which, in spite of many repetitions from the raconteur, his attention never wanders.

She's still mid-story when Stephen marches in. He's dressed for the office – crisp white shirt, grey silk tie, expensive leather shoes and the look of a Rottweiler on the scent of a good steak.

'Morning, Daddy,' says Marcie, but Stephen's not in the mood for pleasantries and ignores her.

'Jamie, this is no time to come visiting,' he barks, brushing past him and heading straight for the refrigerator. 'I'm due in the office in five minutes. I don't have time to talk now.'

'But you said eight o'clock,' says Jamie, nervously brushing the mop of hair away from his forehead.

'I don't believe I did,' Stephen snaps. He's now searching through drawers in the fridge. 'Maria,' he yells in the direction of the hall, where the housekeeper is dusting. 'Maria, where's my smoothie?' Maria comes running.

'But Pearl called to tell me eight a.m.,' says Jamie.

'Well, I haven't got time to talk to you now. You'll just have to book another appointment with Pearl.'

Disappointment spreads across Jamie's features, making him seem brooding and pained. Stephen glugs back the pink-coloured smoothie, and I'm just about to haul Logan out of his high chair and take him for a complete change of clothes when there's a buzz on the intercom. Stephen presses a tiny TV screen on the wall, and a black and white picture from the security camera at the gate shows a white Mercedes waiting to be allowed in.

'Stephen. Have you changed the security code?' comes Candice's voice. There's a don't-mess-with-me impatience about her tone.

'Mummy,' cry the children in unison. 'She's back.'

'Yes, I have,' says Stephen with a face suddenly so terrifying you'd want to put it in a horror movie. 'You don't live here any more.'

This is obviously news to the children, who fall silent. Fear passes over their faces. Craig reaches for Jamie's hand and suddenly he's not the bad-tempered eight year old any more, he's an innocent, doe-eyed baby, struggling to make sense of this. Marcie holds her hands to her ears, as if she doesn't want to hear anything. Even the toddler goes quiet.

'Stephen, let me in. Don't be so ridiculous,' Candice orders.

'No. You can get your sorry ass off my property.' Stephen's shouting into the intercom now and spitting as he does so. 'And don't even think about coming back here, you filthy whore. After all I did for you.'

'But I want to see the kids,' comes Candice's now tearful voice. 'You can't take them away from me.'

'I can and I will. You don't deserve them.'

'But Stephen—'

Stephen switches off the intercom. Marcie begins to cry. Craig takes a deep breath and boldly steps forward into Stephen's path: 'Dad, you've got to let her in,' he begs. 'You've got to.'

'Don't tell me what to do, young man,' Stephen snarls back, and pushes him roughly out of the way. 'This is my house. I say who comes and goes here.' He's pacing now up and down the kitchen. Clearly Candice's arrival was expected, and he'd been planning this. But he's unable to contain his fury.

'Silly bitch,' he's shouting to anyone who's listening. 'Silly, silly bitch. Thinks she can come walking back in here.'

Jamie seems as shocked as the kids and wraps a protective arm round Craig's shoulders. Then suddenly Stephen becomes aware that his behaviour isn't appropriate in front of the children. Either that, or he just can't stand seeing them any more. Either way, he wants them out, and I've met enough ogres to know not to mess with him.

'Isabella, get the kids outta here,' he roars at me, as I pick up Logan. 'Get them to school. GET THEM OUTTA HERE.'

I reach for Marcie's hand.

'But I want to see Mummy,' Marcie screams. 'I've got to see Mummy. She's my mummy.' She starts running towards the front door, but Stephen blocks her way. She falls to the floor in tears and refuses to get up.

'Come on, Marcie,' I say and try to pick her up, but she's heavy and now the toddler's crying too. Thank God for Jamie, who picks her up kicking and screaming. I carry the toddler and Craig simply follows, tears streaming down his face, hands sunk deep in his pockets.

Poor kids. At least my parents loved each other.

'Is he always this mean?' I ask Jamie as we retreat to the kids' rooms.

'I'm afraid so,' he says softly.

Once the older children are in school, I have my first chance to look round my new neighbourhood in daylight. The baby is in his child seat in the back of the car – a feat in itself. Rebuilding the QE2 would have been easier than getting an infant into all those belts and buckles. The sun is out. The sky is majestically blue. And Beverly Hills is another world – though a strangely familiar one. I feel I know the place already, but only because I've seen it at the movies. I'm on the Beverly Hills 'flats' now. These are the superwide avenues, lined with palm trees, that you've seen in every film. All I need is something catchier than 'Row, Row, Row Your Boat' on the sound system and I could be Eddie Murphy in *Beverly Hills Cop*.

It feels fantastic to be here. Understatement. It feels extraordinary to be here. I feel like Dorothy walking into technicolour after black and white Kansas. Last week, I was sleeping in a grey dormitory in a grey convent where my prospects were about as bleak as the cooking. Now I feel anything could happen. I hadn't fully realised at the time how big a break that little ad in *The Lady* had been. The break I'd been waiting for. It was my escape route to prosperity – my chance for the big time. You can smell money in the wind round here. Heck, it's hard to miss it. And money means not being pushed from pillar to post. It means no more convent cooking. I just hope I can pull this off. It would be so fabulous not to have to go back there.

For all the wealth about, the streets of Beverly Hills still have something of *Brookside* about them. It's like a modern housing estate with schizophrenia. Every house is right bang next to its neighbours. But instead of looking the same, they're all a different style. Not only that, they're all a different era too. And none them are small. Hell, no. I'm sailing past a Roman edifice now that the Emperor Nero might have felt at home in. Next door is a French period château that Napoleon Bonaparte wouldn't have turned his nose up at. Next door to that is a half-timbered Tudor mansion where Henry VIII might have kept one of his wives and beyond that is a vast plantation homestead like Tara in *Gone With the Wind*. It might as well be Disneyland. I think I'm going to like this place, schizophrenic architecture, scary employer and all.

Back at the Shawes', I take Logan for a walk round the grounds, fearful of bumping into Stephen. Pearl's jeep is in the drive, and I'm just wondering if I'll see her when she wanders down across the lawn to the sandpit we've found.

'I'm sorry I left you last night,' she says, and I could see she meant it. Her eyes were red and she had even bigger rings of mascara under them than me.

'No worries,' I say. 'Gave me a chance to chat to Adam. Nice bloke, isn't he?'

'Yeah. He's a friend of my brother's. Known him for years.'

'A brother. Must be nice to have a brother,' I say.

'Got a sister too, but I don't see much of her.'

She sits down next to me and Logan in the sand, and starts filling up a bucket for him. I can see she wants to talk, looks like she could use a good girlfriend, but I don't know how much I'm supposed to know. See, I might have had a few, but I've never been so drunk I can't remember anything in the morning and Adam told me quite a bit about Pearl on the way home. Her dad is Gavin Sash, a rock legend, who I can remember even Mum listening to on the radio. And it's not like it's a secret or anything, but Adam says she's got this thing about not telling people. She wants people to like her for her. Says people only like her because her dad's dead famous and she can't do anything in this town without everyone giving her dad the credit. So she tries to keep it quiet. Tries to live a normal life. And that's the joke right there. She's got Austin Powers for a boyfriend and Jack Nicholson from *The Shining* for a boss and she thinks this is normal. Boy, this girl needs a friend. Either that or a psychiatrist.

'How's your man?' I venture.

'He's such an asshole,' she says, turning the bucket out to make a perfect sandcastle and then smashing it with her Prada boot.

'Dump him,' I say, sounding resoundingly sensible.

'I can't,' she says. 'It's hard for anyone else to see it, but we've got a really special relationship. We work together.'

Like doormats and dirt, clearly. But I don't say anything. There's not much you can say. So we stare into the sand and watch Logan dig holes.

I'd like to ask her more. How can a girl who's this pretty and this far up the Hollywood vine go for someone who cheats on her? And why, if her dad's that famous and rich, would she choose to work? I wouldn't. Her whole body, slumped with despair, says she's hurting. But I don't like to intrude. Sometimes it's best to not get too involved.

'What about you?' she asks eventually. 'Gotta guy?'

'Nah. I'm here on my big adventure. Wouldn't mind finding one . . . but as we all know "a hard man is good to find." '

She giggles. I ask her about Candice Shawe and she rolls her eyes to the sky, as if to say 'Don't you know anything?' And I remind her that I don't.

Candice had grown up in a trailer park in Texas. Her mother ran a beauty salon in a small town outside Dallas. Candice had spent her childhood in front of a hairdresser's mirror, doing manicures and shampoos and playing truant from school. At eighteen, using all that she had learned in the beauty business to good effect on herself, she presented herself to American

Airlines and became an air hostess. Stephen was one of her first-class passengers.

'See, there's an up escalator in this town,' Pearl explains. 'And a down escalator. And they both move pretty quick when you're on them. Candice moved up pretty fast when she married Stephen. Went from "Would you like peanuts with your drink, sir?" to the best table at Spago. Now she is on the fast track down. She signed a pre-nup, too, so she's as good as living in a Motel Six.'

'What did she do?'

'Got caught.'

'Doing what?'

'She was messing around with some guy.'

Candice's future is looking bleaker than solitary at Her Majesty's. Pearl explains to me that Stephen Shawe is as powerful as God Himself in Los Angeles. Probably even more so, because God probably couldn't put Brad Pitt's next movie deal together as fast as Stephen Shawe. And he probably wouldn't take as big a percentage either. Stephen Shawe knows everyone. He's the super-agent who makes and breaks careers from his towering offices in Beverly Hills every day. There's scarcely a film that gets made that doesn't have his clients involved, and that's not just actors, but writers, directors, musicians, editors, every one of them handing over a percentage to him. He has a staff of over a hundred, and a personal bank account that puts him on the Forbes list of the richest in America. By marrying Stephen, Candice got the crown jewels.

She also got the personal trainer, the charity functions, front seats at the runway shows, and the

Brazilian waxer to the stars – just an average shopping trip for her weighs in at around thirty thousand dollars. But three children into the marriage, she gets bored. Stephen's a workaholic, not to mention controlling. I only had to see the scene at breakfast to know that. If things don't go the way he wants them to, he flips. He's affable Richard Attenborough in *Miracle on 34th Street* one minute and the Terminator the next. So Candice starts to mess around, because if you live like this you don't feel you're part of the real world anyway. And it's not like she's short of offers – everyone in Hollywood wants to be touched by power.

Now her punishment is isolation. It's what happens to all the Hollywood wives who transgress the code. Stephen's too powerful for anyone to sip lattes with her. No one can afford to cross the cash cow. Pearl says Stephen's so controlling there was even a clause in the pre-nup which said that if she gained twenty-five pounds in weight, then their marriage was over. The best she can hope for now is for him to take pity and give her one of their homes. But there'll be a fight over the children.

I feel sorry for Candice. But surely she knew she was jeopardising everything? To have come so far, to have married so much money, to live so grandly, and then to blow it with a dalliance? To risk it all, even her own kids? She must have been out of her mind. I realise now what it was that clicked between us when we met . . . she knew about searching for security too. But she'd been stupid. And now the kids would suffer. They didn't deserve this. It wasn't their doing. And what strange dog-eat-dog town is this where a man can be so powerful that the mother of his children can be ostracised so easily? It sends a shiver down my spine.

Having eaten half the sand in the sandbox, Logan's now ready to leave and wants his lunch. We get up to walk across the lawn towards the house and Pearl asks about my family. I often think that being an orphan is a bit like having a scar on your cheek from a car accident: you feel you've got to tell everyone how you got it. I tell her. And I can see, just by the way she looks as if a number seventy-two bus has just run over her foot, that she's feeling sorry for me. It always works. She invites me to a dinner party at her house with her family at the weekend. My first invitation.

There's a certain look that people have when they feel sorry for you because you've got no parents. First there's the steamrollered by a bus expression. Then comes constipation, all furrowed brows, concentration and an inability to say anything. Melodrama usually sets in – some people even cry, which I always think is odd because it's not like they knew my parents. 'I'm so sorry,' some people say, as if it's their fault. No one laughs.

But there's a lot to be gained by having no parents. You can casually let them know at the local newsagents and they'll give you free magazines and chocolate. You can tell them at the chip shop and they'll usually pile on extras. The school dinner ladies always slipped me extra puddings. Some charities will even send you money if you write a good enough letter.

The truth is, it was pretty horrible after Dad died. Two policewomen came to collect me from school. We all went into the headmistress's office where she put on the kind of face that raises funds for children in Africa in the telly adverts and broke the news. Then they took me home and handed me over to some social workers. I can't even remember what they said. But there was a lot of talking, ever so calm, ever so sympathetic, ever so nice. And the house was really quiet. I remember hearing the mantelpiece clock clicking. All around me, everything seemed absurdly normal. Cushions on the sofa. Tetleys in the tea caddy. Milk in the fridge. Post by the front door. Nothing seemed changed, except there were these strange people standing in our living room. I think I might even have offered them tea.

But inside my head, there was a typhoon breaking loose that would have decimated cities had it escaped. My dad is dead? My dad, who's been alive ever since I can remember? My dad, who brings me Cadbury's chocolate? My dad, who told me he was going to live for ever? He told me he wouldn't leave me alone. He promised. There's got to be a mistake. There really has. 'Let me see that he's dead. I don't believe you,' I think I said to them eventually.

I'd always had a great relationship with Dad. He always said we were a team, him and me. We'd do the supermarket shopping together on Saturday mornings, leaving Mum behind. And on the way home we'd sneak into the Coach and Horses for a 'swifty' as he called it and we'd sit in the games room at the back where they allowed children, and I'd sip a Coke and eat salt and vinegar crisps. And we'd play darts and he'd teach me chess and we'd make up excuses for what we'd say to Mum when we were late back, which we always were. And we'd have our own little private jokes between us, which we'd never let Mum in on. Not that we wanted to exclude her, but it was nice to have something special between just us. I couldn't believe he'd betray me.

I had to collect my belongings because they were

going to take me to a home while they contacted my relatives. We went to my bedroom. The social worker asked me what I wanted to take. She had a kind face. You could tell she really cared. 'This is a nice teddy bear. Shall we pack him?' she'd asked. 'What's his name? What about your clothes, which ones are your favourites? Got a book? Got a favourite toy? Shall we put in this little painting?' she'd suggested, picking out the one of the sea front at Torquay. It had been our last family holiday before Mum died, and Dad had sat on a park bench for hours doing it, while Mum and I played on the beach. 'And what about this photo?' It was Mum and Dad on their wedding day.

Perhaps she knew what was in store for me. Because apart from what we packed that day, I never saw any of my belongings ever again. Was never even allowed back into the house. Once it was discovered how much money my dad owed, it was all hauled away by the bailiffs. I didn't have time to worry about it at the time. But now and then I think about what might have happened to our little knick-knacks – my baby pictures, Dad's paintings, our orange teacups, Mum's opera books. Is there a family somewhere eating sausage and chips off our kitchen plates, some transvestite wearing Mum's knickers or perhaps someone finally appreciating Dad's art?

I got sent to a home where they take care of the children that no one wants. It smelt of disinfectant and school dinners, floors were tiled not carpeted, walls were covered in noticeboards not pictures, the furniture was plastic, the lights were harsh and it was run by a matron with a bosom like Mount Etna. I got to share a room with three other girls. One of them had been spotted living on the streets around Waterloo station, another had found her way here when her stepmother kicked her out of the house, and the smallest had been taken into care when her mother was caught for shoplifting.

There was a poster of Johnny Depp on the wall that a former inhabitant must have left behind. He looked down on us, smiling warmly, sexily, caringly. But there wasn't any love between any of us. This was a place of stony silences, distrust and internal torture. The other girls kept me awake with their nightmares every night. And during the days I got packed off to school – not my nice private school where the fees hadn't been paid and I had friends, but the John Donne Comprehensive where my accent stood out like Liza Doolittle's at the races – except I was the one with the nice rounded o's and short clipped a's.

They never did take me to see Dad. Said his body was too mangled to let a child near it – even a thirteen-year-old one. There was a cremation service. I didn't cry. I didn't want anyone to know that I cared. I remember sitting at the back of the church, larking about and telling jokes. I didn't want to stand up and act like it bothered me. I wanted to show everyone I was tough.

I don't think I've ever really believed that he died anyway. I'm still convinced he wouldn't have left me like that. I mean, what kind of father leaves his daughter? A cruel father, a drunk father, a wicked stepfather. An abusive, ugly, stupid father. But not mine who loved me so. I used to look for him. Used to search the parents waiting outside school at the end of the day for his face.

I kept expecting him to come bounding up the path to the home, ring the bell and tell me it had all been a terrible mistake. I imagined that perhaps he'd even staged the whole thing just to clear his debts and he'd secretly contact me one day with a new name. For a while I used to keep an ear out when the telephone rang in the home, imagining he'd call and try to let me know he was alive. Sometimes I still wonder if he might turn up and come and rescue me . . . but it's been a long time now. Dad, if you're still out there, the joke's wearing thin.

Pearl has taken me under her wing. I get the feeling I'm her latest hobby, and I confess that I rather like it. Last time anyone made this much fuss over me, I was being packed off to my posh private school. She's even giving me all her old clothes. Tells me mine aren't hip enough. Even my jeans, which I'd bought from Gap and imagined I looked rather Californian in. 'You can't wear jeans like these,' she says, pulling them out of the wardrobe in my room and looking at them as if they might give her a disease. 'They're so, so . . . well, they're so ordinary, so dull. No one wears baggy jeans any more. You need to have a pair of Missoni's, or at the very least a pair from Guess. You've got such a cute ass, you need to show it off.'

'Leave my arse out of this,' I tell her and laugh because I know she means well, and if I'm to get ahead in Hollywood, I need these lessons. Stephen is out for the afternoon, the older kids are in school, Logan's napping, and Pearl and I have retreated to my room for an hour or two for her to give me a makeover. It was her idea and she had arrived at work this morning clutching a huge suitcase, which she'd struggled to carry in.

'Your arse, as you call it,' says Pearl, mimicking my

accent, and unable to keep a straight face, 'will get you noticed. As will a new wardrobe.' She looks me up and down, taking in a Marks & Spencer polyester blouse, my reliable and favourite on-the-knee black skirt, and flatties. 'Bella, you've got the cutest face there is, your figure is to die for – I wish I was as tall and curvy as you – but you dress like an old woman.' She's half laughing as she says it, but I can tell she's serious.

'No, I don't. I dress like a respectable young woman.'

'Honey, Zsa Zsa Gabor dresses younger than you.' She turns her attention back to the few precious items I have hanging up in the wardrobe. 'And what's this?' she says incredulously. 'A suit? No one wears suits in LA. You can take that to the thrift store.'

'The what?'

'The charity shop.'

'I'll do no such thing. Do you know how long I saved for that?' I say with mock outrage, but her head is in the wardrobe.

'And what about this?' She emerges holding up a white handbag I bought from Top Shop on one finger. The look of disdain on her face would be hard to match. 'Sweetie. You've got to have a purse made by someone.'

'That one has been made by someone,' I say. 'Probably someone in Taiwan.'

We both giggle. 'I mean a designer name. A Kate Spade.'

'A who?'

Pearl is enjoying this. She opens the suitcase with a flourish, like a magician producing a rabbit from a hat. Cropped T-shirts, miniskirts, jeans, jewellery, all burst out on to the bed. There's even a pair of Jimmy Choos.

'Now let's see what works on you,' she says, with that indulgent headmistress look she does so well on her face again. She begins riffling through the clothes.

'But Pearl, I can't take your things.'

'Course you can. I never wear these anyway. I've got another three wardrobes full at home. Besides, it saves me having to look at you dressed like Mary Poppins. Think your boobs could fit into this?' She produces a low-cut leopard-print top. I reel in terror at the prospect of showing so much cleavage. 'You've got more up there than I have. You should show it off.' She throws the top at me and I try it on.

Of course I'm a girl who likes to shop. What girl doesn't? And I'd always thought I knew a thing or two in the fashion stakes, but it becomes obvious that I know nothing. There are designer names here that I've never heard of, never even had a chance to dream about owning. When you've got nothing – and I don't use that term lightly: when the most valuable thing you own is some amateur painting of your dad's – a suitcase of designer clothes is a jackpot score.

But they're clothes that are super-flashy. Clothes that reveal much more skin than I'm used to showing. Clothes that make a statement. They're brighter-coloured, closer-fitting, and harder-edged than anything I've ever worn before. I'm also far taller than Pearl, so all her hems come up much higher on me. My ideal wardrobe used to be one that made me blend in with the wallpaper. It was useful back in England. Being pretty, as a foster child, only caused trouble.

'Sweetie, I love this on you,' says Pearl, having forced me to try on a sequined halter top with a leather miniskirt and knee-high boots. I feel like the hooker Julia Roberts once was in *Pretty Woman*, and super self-conscious.

'But I can't wear this. It's so . . . so . . .' I struggle for a word that won't offend Pearl. 'It's so loud,' I plead. 'Besides, I'll look like a right idiot collecting the kids from school. When will I ever wear something like this?'

'We'll find an occasion,' says Pearl knowingly. 'Bella, you look beautiful in these clothes. You could be a model, you're so tall. Wear them. Enjoy them. Besides, you'll need something for your date with Ashley.'

As well as taking care of my appearance, Pearl is also set on taking care of my love life. She has got it into her head to set me up with her older brother, Ashley, whom she insists I'd be perfect for. He needs a girlfriend and I need as many connections as I can make. I am to meet him at the family dinner she invited me to on Saturday night.

'Don't be put off by his size,' she warns as she hangs up my new clothes in the wardrobe. 'He's adorable really. He's the most beautiful person I know. He's got a good heart, and he's blessed with so much inner beauty.'

Sometimes I think Californian is another language.

'But . . . how should I say this?' she continues, just a little too coyly for my liking. 'He's an epicurean.'

'A what?'

'Loves eating,' she carries on. 'Knows all about wine and good eating. He's a real bon viveur. It's just he does it rather a lot. And he's . . . well, he's . . .'

'Come on, tell me all the afflictions.'

'Well, he's really shy with girls. But you'd be so great together. He's a really nice guy. He really is.'

*

I'm a vision of laddish fantasy when I turn up at Pearl's house for dinner. I'm shrink-wrapped into an oh-so-tight black dress, cleavage oozing and legs going on for ever thanks to those heels. No one ever really likes the way they look – even models like Kate Moss and Gisele Bundchen will tell you they don't like their elbows or their toenails or whatever. And I could go on about my knees – I hate my knees, they're really knobbly. But people tell me I'm beautiful. It caused me trouble back in the home – other girls were jealous of me always standing out. And at the convent, the nuns looked on it as some sort of crime. But we can't help the way we look. DNA, as we know, is everything. Before he died, Dad used to say I was a carbon copy of my mother. I have her long, curly blond hair, which looks Pre-Raphaelite on good days, but has a tendency to turn into dreadlocks if I don't reach for the hair conditioner in time. I have deep-set, long-lashed eyes like hers, though mine are blue, and my father used to say I had her smile, the one that could sell toothpaste.

I walk the same way as Mum did too – head up high, with a posture that a Victorian governess might pile books on the heads of her charges to achieve. The children at the foster home used to call me haughty, said I looked down my nose at them. And maybe I did. But Mum used to tell me that it's important to walk that way and always look confident, even if you're not feeling it. She told me you need to look as if you've just swallowed a confidence self-help book. 'You have to believe in yourself,' she'd say, 'or no one else will.' And so I try to remember her self-assurance, the fearlessness in the way she talked to people – always direct, sometimes brazen and never hesitant.

Pearl's family home is another enormous mansion – this one's got a touch of the Gothic baronials. There are exposed beams overhead, latticed windows, stone archways, and floors that send echoes everywhere when you clip-clop across them in heels. Pearl leads me into the lounge, which reminds me of a medieval church, except with velvet sofas everywhere, giant festoons of curtains and a grand piano in the corner covered in photos in silver picture frames. Pearl's dad has a collection of crucifixes – silver ones, brass ones, genuine Renaissance ones covered in paintings of Christ that Pearl says are worth a fortune. They cover every possible surface in the room, alongside crystal. Pearl's stepmum collects crystal – chandeliers, picture frames, even those tacky little animals you see sparkling in shop windows. And all of it is glittering like Christmas because there are candles burning everywhere.

'Everyone, I want you to meet Isabella,' Pearl says enthusiastically. Adam comes over straight away to kiss me like I'm an old friend. And I can only say I'm grateful because I'm feeling just a wee bit nervous.

'N-n-nice to see you again,' he stammers.

Brett, Pearl's boyfriend, is leaning up against the mantelpiece over an unlit fire, and doesn't move from it. When I first meet someone, I can usually tell, within a few moments, certain things about them – whether they're trustworthy or deceitful, whether they're happy in themselves or disappointed with life. It's a knack I've always had, but time in a care system, observing people, has really honed it. Brett looks me up and down like I'm some sort of lowlife. He's suspicious of me for some reason. And so am I of him. His face is sneery, snarky – it has the look of someone who thinks they've already won, like there's some intangible battle between us. I sense a frustration in him, as if he feels he always has to prove something to everyone around him. And for all his movie star good looks, there's cruelty in his eyes. They show craftiness and ambition. But it doesn't bother me. It's not him I'm here for.

Ashley is my big date. He moves forward to shake my hand, while Pearl disappears to fetch me a drink. You'd never know he was Pearl's brother – he's enormous. 'I'm Ashley,' he says in a surprisingly deep voice. Big? He's got a backside the size of a small American state moving in on the Canadian borders. Huge jowls hang down his face like a bloodhound's, and he has a look about him that brings Mr Toad from *The Wind in the Willows* to mind. 'Nice to meet you, Isabella. How are you finding Los Angeles?' he asks cautiously.

'Oh, I love a place where you inadvertently learn to speak Spanish just by driving around,' I say breezily. Just about all the street names here are Spanish.

He laughs politely, and out of the corner of my eye I notice Brett smirking from his vantage point by the fireplace. But I don't take my attention off Ashley. He needs to be made to feel special. He's got nice eyes, I notice.

'So why are you here?' demands Brett, who clearly can't bear to not be the centre of attention. There's a scathing tone to his voice.

'Well, Pearl invited me,' I say innocently.

'No. Why are you in LA? What kind of reinvention are you here for?'

I look at him blankly. 'Reinvention?'

'Yeah. Everyone who comes to LA is here to reinvent themselves. It's what the city is all about.' He puts on a deep, booming voice as if he's on a television commercial. 'It's where to turn yourself into something . . .'

He has the floor now and the others chortle.

'Don't tell me you're another wannabe actress?' he asks, now in a bored tone. 'Come to join the throng?'

'Actually, no.'

'No? Don't deny it. All the dumb blondes want to be actresses.'

'Dumb blonde, am I?' I say icily.

'Look blonde to me.' He laughs.

'And you're so smart your flies are undone.'

It's a pathetically childish trick. But it works. He looks down to check, and Ashley and Adam smirk. A small triumph. Brett is not amused.

Pearl arrives back in the room with a Martini – mercifully no vegetables floating in it – and her dad shuffles in after her, clutching a mug of tea. It's odd meeting famous people. Gavin Sash had hits about ten years ago. He was on *Top of the Pops* all the time when I grew up. He doesn't look any different now – except older. He's even still got the same just-got-out-of-bed hairdo and that unwashed look that only pop stars seem to perfect – all torn jeans, stubble and a sleeveless T-shirt. He's got Ashley's and Pearl's names tattooed at the top of his arms. Sweet. Although I wonder why there isn't a tattoo of Pearl's sister's name there. Pearl kisses him and he hugs her so close, you can see he loves her. I remember hugs like that with Dad.

'How you doin'?' he asks me, in that gravelly voice that's so familiar. He's actually a Geordie. He was born in Newcastle, but has been here so long he speaks with a strange mid-Atlantic accent that's neither English nor American.

'I'm doing fine,' I say, but no one in this town ever listens to your answer. They've got no attention span. Now he's talking to Brett.

No matter. It's Ashley I want to impress. Pearl has fully briefed me. Ashley is an attorney – a high-flying one. Earns enough to never have to bother his dad for spare change. He doesn't live here like Pearl. He has his own penthouse apartment in a tower block in West Hollywood. He's a senior partner at Maxwell, Zucker and Sash and takes care of loads of celebrity clients. Truth is, I don't really care what he looks like. I'm not looking to fall in love with him. 'Love conquers all things, except poverty and toothache,' according to Mae West. And that's no use to me. I need a marriage that not only conquers poverty, but nukes it into a faraway wasteland. I'm here to marry money. I'll be a good wife, better than Candice was to Stephen, but I'll be a wife who can afford to sleep easy at night.

'What about you? Have you always lived in Los Angeles or are you a reinvention?' I ask Ashley, looking straight at him, which I notice he has difficulty doing back. Pearl disappears to the kitchen again.

'Born and raised in LA,' he says flatly.

'Ashley, Pearl and I are r-r-r-rarities around here,' says Adam, throwing himself into a sofa and spilling his Martini in the process. 'We're all true Angelinos.'

Adam is easily the friendliest person in the room, so I sit down next to him. He's softly spoken. He tells me he is an old school friend of Ashley's. They've been friends ever since the time when a group of kids cornered him in the bathroom in his first year at high school and were about to flush his head down the lavatory. Adam, being something of a bantamweight, with a delicate disposition and glasses, stood no chance. Ashley on the other hand, who is tall, wide, impressively strong and has an urgent sense of justice – not to mention an urgent need to use the lavatory at the time – sorted the matter out in minutes. Together, they look like Laurel and Hardy, but I can see how the two would get on. Both are gentle people. And like Pearl, Ashley likes to brings home strays.

'I . . . I . . . I . . . grew up here, but now my family have moved to a neighbourhood in Orange County,' Adam explains, drawing hard on a Marlboro Light, while we wait for Pearl to tell us that dinner is ready. 'That's the boring wasteland that stretches south.'

'Down by the airport?' I ask cluelessly.

'Way, way beyond the . . . the . . . the airport. You've got to remember how big this place is. Anyway, there's no reason to ever go there. There's nothing there but car showrooms and bland suburbs.'

Adam's too modest to tell me that he stayed on in LA because he got a scholarship to study scriptwriting at UCLA, where if you're successful you can sell your homework for millions of dollars to the film industry, so Ashley fills me in. Trouble is Adam hasn't sold a thing, so he lives in a tiny studio apartment, which is fancy talk for a bedsit, and pores over a computer every day.

We eat dinner in the kitchen, which is big and cosy, with terracotta wallpaper and granite worktops everywhere. Pearl's stepmother, Heather, joins us round a pinewood table that is laid for seven. She's another blonde clone wearing the uniform: manicured nails and a pink Juicy Couture tracksuit. She's less than half Gavin's age – his third wife. She brings to mind the old joke about Californian blondes: 'I wouldn't like to say she's vacuous but if she spoke her mind she'd be speechless.' She sits next to Gavin at the table and rests her hand proprietorially on his knee.

'Gavin, don't you just love her accent?' she drawls, nodding in my direction. 'It's not like yours, Gavin. It's much sweeter. What did you say your name was, honey?'

'Bella.'

'Bella.' She sounds it out like a toddler learning a new word. 'Say something else, honey. I just love to hear it.'

I oblige. 'It's lovely to be here. Thank you so much for having me.'

Heather screeches with delight. If only the audience I'm here for could be so easy to please. Talking to Ashley is like wading through treacle.

'Working on any interesting jobs?' I ask him, as I try to tackle a burger which I've overloaded with too much ketchup.

'Kinda.'

'Must have some interesting clients.'

'Yeah. Like me,' Brett interrupts, unable to pass up an opportunity to talk about himself.

To say that conversation around the table flowed would be like describing a muddy dried-up stream as a raging river. Ashley makes it clear he can't talk while eating. Pearl listens agog to anything that Brett says. Adam spends the whole meal gazing wistfully at Pearl and both Gavin and Brett drone on about their favourite subjects: themselves. I feel like I'm living out one of those Venn diagrams they make you do at school with circles that overlap where there is common ground. Except my two circles remain entirely separate on the same sheet of paper with no overlap at all.

Brett: 'I've been asked to give an interview in Los Angeles magazine this week. Think I should do it?'

Gavin: 'I've been thinking I might get a new tattoo next week.'

Brett: 'I wonder if they're going to give me the cover.'

Gavin: 'Think I could squeeze another one on my ass?'

Finally, when the plates are clear – and we're all dizzy from the sparkling repartee – Ashley brings out a packet of white powder. He lays it out on a silver platter and carefully divides it up with his credit card into neat little lines. It looks like something I might do with Logan in the sandpit. Then he takes a hundred-dollar bill from his wallet, rolls it up into a neat little tube and offers it round like a plate of sweeties. Everyone takes a snort, except Heather, and Gavin who doesn't touch the stuff since he joined Alcoholics Anonymous eight years ago.

'You will have some, won't you?' Ashley asks when the plate reaches me.

I've never moved in rich enough circles to try coke before. Not that I've ever been into drugs. I was never interested in the weed I got offered in the home. I had better things to do than get wasted with the lowlife who used it. But now trying coke suddenly seems like a good idea.

Two hours later I have no idea where I am, but I'm feeling just grand. It's a party somewhere in the hills that Pearl has dragged us all to after dinner. The house looks like it should be in *Hello!* magazine. The swimming pool is sparkling, bartenders are shaking cocktails, DJ Funkmaster Flex is sending out rhythms that thump loud in my head and I think I'm Jennifer Grey in *Dirty Dancing*, though possibly more Bridget Jones after the amount I've had to drink.

There's a big crowd that is heaving like a giant amoeba inside. It oozes and sways and I dance like a dervish. The sweat's pouring. Someone in a stiletto is standing on my toe, but I feel no pain. Someone else is grinding an elbow into my back, but I don't care. I seem to have lost Pearl. Even worse, my drink. But I dance on regardless.

Eventually Pearl's face reappears. 'Come on,' she mouths to me above the din. And I follow. She leads me to the bathroom where she says we can do more coke. I'm not sure it's what I need right now. And there's a queue of girls waiting to get in anyway. We join it only to discover something wet splashing up our legs. Girls are rolling up their trouser legs. What's this? We are standing in three inches of toilet waste which is oozing its way across these multimillion-dollar hardwood floors from a flooding lavatory.

'Now you know why everyone wears five-inch heels around here,' says Pearl, laughing.

And I thought Hollywood was glamorous. We try to search for another bathroom. But the crowd is so thick I can't move through it and suddenly I'm in the middle of it, Pearl's gone and the world starts to spin. I have my face pressed up against someone's bare chest hair. Ugh, it's not a chest – it's an armpit. Now there's a bearded face leering at me – or is it more chest hair? I can't tell. Body parts are merging. I'm penned in on all sides. Oh, God, I think I'm going to be sick. How to get out of this? I push against a bloke who must be double my size, but he won't move. There's another bloke behind me who I'll swear is grinding something he shouldn't into my back. And another leaning right into me like I don't exist. It's hard to breathe. Fuck, it's really hard to breathe. Where's the air? 'Give me some space,' I say, digging a sharp elbow into the bloke in front of me. But he can't hear me. I think I'm going to faint. More to the point, I think I'm going to be crushed to death here.

Panic is rising when a hand grabs me and pulls. I cling on, desperately. As it pulls, the crowd parts reluctantly. Only inches, but enough to squeeze through. The hand leads me through the tangle of bodies towards a door. I can feel a taste of fresh air for the first time. I push on, digging a fist into any bodies that won't budge, and eventually I'm out in the garden.

'Thank you,' I say, looking up to see Brett. I gulp the air gratefully and find a patio chair to sit on. 'Talk about sardines. I thought I was a goner in there.'

It takes a while for the world to stop spinning and the

desire to vomit to pass. 'I lost Pearl in there. Did you see which way she went?'

'I think she went into the VIP room upstairs,' Brett says. The coke seems to have mellowed him. He seems friendlier. 'She'll be okay. She knows how to take care of herself. Here, come on, I'll show you the view.'

He leads me up a flight of uneven garden steps, through some thick oleander bushes, to a viewing deck overlooking the city. There's no one else up here and the party seems a long way beneath us. I breathe deeply and survey the panorama, leaning on a balcony railing. It's very pretty. From here it's possible to see the long straight lines of streets charging off into the distance lit up by the lights of the traffic along them. The giant sky-high billboards that take up the sides of whole buildings look tiny. And the high-rise blocks of Downtown loom in the darkness, all twinkling with office lights. I wonder if people are still working in them.

'Gosh, this town is so much prettier by night,' I say.

'Yeah, I'll admit it's kinda ugly by day,' says Brett. 'Still, it's not the view people come here for.' He sidles up next to me, so that his arm is touching mine where I'm leaning against the railings. I involuntarily take a step sideways. I'm not fond of space invaders.

'Which street is that?' I ask, pointing to the prominent one beneath us.

'That would be La Brea,' he says without looking. I am aware that he is scrutinising my face. 'So how are you liking it here?' He's slurring his words, probably quite drunk.

'Beats the rain back home.'

'Can't argue with that.' The crickets chirrup in the silence. 'Where are you from, anyways?'

'Oh, I doubt you'd have heard of it.'

'Try me.'

'I come from a town called Guildford.'

'You're right. I've never heard of it.' He lets out a burst of laughter, and I remember why I don't much care for him. I contemplate walking back down to join the party, but in the interests of good politics I can see it would be wise to get on with Pearl's boyfriend, so I look round to find a chair.

It's then that I notice that Brett's got a strange look on his face that I don't fancy much. It's the same predatory look an alligator has when it's about to move in for dinner time. He begins stroking my arm.

'Such a cute accent,' he croons.

'Nothing I can take credit for,' I say and pull my arm back. Think I will join the party, after all.

'Oh, come on, don't be like that. I'm just trying to get friendly.'

'Friendly is fine. But carnal is not. Look, you've got a lovely girlfriend down there, and I wouldn't want her to get the wrong idea.' I move to take a pace towards the steps back down, but he's fast.

'Oh, Pearl doesn't mind me messing about a bit,' he says, blocking my path.

'Really? Well, you must find someone else to mess around with,' I say firmly, imagining he'll get the message. But Brett is clearly not a man who is turned down often. His mouth tightens so that his lips curl meanly. His cruel eyes stare sharply at me.

'Not so hoity-toity,' he says and grabs my upper arm

and clenches his fist round it. His nails dig into my skin. I try to pull away.

'Where are you going, Little Miss Hoity-Toity?' He's got both my arms now and pulls me so close, I can smell the garlic on his breath. 'Where are you going so fast? Come on. I've never met a girl who didn't want it with me.'

'Not this one, I'm afraid. You got the wrong girl here, mate.'

He's strong. Very strong. In an instant he has me pressed up against the railings, one of his arms pinning both my wrists together, and his other hand is up my dress, pulling at my underwear.

'Mmm, nice,' he says and I can feel his fingers sliding into me.

Well, I didn't spend all those years in foster care without picking up a trick or two. I pull my knee up fast and sharp to his groin and just for good measure I bite into his shoulder as hard as I can.

'Wanker,' I yell over my shoulder, spitting out the taste of blood.

He's bent double when I leave him and race downstairs, noticing en route that there is a yellow cab waiting outside the front of the house.

'Are you Schribinger?' says the taxi driver. 'You ordered the cab?'

'Yes, I sure am,' I say.

I never really considered myself pretty, growing up. My parents told me I was. But that's like the football manager telling his team they're champions when they're bottom of the fourth division. Cheerleading is his job, so it doesn't count. When you've got silver railway tracks slashed across your teeth in the form of braces, it's hard to use the word 'pretty' in the same sentence as 'face'. Then there were the spots. They landed on me early, around my twelfth birthday, like aliens from a strange planet and then proceeded to reproduce themselves with all the speed and efficiency of germ warfare. My figure wasn't exactly cover model material either. Before I lost everything, I had a rag doll called Lilly Longlegs because she had these long gangly legs – I was Lilly Longlegs: skinny, gangly and floppy.

But then something happened while I was at the home. I looked in the mirror one morning and found someone had left a pair of breasts on my chest. Hair began sprouting in unaccustomed places, curves formed, even the spots disappeared. I grew tall, and, although slim, quite curvy too.

My face grew to have a sophistication to it. It was attractive, but not in the angelic, cutesy way it was when

I was small. My features emerged as more defined and prominent. My cheekbones became pronounced, my eyes deeper set, and I soon realised my lips could be made to smoulder with a touch of lipstick. Quite suddenly, almost overnight, I discovered that I was of interest to the opposite sex. And, more to the point, they were of interest to me.

I already knew about the mechanics of sex. My mum had revealed the secret – over roast beef during lunch one Sunday. I was ten. I didn't believe her. Couldn't understand how it could be so messy. And it still didn't explain how Ariel and her prince got it together in *The Little Mermaid*. Disney never got down to the nitty-gritty of how mermaids have sex and it seemed to stump my mum too. But I must have stored the basics away, ready for easy access later. Who knew then how handy it would be to keep a gang of delinquents at bay.

Jay Altenough controlled the gang at the home. There were about seven or eight of them – all boys. You couldn't live at that house without Jay's people getting at you. They'd steal your things, pee in your bed, poo in your shoes, cut your hair while you were asleep. All those really nice things that teenage kids do when there's no one to stop them. Their favourite game was terrorising kids in the bathroom – they'd make anyone new to the home take off all their clothes and stuff them down the loo, leaving them naked and forced to run back to their rooms with no clothes on. They were just bored really. The matron tried to keep order, but there weren't enough staff to watch us all the time and Jay was on a power trip. I don't even know what his story was. Parents beat him up, or something. There were so many hard luck stories at the home, they all merged into one. Hell, there were some kids there who had asked to come to this place – they thought it was a holiday camp after what they'd been through.

Well, Jay was fifteen and never been kissed. And I could see he was curious just from the way he'd check me out in the canteen. Frankly, I was curious too. All those happy ever afters we got on movie nights in the common room with the heroine falling into the man's arms without a care for bad breath or spinach between her teeth. It seemed worth a try.

So one day, I caught him in the corridor on his own.

'You bored of the movie too?' I'd asked him. It was a Sunday afternoon with *The Wizard of Oz* on the telly again, and I'd watched it a million times before.

Jay wasn't so frightening when he was on his own, away from his henchmen. He was almost good looking. Bit pimply, but tall, and he had long curly hair that made him look a bit like Jesus. I smiled and brushed a fleck of dandruff off his black *Star Wars* T-shirt and twirled a lock of my hair round a finger – I'd seen enough movies to know what to do.

'Boring here, isn't it?' I said coyly, pouting hard. 'Never anything to do on Sundays.'

'Yeah,' says Mr Loquacious, standing there like a confused gorilla.

'I wonder if there's something we could do together that wouldn't be so boring?' I offered, which I know isn't the most witty of pickup lines, but I wasn't exactly dealing with Einstein.

Jay looked distrustful. I reached up to tame a tendril of his hair. Clearly he hadn't done this before, and since

I only had a repertoire of Hollywood moments to go by, it was a case of the blind leading the blind. But slowly he picked up the plot.

'Come on. Why don't you come with me and we'll see how we can pass the time?'

We snuck into the boys' bathroom. On Sundays there were less staff about. We kissed in the showers, messily. Jay slobbered like a dog, and we both groped each other uneasily. We didn't even take our clothes off.

Quick? Jay could have won a gold in the love-making Olympics. No sooner was he done than he was zipping up his flies and tossing a 'Thanks' over his shoulder as he departed. Tender? Loving? Well, let's just say it wasn't what I'd seen at the movies. And there was no riding off into the sunset discussing pension funds, children and wedding dresses. Possibly too much to expect of a spotty lad from Leeds. But the post-coital glow lasted long enough keep his gang off my back until I got out of that place.

Today is a joyous and historic day. I have been in Hollywood four months, and so far I haven't got the sack. I have a best friend, a job and a boyfriend, and tonight I am going to walk down a red carpet. I'm so happy, I'm frightened that this might just be a dream and I'm going to wake up any second back at the convent. I am to go to the premiere of a children's movie at Mann's Chinese Theatre. Stephen can't go. Wondered if I'd like to take the two older kids. There are going to be celebrities, paparazzi, nibbles in the foyer. Marcie is almost as excited as I am, and has spent the whole week deciding what she is going to wear. I have too, though even with Pearl's hand-me-downs I have less choice. Craig has seen it all before. How can you be jaded at eight? But I'm not going to let him spoil my fun. And after the movie, when I've got the kids tucked up, Ashley is picking me up and we're going to go to a new nightclub that's just opening.

Things have calmed down a lot at the Shawes. Candice is living in a rented house not far away and I drop the kids off there two nights a week and every other weekend. This means I get a whole lot more time to myself, and no one has suggested cutting my wages

yet either. Stephen seems thrilled that I've possibly seen
more movies than he has. He keeps bringing DVDs
home for me to watch – films that haven't been shown in
the cinemas yet. He gets them all sent to him at his
office, and some evenings we even watch them together
on a TV set the size of Arizona in a special screening
room at the back of the house. I think he's grateful for
the company. 'This is a film that should never have been
released,' he'd say. 'Not even on parole.'

What surprises me most about Stephen is how
desperate he is to appear normal, which, as we all know,
is no more than a setting on a microwave. He's at pains
to tell me he's a self-made man and he grew up having
to make his own bed in the morning and that's what he
wants for his children. The joke is you could actually
mistake him for being normal. He does all the things
that ordinary people do – watches sport on the TV at
weekends, eats breakfast in his dressing gown, cracks
jokes. He'll occasionally play football with Craig in the
garden, hoist Logan on his knee to play horsey and even
sometimes bother to listen to Marcie's stories that never
end. But the truth is he mostly ignores the kids. He goes
to work early, comes home late, and whatever affection
his children get is parcelled out in small doses, just as it
was for him. He's a compulsive worker, has to be in
control, must always be the crowing cockerel in his own
home to whom everyone else must defer. And he has a
mean streak that strikes out unexpectedly – usually at
Craig.

The other big joke is that he likes to think he's an
environmentalist. Says it's important to stop global
warming and save the planet for our children. So he's

always going round the house turning off the lights, yelling at anyone who leaves them on and whining about the size of his electricity bills. Get that. A billionaire who whines about his lecky bill. And he's ever so proud that he was one of the first to buy a Prius, a hybrid car that doesn't always have to run on petrol. But what he usually fails to mention to those he's crowing to is that out in the garage there also happens to be the Jaguar, the Porsche, the SUVs (several) and let's not forget the private jet that uses nearly as much fuel to transport one rotund billionaire as a commercial jet might to ferry three hundred average joes.

Stephen's parents were farmers in Idaho. He grew up in a strict Baptist household, where everyone went to church on Sunday and read the Bible after supper each night. 'Repression and puritan roots run deep in my family,' he likes to tell people. 'There wasn't any affection,' he always adds, as if this is something to be proud of. He was always driven. Wanted to be a movie director and moved to Los Angeles when he was eighteen. He got a job as a director's assistant, but quickly realised there was more money to be made as an agent. Within ten years he had a roster of big names and his own business.

For all Stephen's weirdness, I like living here. When I was at the children's home I used to think to myself how nice it would be to have a chance to prove that money wouldn't make me happy. People always tell you it won't. But it seemed unfair to never have the opportunity to find out for myself. To test the theory, so to speak. Well, let me tell you, as one who has now experienced living up close to it first hand, you can't overestimate the sheer pleasure of having it around you. It really wasn't that hard to get used to at all. Am I happy? I'm effing delirious.

Of course, the money's not mine and I'd been a bit stunned to begin with by the scale. I mean, Pearl goes out and spends a thousand dollars each week, just on flowers to put in vases around the place. Imagine looking at a vase of wilting foliage and thinking, 'Those petunias cost more than me.' And all around me is excess: Maria, the housekeeper, spends another grand each week just on food for the fridge, most of which goes off because there aren't enough people here to eat it all. And when Candice moved out, it took two rental trucks just to move her clothes – most of them had never even been worn, their labels flapping in the wind. So anyway, here I am wiping my arse on some of the most expensive toilet paper that money can buy, and frankly, I've got no complaints.

A rich boyfriend is not that difficult to get used to either. Dinners out? Nightclubs? Movie tickets? Shopping trips? All paid for. I called Ashley the day after the party to ask him if he'd like to show me round LA. It was a bit brazen, I know. But I knew I'd be waiting for ever for him to pluck up the courage to invite me out. Pearl had warned me I'd need to be a bit proactive with him. So on our first date he showed me a few sights and we ended up at a Chinese restaurant. Mr Chow's is the fanciest Chinese that I've ever eaten at. Never mind the egg rolls, it was the best of sweet and sour society right there. Every celebrity facelift in town seemed to be chowing down (pardon the pun) at this spot.

Ashley's big on politics, I'd discovered. He'd droned

on about the weaknesses of the Democratic party for nearly an hour. Now, I know how to nod appreciatively in all the right places, but there comes a point when enough is enough. So between courses of the most delicious Chinese food I'd ever tasted, I tried to vary the conversation.

'So what was it like growing up with a famous dad? Bet I'm not the first to ask,' I asked, watching him knock back a vodka cocktail like it was lemonade.

'No, everyone asks,' he said. 'It's okay. It's kind of a pain sometimes, but I don't mind you asking.'

Silence.

'So?'

The waiter brought another course and he tucked into the Peking Duck like a refugee from Somalia.

'So what?'

'So what was it like?' I asked again.

'Oh, well . . . well, it seemed pretty normal to me.'

Is that it?

'Come on,' I said, fully aware that no one has any idea what normal is in this town. 'How could it be normal having a dad singing on the radio every time you turned it on?'

'Well, I didn't think about it really. Besides, everyone's got a famous parent around here. Dad was on the road lots of the time, so we didn't see him that much. Mum used to stay with us, but she had her own career – she was a model, you know – so she was kinda busy.'

He took another bite of Peking Duck and slooshed down another Martini. He was easier to talk to when there was no one else around and he had food to look at.

'But we were very privileged. We were totally

provided for. We had very good care and we never wanted for anything. Dad was very strict.'

I stifled a giggle.

'That makes you laugh, doesn't it? Everyone thinks, rock star? Got to be laid back.'

'Yeah, I suppose so.'

'But solid morals and education was what Dad was all about. Told us we had to treat other people with kindness and respect. If we were rude to anyone we were sent to our rooms. Didn't stop us mooning at the tour buses when Dad wasn't there, though.'

I giggled, horrified at the thought of Ashley's large spotty derriere on display to passing coachloads.

'The tour buses used to stop right in front of our home. Still do, I think. But I haven't been looking out for them recently. We'd hear the guide say, "And this is where Gavin Sash lives." And everyone would stare at our house, so if us kids were ever in the front garden, we'd pull down our pants and moon at them. All over the world there must be pictures of my ass.'

He was quite funny once he loosened up. At the end of the evening, as he drove me back to the Shawes', he asked if he could see me again, and I said of course, as long as he didn't start mooning in public. We both giggled and left it at that.

But he called the next day and invited me to the beach the following Sunday. LA's a romantic place, when you've got money and you're not looking at the smog. He took me to a beach called El Matador where rocky cliffs hang spectacularly over the sand. Seagulls soared, the air felt fresh and the waves pounded ferociously. We walked for miles, until we came to a group of seals who argued vociferously in front of us. He asked me about England, and I told him my story, warts and all. He didn't say anything. Not everybody does. And later, he took me to a surfers' shack, way beyond Malibu, where we picked out our own live lobsters from a tank and then ate them watching the waves.

Over the next few weeks, we spent more and more time together – eating more and more meals. He took me to The Ivy where we sat in a garden in the shade of umbrellas and ate crab cakes watching the movie stars. He took me to Yamashiro, a Japanese palace in the hills, where we ate sushi and watched the goldfish in a pond. He took me to Barney's, the most expensive department store in town, where we ate smoked fish in the delicatessen on the fifth floor and then I looked at the clothes. He took me to Spago, where we ate blinis with caviar that cost a hundred dollars a teaspoon and I watched the bill mount up.

Back home you'd know a bloke was in love when he lost interest in his car. I wondered if there would come a time when Ashley lost interest in food. There didn't. Me? I liked Ashley. I could grow quite fond of him. He was a gentle giant. He wasn't the most confident of people, but he was a good listener. And he had qualities I could grow to love.

I believe you can grow fond of anyone given a long enough period of time. Look at all those Asian weddings where the couple haven't even met before their parents march them down the aisle. Look at all those marriages of convenience in Jane Austen novels. Love is a privilege that only the rich can afford, and I realised long ago that I wasn't in that league.

I also realised that there's only one surefire way to acquire oodles of immediate and excessive wealth overnight (besides winning the lottery, which most people forget you actually have to buy a ticket for in order to stand a chance) and that's to marry it. Call me a gold-digger if you want. But that's just a modern label for something people have been doing for centuries. In my mum's day they called it social climbing. In Dickens's time, they called it an arranged marriage. In Neanderthal man's day, they called it survival of the fittest. I call it common sense.

It's deeply unfashionable to admit to wanting to marry into money, of course. It's the implication of calculated greed that people don't like. But all women will weigh up a prospective partner's wealth if they're really honest. Which would you rather, the date who takes you somewhere fancy for dinner and picks up the tab, or the geezer who takes you down the pub and tells you it's your round? I mean, come on. It's a no-brainer. Some psychologists will even tell you that women are biologically programmed to look for a man with money. Not all women are chasing billionaires, but unconsciously all women look for a mate who is strong, reliable and able to support their children. Ultimately, it's got nothing to do with love and everything to do with a biological urge: find a man who can provide for you and your nippers. Only thing is, I must need a lot of providing for because my urge is for a man who's super-wealthy.

Ashley was perfect. He was generous, wealthy in his own right, rich in what he stood to inherit; he didn't look like an axe murderer, and although he was bordering obsessive about food, he had a heart. It was also quite clear that Ashley needed a wife. A man who already has everything in Hollywood needs only one thing more: a beautiful wife. She's as much a status symbol as the car. He knew it and I knew it. Even Jane Austen knew it: 'It is a truth universally acknowledged, that a single man in possession of a good fortune must be in want of a wife,' she wrote. I would be Ashley's wife. I was quite determined.

We had sex on our eighth date. I waited until after he had bought me a Cartier gold watch that must have cost him more than I would earn in a year, and flown me to Aqua, a restaurant noted in the guide books as being solely an expense-account destination, which just so happens to be in San Francisco. Ashley was uncertain but gentle. Too many jokes about his weight over the years had made him nervous and self-conscious, but he warmed up once I showed him I didn't care. Money and power are more potent aphrodisiacs than muscles, and his exploration of my body wasn't entirely without its moments of pleasure.

Pearl is thrilled that her brother finally has a girlfriend. She keeps telling me so. 'You know you've made Ashley so happy,' she's been cooing almost every day. 'Love is such a beautiful thing. Isn't it? Oh, isn't it, Bella?'

Yeah, yeah, yeah. Pearl is a hopeless romantic. Thinks there is nothing more important in life than love and passion. Thinks that when Brett sends her the odd bouquet of roses from where he's making a movie in Canada, it's because he loves her. I'd take a guess that it's because he's shagging someone else up there, but what do I know?

I've become very fond of Pearl – in fact, I think you could say we've become close. We see each other every day. She tries to time her lunch break with Logan's naps so we can eat a sandwich together. We usually disappear into the garden and sit on a bench in the shade of a Chinese elm overlooking the view. There, no one can overhear us and she talks about things that I have a feeling she doesn't talk about with anyone else. She tells me about growing up in LA and a stint she had at an English boarding school, when her dad thought she was getting out of hand. Apparently she was quite a wild child. Her sister was too, but she doesn't talk about her much. She lives on the East Coast now. But she adores her dad. Hero-worships him, even, although I get the impression that he's too busy with his own life to really notice her. He's tight with his money, too. That's why Pearl has to work. Imagine coming from a family with all that wealth, and still having to pick up the phone for someone else. Her dad says she has to make her own way in the world, same as he did. I think that's what makes her such a good person.

Pearl is the definition of good. She goes to charity benefit balls, she eats organic, she makes downward dog look easy when she's doing yoga, she talks about auras and karma and all that Californian nonsense. She even reads romance novels – she's got tons of them.

But all that goodness comes wrapped up in naivety when it comes to her choice of men, and it makes me sad to see all that wholesome romantic generosity directed at such a sponge. There must be a better man to take care of her than Brett. He doesn't even bother to call her from Canada. It's always her phoning him. I sometimes wonder how anyone can be so besotted with someone who is so clearly not interested. Maybe it's the thrill of the chase. Maybe she always goes for wild cards.

Of course Adam is in love with Pearl, that's for sure. He follows her everywhere like a loyal dog that just doesn't notice she's not throwing him any bones. Every time we go out – and there have been quite a few nights together out on the town – Adam strings along. I'm always grateful because he's easy company. He also knows lots about the movies, more than Pearl does, and he has always seen all the latest films. That's the thing about this town that I love – everyone is involved in the movies and no one gets tired of talking about them. People talk about films here like my parents used to talk about politics at home – what's being made, what ought to be made, favourite scenes of what has been made, and, best of all, poking fun at what's awful.

'Have you seen *Cat People* yet?' says Adam over dinner. 'Talk about impurrrrrfect. Heads are going to roll on that one. It's soooo bad.'

'Mee-ouch,' says Ashley, rather pleased with the pun. 'As bad as *Plan Z from Mars*?'

'Worse.'

They know all the really obscure films. And there's tons of celebrity gossip too. Because everyone knows someone who works in the business, there're always snippets about movie stars that you just know are true – those who demand extra private jets to transport their luggage, those who complain if their ice comes cloudy, some who are mean, others who are genuine – the stories of all their excessive demands are hysterical and I love to hear the talk.

Ashley, Adam, Pearl and I make a good foursome. With Brett out of town, Pearl seems grateful for friends to hang out with. In the last few months we've done dinners, clubs, cocktails, but our favourite is always the movies. I always sit next to Ashley, our knees touching and his arm wrapped proprietorially around me, while Pearl sits next to Adam – not touching.

'No making out in the boring bits, you two,' Pearl warns Ashley and me every time with a giggle.

I just wish she'd consider Adam. They say the only love that lasts for ever is unrequited. I suspect Adam's is going to be lasting for some time.

'Pearl, when are you going to break it to Adam that you're not interested in him?' I asked her one lunch time while we were tucking into salads on our favourite bench in the garden. 'Don't you think it would be kinder to put him out of his misery? You know he's besotted with you.'

'Oh, don't be silly. He's not in love with me.' She sighed. 'We're just friends. We are. Truly. I've known him as long as I can remember.'

'Yeah, but I think you mean more to him than just a friend.'

'Oh, you're so sweet. But you're wrong, Bella, you really are.'

Tonight's premiere is the opening of a Dreamworks cartoon, which Adam assures me is likely to be good. In truth I don't really care how good or bad it is – I've never been to a premiere before. There are going to be lots of famous names there who are the voices behind the characters.

I'm up in the children's suite, persuading Craig to put on a tuxedo and bow tie, as insisted upon by his father, when there's a knock at the door. It's Pearl. She doesn't usually come up here to the children's rooms, but I haven't got time to talk now. Craig is refusing to wear the monkey suit. 'I look stupid,' he's yelling at me. I don't blame him. He does look ridiculous in it. But I have my orders and I'm in the middle of bribing him with a trip to the toy shop when Pearl becomes quite insistent.

'Isabella, I've got to tell you something,' she whispers. She's very excited, clapping her hands together like she's younger than Marcie. Craig makes a run for the bathroom and locks himself in.

'What?' I follow her out on to the landing outside the children's room.

'You'll never guess what.'

'What?' I say again, just a bit tetchily. I've only got an hour to get ready and I've still got to get Logan ready for bed, besides wrestling with the monkey suit.

'God, you're never going to believe this.'

Sometimes I think Pearl doesn't live in this world. She'd be better suited to an Enid Blyton novel, where everyone drinks lashings of ginger beer.

'What is it?'

'I think Ashley's going to ask you to marry him.'

The news winds me. It's what I'd been hoping for, of course, but I wasn't expecting it to happen quite so soon. We've only been seeing each other for three months and although things have settled into an easy familiarity between us, and there's an expectation that every week-end will involve spending some time together, it hadn't occurred to me that he would claim the rest of my life just yet. I feel a huge thud inside my chest as if someone had just punched me there. This is more than I had ever dreamed of. Is it just the shock, or could this be love after all?

'Are you sure?' I ask Pearl. 'How do you know?'

'I heard Dad telling Heather. Ashley's obviously told Dad. It's the kind of thing he would do. But you'd better act surprised. He'll kill me if he knows I've told you. I think he's going to ask you tonight.'

The premiere is a blast. But, oh my God, it's impossible to describe just how terrifying a red carpet is. I don't honestly know how the celebrities can bear it. You see pictures of them on it all the time in magazines. They look as casual as if they're nipping to the shops. A bit more dressed up than you might be if you were off to Sainsbury's for a tin of beans, but they somehow pull off relaxed and carefree, as if the only thing on their minds is something easy for dinner. I think the only thing I pulled off was my shoe, which fell off as I clambered out of our limousine.

It's the noise that hits you first. See, all down one side of the carpet is a barrier. And behind that barrier are just hundreds and hundreds of photographers. And they're all crammed in so tightly that if they were animals in a cage – and they do look like animals in a cage – you'd be calling in the RSPCA. The noise is the sound of their cameras going off. It makes an enormous din, and coupled with that are all the flashes. There's so much bright light, it's like standing in a field with lightning crashing down around you – except even brighter, and possibly more dangerous if you've not had a stylist dress you for the night.

Craig and I just make a beeline for the theatre entrance and get ourselves in as quickly as possible. But Marcie . . . Marcie can't help herself. She's posing, she's flirting, she's asking the photographers to take her picture even though they haven't got a clue who she is.

Eventually she makes it inside and we take our seats, but it's impossible to concentrate on the movie. All I can think of is wedding dresses – designer ones, naturally – honeymoons in unpronounceable places, especially that one in all the travel brochures with the white sandy beach and palm trees leaning over so low it looks like you could just pick yourself a coconut, first-class air tickets, luggage that's all the same colour, a personal shopper, pedicures, massages, an investment portfolio, a home to call my own, and never having to work again. Of course, I will actually have to say yes to Ashley. I will actually have to marry him. But that's okay. He'll do just fine. Never mind the movie, I'm walking off into the sunset all on my own.

When the movie is over, I am naturally keen to get the kids back home as quickly as possible so I can get on with the life I've mapped out right down to the colour of my luggage, but the limousine driver is the slowest on record. We crawl along the Sunset Strip because there's the usual late-night traffic jam.

'What does S-T-R-I-P-P-E-R-S spell?' Craig asks as we pass one establishment. I tell him.

'What's a stripper?'

'A lady who takes off her clothes and dances.'

'Can we go and see?'

'Hell, no.'

'Why not?'

'Got to be eighteen.'

'When will I be eighteen?'

So many questions. And it takes simply hours to get home. It takes hours to get the kids to bed too. And it's only then that I realise I've forgotten to turn my phone back on after the movie. There's a message from Ashley.

'Sorry, Isabella. I've got to cancel this evening. A job's come up in New York. I'm catching the red-eye tonight. Speak soon.'

10

The Fields were my first foster family. Their house was like a builders' site, cars jacked up on bricks in the driveway, children's toys spilling out on to the pavement, rubbish bins lying on their sides, and old door frames and windows jammed into the tiny front garden. The street was lined with ex-council houses, and the Fields' home stood out a mile. I remember thinking to myself as a social worker drove me there, 'Please don't let it be that house. Let it be the one with the flowers, next door, or even the one with the garden gnomes and plaster-of-Paris bunnies.' But of course it was that one. Given that the only luck I seemed to have was the bad variety, of course it bloody was. It was my fourteenth birthday. But no one even mentioned it.

Lesley Field was a mean-looking redhead, who was holding a toddler sucking a dummy when she came to the door. She wore jeans over which spilled her rolls of flab, made all the more noticeable by the skin-tight T-shirt. She had four children already, but taking in foster kids gave her extra income.

'She's a good-lookin' one,' she said to the social worker accusingly. 'Don't usually see them that handsome round here.'

She led me through a hallway piled high with old shoes, newspapers, cheap plastic toys and random pieces of clothing, and then upstairs to my new bedroom at the back of the house which had a camp bed and a net curtain hung across the doorway.

Lesley and Paul Field were my first taste of family life since Mum died. It wasn't anything like I remembered it. They ate all their meals in front of the telly, which was permanently on, argued with each other, slapped their children, drank beer from bottles which they left around the house, and never washed up.

That was my job. As was the babysitting, cleaning and laundry. I'd come home from school and face nothing but chores. The older kids resented me. 'Touch any of my stuff and you're dead,' the boy had warned on the first day. And it never got friendlier than that. He was thirteen and looked about twenty. The two older daughters would make up stories about me. They'd tell their mum I was stealing from her. That, and less, was all it would take for Lesley to imagine she was some kind of welterweight and I was the punch bag.

But the best part about living at the Fields' was the money. On my second day there Lesley marched me into a hardware store in the high street where a friend of hers worked and got me a weekend job. Said I needed to earn my keep. The pay was crap and Lesley took half of it. But the rest was mine. And you've no idea how good that felt.

California suits me. Every day the skies are cobalt blue. 'Beautiful day,' people say to each other like it's a surprise. 'It's going to be sunny, sunny, sunny,' crow the weathermen, 'have a grrreat day.' Who could not love that? The optimism. The positivity. The sheer sunniness of it all.

I'm learning to like the children too. It wasn't easy to begin with. I'd often felt they ought to come with instructions, but there was no insert A into B and you'll find yourself with C. And there were often days when I thought I might have made a terrible mistake: like thinking I could marry Prince William when I've never even been to Buckingham Palace – not even to watch the changing of the guard. I was often overwhelmed, but I guess you could say I've adapted into the role.

I've learned that American children inexplicably call snot 'boogers'; that for peace to reign there needs to be an identical toy available for each child at all times; that all food items need to be sliced, measured and counted out into exactly equal portions, even raisins; that everything about children is sticky and slimy, that everything is a battle and that absolutely everything –

EVERYTHING – is a negotiation. 'Hey, kids, would you mind sitting down for dinner please?'

'Nah. I'm watching TV,' says Craig.

'Come on, kids.'

'But Bella, can't we just wait until the end of this programme?' says Marcie.

'But we've just waited until the end of the last programme. And after this one there'll be another.'

'But just this one. Please.'

'No. This is not negotiable.'

'But it's my favourite show.'

'And so was the last one. Now sit down please or I'm coming to turn it off.'

They troop in.

'Oh, no, it's peas. I hate peas,' says Craig.

'Me too,' says Marcie.

'Eat your peas.'

'Why should I?'

'Because I say so.'

'Can we have ice cream for dessert?'

'Only if you eat your peas.'

And on it goes. But in spite of all this, I feel part of this family. I can see a place for me. The kids need me.

I wish I could say the same for Ashley. It's been two days since the premiere, and he hasn't return any of my calls. Usually he calls me back straight away. My messages have been increasingly pleading. But I guess he's either busy or tired from the red-eye. Far more worrying is Pearl's mood. She's refused to have lunch with me, feigning too much to do. Frosty? You could carve a middle finger in an ice sculpture out of the atmosphere. Every time I see her, she looks at me like

I've just murdered her mother. There's a worry at the back of my mind that her mood and Ashley's silence are connected. So eventually I go to her office. You've got to take the bull by the horns, my dad used to say. Logan's napping and Stephen's out.

'Pearl, would you mind telling me what's going on?' I say, trying my hardest to sound sympathetic rather than confrontational.

'I'm kinda busy right now,' she says, refusing to look up from her computer. Her eyebrows are knotted together in concentration.

'Look, I know something's bothering you. What is it?'

The silence is deafening. I can't bear to lose Pearl as a friend. In truth, I'm more worried about losing her than I am about Ashley.

'Pearl, I'm so grateful for everything you've done for me. You've done more than any friend I've ever had. I can't bear it that I've upset you. I really can't.' I'm not the sort to cry, but I sense that now would be a good time, if only to show that I mean it. 'Please tell me what I have done?'

'Done? Done?' she says fiercely. She gets up off her chair and puts her hands on her hips. 'Done? You deceived me, that's what you've done. And you deceived Ashley.'

Well, there's nothing to say to that, because I don't know what she's talking about. My mind is racing to all possibilities, but reaching blanks every time.

'Pearl, what are you talking about?' I say calmly.

'Why didn't you tell me about you and Stephen? I'm your best friend. You should have told me.'

'Me and Stephen?' I'm flabbergasted.

'I feel so stupid that I hadn't seen it,' she says, brewing up righteous steam. 'And there I was building up Ashley's hopes. He really liked you, you know.'

'And I liked him. Pearl, I don't know what you're talking about.' And I really don't.

'You and Stephen.' She's shouting now. 'How could you string Ashley along like that?'

I sit down in the chair in her office because my legs have gone all floppy like Lilly Longlegs's.

'Pearl, I'm sorry. I still don't know what you're talking about.'

'You should have told me you were involved with Stephen.'

'With Stephen? Are you out of your mind? Of course I'm not bloody involved with Stephen.'

Pearl looks at me questioningly. Suddenly there's hesitation in her eyes. Her face softens marginally. It's not the reaction she's expecting.

I take a deep breath. 'What is all this about?' I ask her gently.

'I've heard you're sleeping with Stephen.'

This is ridiculous. 'When have I had time to be involved with Stephen?' I ask her. 'I've spent every last weekend with Ashley, and all my evenings off with you. Wouldn't you of all people have noticed if I was having a thing with Stephen?' I pause to draw breath and think. I can see she's taken aback. 'Who told you this? It wasn't Stephen, was it?' It seems unlikely, but it's my only lead.

'I can't tell you,' she says.

'Course you can. I'm your mate.'

She sighs, realising perhaps that she's misjudged me. 'Brett.'

'Brett? Brett? Why would Brett make up something like that?' Then it dawns on me. He's clearly more dangerous than I've given him credit for. My victory in the oleander bushes hasn't gone unforgiven. 'What did Brett tell you exactly?'

'He didn't tell *me* anything. Ashley rang him while you were at the premiere and told him he was planning to propose to you, and Brett told him to forget it, you were dating Stephen . . .' She breathes deeply and examines her nails. They're painted a beautiful pale pink, but one is chipped at the edges. 'But I don't understand why he'd make it up if it wasn't true?'

'I don't think Brett likes me very much, that's why.'

'But he'd never do anything that malicious. Brett's not the malicious sort, Bella. He might be arrogant, but he wouldn't lie.'

I consider telling her exactly how malicious and arrogant he'd been at that party, but I can see she wouldn't believe me. And even if she did, it would hurt her too much.

'Perhaps he just misread the situation,' I suggest. My mind is now racing to find a way of salvaging this. But what I don't understand is why Ashley believed him. I ask Pearl.

'What you underestimate, Bella, is how powerful Stephen is in this town,' she says sternly.

'What's that got to do with anything?' This is beginning to feel like a crazy dream.

'For someone in Ashley's position, to be found messing around with Stephen Shawe's girl is career suicide. He wouldn't have gotten any more clients if Stephen got wind of it.'

'Yes, but it wasn't true.'

'But he didn't know that.'

This is absurd. 'Look, you do believe me, don't you?' I stare Pearl straight in the eyes.

She wants to believe me. I can see it on her face. But she's not sure. She's so infatuated with Brett, she can't imagine him lying. I make it easy for her.

'Look, I'm sure Brett just misunderstood the situation. Perhaps it was something Stephen said to him. It was probably just a simple mistake.' Pearl nods slowly. 'But I've got to talk to Ashley to explain everything. Can you get him on the phone for me? He won't pick up when I call.'

Pearl dials the number. She gets his voice mail and leaves a message asking him to call her back straight away.

Saturday is Marcie's birthday and I've got to organise the party.

'Just give her what she wants,' Stephen had yelled at me as he left for the office earlier in the week.

Being the socialite that she is – and a desirable one to invite to parties because of Daddy – Marcie has already witnessed more gardens turned into private carnivals, complete with ferris wheels, pony rides, and whole armies of clowns, than I've had hot lunches (and thanks to Ashley my tally in that regard has gone up quite a lot recently). She's also encountered enough life-size cartoon characters to believe that Barney the purple dinosaur really lives at her friend Aurora's house (yes, someone really did name their child Aurora) and that a four-man stilt-walking rock band is an everyday occurrence.

So after school, which I have discovered doesn't leave you much change out of fifty thousand dollars a year, we go to a kids' party planning shop, where we sit among balloons and goody bags to look at videos of other kids' parties.

'I want an ostrich, a real one. Not one of those stupid cartoon birds,' she announces. 'And I want elephant rides, and a petting zoo with a snake. That'll be way cool.'

I add it to the list, on which there is already a princess makeover tent, a human hamster wheel, a flea circus, a 'Vegas-style' magic show, and several tons of snow to be produced by a snow-making machine to form a toboggan run. This being Los Angeles where the temperature rarely drops below seventy degrees, snow is the ultimate birthday party addition, I am told by the assistant helping us. The total cost, excluding food, birthday cake, goody bags, photographer, and marquee rental, is already nearly twenty thousand dollars.

'Whatever happened to boring old cake and balloons?' I say by way of a joke. But the assistant is not laughing. She's making too much money out of this.

Organising a kid's party is more work than I had ever imagined. I'm more nervous about it than if it were my own wedding (not that that's too much of a concern). Because it's not just kids who come, oh hell no. We've got the cream of LA society coming – every movie producer, director, actor and agent with offspring is going to be here. And about every ten minutes I'm getting a call on my phone from PAs to RSVP.

Marcie has also insisted upon fancy dress which so far has meant ten separate trips to costumiers around town. She finally settles on Cinderella, for which we've seen a dozen costumes in every shop, but she wants the costume that we saw in the first shop because it had the best plastic – sorry, glass – slippers. So back we go.

'And you and Craig can be the ugly sisters,' she announces, wafting around the shop looking like a cloud of pink candyfloss. She picks out two costumes with fat suit padding that would impress an elephant in search of a mate.

'No way,' says Craig, understandably. And the costume is too big for him anyway. As luck would have it, it fits me perfectly.

'Well, Daddy can be the other one,' says Marcie emphatically, and I pay for both.

Stephen Shawe is surprisingly excited by the event. 'Who's RSVPed?' he keeps asking me. 'And what's my little princess going to wear?'

It's sometimes hard to imagine Stephen as a powerhouse when he's at home. He likes to pad around the house in these sheepskin loafers, a maroon sweatshirt that's too tight and sweatpants that do nothing for his overhanging belly. His favourite spot in the whole house is leaning on the door of the fridge in the kitchen and drinking milk straight from the carton. He often invites me to eat dinner with him in the kitchen when the kids are in bed, and the house has gone quiet.

'Come on, Isabella, come and sit with me,' he says, surveying the plates of cold meats and salads lined up in the fridge. 'I've had such a tough day. Tell me something fun. Tell me about your day. Have my kids sent you crazy yet?'

I usually sit with him at the kitchen table, drinking wine (a more appealing option than what he's left in the milk carton) and eating nachos with cheese – his favourite food. I tell him about Craig's tantrums and Marcie's quarrels and Logan's latest words. And he laps it up. Wants to hear every detail.

'And what about you? You liking LA? You're not going to find yourself a boyfriend and run off with him, just as we've got used to your accent and understand what you're saying?' he says.

I promise him I won't. He's really not such bad company. Sometimes he talks about his business: new celebrities he's taking on, employees who are acting up, stars who are driving him nuts. I wouldn't say he's exactly easy to be with, but he can be quite personable and it's fascinating to hear about his world.

But there are also times when the Nazi commandant in him awakes, and he's suddenly unrecognisable.

'Who put this Natalie Imbruglia CD back in the Mozart case?' he'd yelled earlier in the week, when I was bathing the kids upstairs. I had all three of them in the bath together. We could hear his voice getting louder and louder as he stormed up the stairs. All the children looked terrified.

'Was it you?' he'd yelled at Craig when he finally found us in the bathroom, his face as red as a prize-fighter's. 'Well, was it? Was it?' He was jabbing a short, puffy finger centimetres from Craig's face.

'Sorry, Dad,' Craig had muttered. 'I didn't mean to. I must have got it muddled up.'

'I've told you a hundred times not to touch my stuff,' Stephen yelled and then took a swipe at Craig's head, hitting him so hard that it knocked him on to the side of the bath. Water sprayed everywhere, Logan burst into tears, and Stephen stormed out of the room.

Craig didn't cry, but it must have hurt. A bump sprang up instantly on his head. I pulled him out of the bath, wrapped him in a towel and hugged him hard.

Pearl and I are friends again. She hasn't told me what she said to Brett, but I think she believed me. She's helping me with the party, anyway, which is a great relief. She's even helped me stuff the goody bags. Ashley is still in New York, but she got him to call me back on my mobile. I told him that Brett was mistaken. Pearl must have told him too. And once the air was clear, he laughed.

'I shouldn't have listened to Brett anyways,' he chortled down the phone. 'Should have known he'd get the wrong end of the stick. Will you forgive me for rushing off like that, Bella?'

This was a good question. I was miffed that I could have been dismissed so quickly. Could I forgive him for totally ignoring me for two days? For abandoning me? Everyone seemed to abandon me eventually. I told him I could, and not to worry, but in my head I wasn't so sure. And what about this proposal of marriage? No one was mentioning it now.

'So when are you back?' I asked breezily.

'Actually, that's a tough one, because I'm involved in a court case, and it doesn't look like it's going to be over till next week. Can you wait that long for me to say I'm sorry in person?'

'Sure.'

He sent flowers the next day. But I was still angry. I was ten pounds heavier thanks to his restaurant fixation, and not because I'd been weighed down by diamonds.

By 2 p.m., the caterers are laying out gargantuan amounts of food in the marquee, there's an elephant crapping all over the lawn, the snow machine is making more noise than a jumbo jet on take-off and Marcie is in hysterics because she's been down the toboggan run three times and now her Cinderella costume is covered in mud. The party hasn't even started. We race upstairs to find something else for her to change into before everyone arrives. Fortunately, she's obsessed with being a princess so we have any number of pink chiffon numbers to choose from in the dressing-up box – not to mention tiaras, wands and enough jewellery to rival anything in the Tower of London.

'Oh, quick, quick, Bella. That's my friend Serenity coming,' she says, hanging out of the window as I'm zipping her in.

Serenity catches sight of Marcie and lets rip a foghorn of a greeting that is anything but serene, and her mother then scolds her with a gesture that is also anything but serene. These kids' names are a joke.

'And where's your costume?' Marcie squeals, suddenly noticing that I'm still in jeans. 'You've got to put yours on. Oh, you promised you'd be the ugly sister. You promised.'

I had quietly hoped I'd get out of dressing up myself. It's a particularly hideous costume too, a sort of eighteenth-century ball gown with sewn-in padding which not only increases my backside by five sizes, but also gives me the chest of an opera singer. It comes with a wig that looks like whipped cream and a hooked false nose that does indeed do what it's supposed to do – make me look ugly. I put it on, in the knowledge that at least I won't be the only one looking this stupid.

Except, it seems, I am. By the time I'm ready, the children are all screaming happily around the garden, so I go into the marquee. There is not a single other adult wearing a costume. In here, it's a party that's straight out of the society pages of *Harpers*. These are people who do not walk, they glide. They are people who do not sweat, but breathe wealth from their pores. Here is the very best in Chanel suits, Gucci handbags and Prada shoes. The women are so well groomed that if they were horses, they'd win trophies. Every one of them is a walking testament to what can be achieved when you've got nothing better to do than spend eight hours with the beautician every day – all are waxed, plucked, pumiced, exfoliated and highlighted. The men are lustrous too – all beige linen suits and sunglasses. Even Stephen looks glossy in a personally tailored suit. He nods at me as I walk in, looking up from a serious conversation he's having with another suit.

'Where's yours?' I mouth at him through the crowd, perhaps a bit unwisely. 'Where's your costume?'

He pretends he doesn't know me. He's got no time for me, of course. This is a party that's all about networking and taking care of business. Children's party? Good Lord, what was I thinking? I'm just beating a retreat when someone taps me on the shoulder.

'Need a prince to take you to the ball, Cinders?' says Jamie.

'Actually, I'm the ugly sister. Marcie is Cinderella,' I say cheerily, trying to maintain composure.

'I never could have guessed,' he says, stifling a laugh. 'Need a drink?' He hands me a glass of champagne, which is impossible to drink because of the honking great nose that is glued to my face. I am feeling decidedly foolish, not least because every time I see Jamie, he is more and more fanciable. He's a dead ringer for Rupert Everett, except not gay, and so personable that I'm almost lost for words, and that's a rare thing. He looks like he ought to be a movie star, except he hasn't got a big enough ego for it. He's too interested in other people to be a movie star. He's a director instead. Twenty-eight years old and the only adult here dressed in jeans.

I hadn't thought he was going to be here. He doesn't live at the house and I hadn't seen him for quite a while. He has his own apartment, down the road in Beverly Hills.

'That's an impressive rear end you've got there,' he says, surveying the costume. 'Looks like you need a licence to drive it.'

'Such flattering pickup lines,' I say. 'I'll bet all the girls fall into your arms with come-ons like that.'

'Didn't know I was trying to pick anyone up,' he says with a smirk.

Now I feel stupid.

'But let's think . . .' he says. 'Pickup lines . . . mmm, I'm sure I could try to think up a few. How about . . . that outfit looks good on you, but it would look a lot better in a crumpled heap next to my bed?'

'You should be so lucky,' I say, cuffing him lightly on the shoulder.

'Or what about ... this is a good one,' he adds conspiratorially. 'How about ... do you believe in love at first sight, or shall I walk past you again?'

'No chance.'

He laughs, and we survey the party like outsiders looking in. 'Got the cream of the trophy wives here,' he says, gesturing to the crowd. 'Young, beautiful, blind to everything except money.' He takes a swig of champagne. 'Of course, Donald Trump has the ideal trophy wife – every ten years he trades the one he has for a younger model.'

I laugh. 'So why don't you get one yourself?' I say cheerily. 'If it's all the rage.'

'Not old enough,' he says, looking pleased with himself. He takes another swig. 'And,' he adds with a huge grin, 'not ugly enough.'

'Says you,' I say.

My phone rings. It's clipped on to one of the fake boobs attached to the dress and Jamie laughs as I try to unhook it. It's the security guard, telling me that the three Power Puff Girls have arrived and where should they go? (These are heroic female cartoon characters that any child under six will have heard of, but you possibly won't have if you're over the age limit.)

'Sorry to miss out on any more of your cheesy lines, but I've got to sort out some people in even sillier costumes than me,' I say.

He puts down his drink. 'I'll come with you ... someone looking sillier than you? This I've got to see.'

The Power Puff Girls are to present Marcie with her cake at some tables set up in the marquee, and I direct them to the kitchen where the monster sugar and cream fantasia awaits. It will take all three of them to lift it, it's so big. I alert the photographer, so he doesn't miss the moment. Now I just have to round up thirty-five screaming children, who are rampaging across the garden like bison on a savannah.

I find Marcie. 'Marcie, we need to get everyone into the marquee for the cake.'

'Yes, yes,' she says. 'In a minute. I'm busy just now.'

I try some of the other kids, but rounding them up is like lassoing water. Fortunately, Jamie knows just what to do. 'Hey, kids,' he yells at the top of his voice. He has the kind of voice that simply commands attention. 'Everyone into the tent, before I count to ten. There's a surprise there waiting for you all.'

They move instantly.

The party is a rip-roaring success, according to Stephen, when he's said goodbye to the last of his guests.

'Thanks, Bella. You did good there,' he announces, putting an arm round my shoulder as we walk into the kitchen. Around us, caterers and cleaners are packing up. 'Nice costume, by the way.'

Marcie is as content as any spoilt seven year old could be. It had taken three people to carry the towering pile of gifts from the marquee into the house. She rips open every package excitedly, but there's little in any of them that impresses her. Dolls' houses, musical instruments, giant teddy bears, jewellery (real, not plastic), painting easels . . . there's nothing that she doesn't already have.

'And you know what's great?' she tells me after they've all been unpacked. 'Next week I'm going to have another party with Mummy.'

'Want a glass of vino?' Stephen asks me, as I pick up the wrapping paper. 'Jamie, get Bella a drink, would you?'

Craig, Marcie and Logan have all now disappeared into the den and plugged themselves into the TV set as if it's been a day like any other. And Jamie brings me a glass.

'For the most beautiful girl in the room,' he whispers, out of earshot of Stephen, and winks conspiratorially.

'I am the only girl in the room,' I whisper back.

'Then you're the only one to practise pickup lines on,' he says.

I used to think there would come a time when I'd feel all right about Mum and Dad not being around. I used to tell myself that if I ignored the stark staring hole in my life and just got on with things, I'd forget all about them. Not that I wanted to forget them. But I thought that one day I'd wake up and forget missing them. I thought the dust would settle and everything would be sane again. But even a year after Dad died, I was still crawling back under the blankets in the mornings and wishing I was someone else. I'd stay there until I'd convinced myself I *was* someone else, someone who was tougher than me.

But the problem with losing parents is that there are always anniversaries to remind you that you're all alone. One minute you're tough as old boots, not caring two figs about anyone or anything, and then along comes Dad's birthday or Christmas or the start of the summer holidays. At the start of the school holidays, Mum always used to take me out for a special treat. Once we even went to see a ballet at the Royal Opera House and had tea at the Ritz afterwards – she said everyone had to have tea at the Ritz once in their lives.

If the anniversaries didn't get to me, events would.

Like the time I won an art prize at school and I'd wished Dad had been there to see it. There I was, up on the podium, collecting my rosette, the whole school clapping, and just for a second I thought, 'Oh, Dad's going to love this. He's going to be dead chuffed when I tell him.'

And for that split second, I'd forgotten I couldn't tell him. It's funny because I really had forgotten. Then the reality thudded in and all I wanted to do was shove that rosette up the headmistress's nose.

There were lots of times like that. And lots of times when I just wished Mum was there to rescue me. Like the time I came home from school one day to find Lesley Fields' fist waiting for my face. It sprang at me, letting loose a loud crack from my nose, and pain like I'd never experienced. The unexpectedness of it had also knocked me hard up against a table where I'd scrabbled to find something to hit back with, but it's hard to do too much damage with an empty can of Coke and a copy of the *Sun* – especially when you can't see out for blood.

Lesley had found her purse in my suitcase under my bed. There was nothing in it, so I don't know what all the fuss was about. Her kids never liked me and of course they had put it there. But I had as much hope of reasoning with Godzilla in curlers as I had of walking away uninjured.

The unfortunate thing was, when she took me round to the social worker's office the next day, insisting she couldn't possibly be doing with a thief in her house, she kept all the money I had saved. I had over three hundred pounds – all my earnings from the hardware store – also hidden under the bed. She said I must have stolen it from her.

I've taken to using the gym in the house early in the mornings before the kids wake up. Until now my idea of exercise has always been a good, brisk lounge on the sofa. I've never had to do it before in my life. But this is California where everyone tells you that you can never be too rich or too thin. And since I'm not the former, I'm having a go at the latter. Although, given that my favourite food is seconds, it's unlikely that I'll ever achieve the emaciated look that's so popular here.

It's also getting my mind off Ashley who became the first man in my life I've ever actually dumped. He was gone nearly three weeks in the end, and during that time, the feeling of being discarded never passed. I was still angry that he hadn't even asked me about what Brett had told him. Just believed a pack of lies and scarpered. I think I lost confidence in him when I saw how easily he was frightened off. I don't need to put up with that shit any more. I want a man with money, but he's got to have some balls too.

I'd been more concerned about Pearl's reaction than his when I'd decided to call it off, given that our relationship seemed to mean so much to her. But in the end it was easy. I told her before I told Ashley. And I couched it in terms I knew she'd understand. I told her that I liked her brother and I wanted to be friends, but it wasn't a big love. It wasn't a true romance. She'd hugged me tight and told me to be brave. Love is always unpredictable, she'd cautioned, along with a roster of other platitudes that she must store up from her library of romance novels. Ashley took it well too – in fact, I think he might even have looked relieved. Perhaps he knew deep down that I was never in love with him. He was probably sensitive enough to tell.

Anyway, the point is, I've realised there are other rich options in this town besides Ashley Sash. Other rich options that aren't going to run off at the first hurdle. Some a lot richer. The place is seething with them. Take Jamie Shawe for instance. He's fun, flirtatious, sexy . . . and tall. I like tall. Got to be tall, because I'm tall. For someone who grew up the son of Stephen Shawe, he doesn't seem to have a screw loose either, which has got to be a miracle. I reckon he's probably a trust fund baby too with a dad like his, therefore rich. And, as I say, I like rich.

I think Candice used to use the gym, but since she's gone the Stairmaster and the treadmill have been gathering dust. Stephen looks like he would no more exercise than give up cheese nachos. So you could hit me with a barbell when I see him wander in in his mauve tracksuit. What is it with the mauve tracksuit?

I suddenly feel guilty, like I shouldn't be there. I get off the treadmill.

'Oh, I'm sorry. Let me leave you in peace,' I say.

'No, no. You're fine,' he says. 'I thought I'd join you.

You know, get rid of a bit of the belly.' He points to his midriff.

'Yes, but it's your gym. I can come back another time.'

'Bella, Bella. It's nice to have a bit of company in here. Candice used to exercise with me. I never do it otherwise. I need someone to chivvy me a bit.'

He climbs on the Stairmaster, and after only a few seconds looks like he's about to croak.

'I hate exercise,' I say.

'Nothing to it,' he puffs.

There's silence as we both pant on. I'm not quite sure whether to listen to my Walkman now or chat. I wonder what the etiquette is.

'Beautiful day out there,' I venture.

'Yeah.'

'It's probably pouring with rain back in England.'

'Yeah.'

After about ten minutes he gets off the Stairmaster and picks up some barbells. He stands in front of the mirror and begins lifting them up above his head, counting to ten. Puce is not a colour that suits him.

'Say, Isabella?' he asks as nonchalantly as a man can who looks like he's about to have a heart attack. He's looking at me through the mirror. 'I've got a function tonight. Got no one else to take. Wanna come?'

'You put it so nicely,' I say.

Americans never get sarcasm. 'It's a charity benefit dinner,' he pants.

'Not fancy dress again, is it?'

'Be ready at seven p.m.,' he barks gruffly over his shoulder as he wraps a towel round his neck and heads out of the door, clearly assuming that I said yes. Then he leans back in through the door frame. 'Got an evening dress?'

'No.'

'Go get yourself something today. Ask Pearl for the cash.'

Jesus, Mary and Joseph. I've got a date with a billionaire.

Pearl is on her headset when I go into her office. This could be tricky.

'Pearl, Stephen says you'll give me some cash,' I say cautiously from the doorway, leaving out what it's for.

'Yes, it's right here.' She hands me an envelope, barely looking up from her computer. Her face is inscrutable. 'There's eight hundred in there.'

Eight hundred! Wow. But does she know Stephen's asked me on a date? Has he told her what the money is for? I can't tell. I decide it's probably best to come clean.

'Look, I know what it must look like, but I didn't lie to you. I haven't been seeing Stephen. He just asked me out this morning.' A police siren wails in the distance outside.

'It's okay. I know you haven't,' she says, turning to face me, and leaning back in her chair. 'But why didn't you, like, tell me that Brett tried it on with you at that party?'

Tried it on with me? Is that what you call it?

'What was the point? Brett was drunk and probably didn't know what he was doing anyway. I didn't want to upset you.'

'I wondered why you left that party so suddenly.' She

pauses. 'Adam says he saw you leaving. And . . .' She coughs awkwardly. 'And saw Brett after you'd finished with him. What did you do?'

'Kneed him in the balls,' I say flatly, not sure if I should be embarrassed or proud. 'But I wasn't expecting him to start wreaking revenge. Did he tell you he'd made it all up?'

'No. I asked Adam what he thought about the whole thing, and he told me what he saw at the party. Brett doesn't take rejection very well. And I realised what must have happened . . . Look, I'm really sorry I was so harsh,' she says sheepishly.

'No, I'm sorry,' I say, not quite sure what I'm sorry for. But then I am British and apologising, even to lamp-posts, is what we do. 'But what about Brett?'

'Oh, he's cool.'

Cool?

'Aren't you angry with him?'

'Yeah, but he was drunk, as you say. He probably didn't mean anything by it, and we'll get over it. We've got over worse.'

I stand in the doorway, not sure what to say next. This girl's crazy.

'So what are you doing going out with Stephen?' Pearl blurts out eventually. 'He's a bit old for you, isn't he?'

'I don't think it's a proper date. He says he hasn't got anyone else to take. I think I'm filling in until he finds someone more suitable.'

'I wouldn't be so sure,' says Pearl. 'Candice wasn't much older than you, and you're far prettier.'

*

I hadn't really considered Stephen Shawe as a prospective date. I've seen better-looking jellyfish. But that's beside the point. Stephen Shawe is the jackpot. Richer than any overweight lawyer and more powerful than the President. Well, almost. In all of my wildest dreams, I could never have imagined someone this well off being interested in me. In me! I was so used to thinking of myself as unremarkable that I'd never imagined this could be a possibility. See, that's the difference between Brits and Americans. Brits don't aim high enough. We settle for long queues at the supermarket, a lousy health system, buses that never come on time, and cold chips as part of our cuisine. We think we don't deserve anything better. We think that aiming at something attainable is the best we can ever do. But Americans always shoot for the moon – they're optimistic, ambitious, and will only settle for second best when they've got no more dreams to live for. And why not aim high? From now on, I'm aiming at the sky. Even jellyfish can have some attractive features when their bank statements go into the billions.

Besides being competitive dreamers, the other thing that Americans know how to do is glamour. You only have to watch the Oscars to know that. But it's not just the A-listers on the silver screen. In Los Angeles, there isn't a street corner without a manicurist or a hairdresser. At home we have pubs, here they have beauticians. You can have silk wraps, glitter tips, acrylic makeovers, French polishes – and that's just for your nails. Never mind what they can offer for your face or any other exposed area. By 7 p.m. my eyebrows are plucked, my complexion is patted and moisturised, my teeth are whitened and my hair is twisted and chignoned. If I was a dog, I'd win a prize at Crufts. I'm also squeezed into the kind of dress that would get me on a 'best dressed' magazine page, if I was someone famous. It's a beaded lace affair from Badgley Mischka that makes the boobs look fantastically plumped, squeezes the waist and then flows in wafts of chiffon. Even though I say it myself, I'm looking the goods.

Stephen says nothing. Not that I'm expecting oohs and ahs. Dressed in a black tuxedo and bow tie, he looks me up and down as we meet in the hall, and kind of nods as if to say 'That'll do'.

He's doesn't say anything in the Porsche either. But I think that's just his style.

'Where are we going?' I ask, smoothing out the chiffon.

'You'll find out,' he says dismissively.

'How do I look?' I try.

He grunts.

'Don't worry, I can take a compliment.'

He grunts again.

The party's in the ballroom at the Beverly Wilshire Hotel. This is the enormous hotel at the end of Rodeo Drive in Beverly Hills where Julia Roberts catches her millionaire in *Pretty Woman*. I wonder if the place will bring me luck too. The ballroom's heaving.

'Stephen, darling,' says a woman bearing down on us whose only body part that hasn't seen the surgeon's knife is probably her toes. She's dripping in sequins and diamonds. 'Darling, how nice of you to come. I've got you on table two. And this is . . .?'

'This is Isabella,' says Stephen gruffly, and wanders off.

'How do you do,' I say, offering a hand to shake. She shakes it limply, but without Stephen by my side, she's not interested.

Well, at least my boobs are my own.

So now I'm doing my deer-in-headlights impersonation. Everyone else in the room seems to know each other. They're gathered in impenetrable groups. Think I'll find the bar. There isn't one – just waiters with trays of champagne. I grab one, and take a big swig. Suddenly the glass seems to be empty. How did that happen? Another waiter goes past, so I grab another and smile aimlessly at anyone who might happen to look my way. An older man with a mane of white hair catches my eye and introduces himself, but the noise of everyone talking so loudly around us means I can barely hear him. I nod blindly, smile and polish off my champagne, and, well, I'm on to my third glass when a gong goes and we are all told by some bloke dressed up to look like an English butler in tails to head to our tables, which are positioned around a dance floor at the other end of the room.

I can't see Stephen anywhere. And which table was it? Four? Five? I can't remember, the old geezer is gone, and I can't see our hostess now either. What to do? A waiter scurries past carrying two untouched glasses of champagne on his tray. I grab them both. No point in wasting them. Now everyone is seated except for me. So I ask a waiter for help, who explains that there's a board up with everyone's name on it, telling us where to sit.

'Stephen, I've been looking all over for you,' I say, possibly louder than I had intended, when I find him.

'All right, all right, keep your voice down,' he says. 'Take a seat, Isabella.'

I'm feeling braver now. There's only one seat left. It's between an Orson Welles in his latter years lookalike, and a younger man who's good looking enough to be an extra on *Will & Grace*. Stephen looks disparagingly at me from the other side of the table, but Orson Welles seems pleased to have me next to him. He stands up to push my chair in for me, and kisses my hand by way of introduction.

'How do you do? I'm Bill Makepeace,' he says, rather pompously, and I can see him checking out my boobs, which I'll admit are worth checking in this dress.

'Isabella Spires,' I say. 'And my face is up here.'

He coughs and raises his eyes with a big grin.

'Of course it is, my dear.' He laughs a little. 'I was just admiring the view.'

Dirty old man.

'Is that a British accent I detect?' he ask.

'Sure is,' I slur.

'Well, let's drink to that,' he says, and holds up his champagne flute for me to clink glasses with.

We clink and swig. I look round the table. On the other side of Bill is a woman who's so thin, she could be trick or treating for Halloween. Best-dressed skeleton I've ever seen. There are a couple of older gals – more plastic surgery and too many diamonds – and across the table is another blonde clearly too young for her date too. The rest are suits – mostly middle-aged and balding. Eight couples in total.

'Shocking champagne this,' I tell Bill. See, I'm good at the chit-chat once I find my feet. And I must be entertaining because everyone else round the table seems to be listening. 'Not that I'm an expert,' I blather on. 'But let me tell you, I know good champagne from bad, and at a do like this you'd think they'd push the boat out, wouldn't you?'

Bill smiles to himself.

'I mean, what do they call this stuff? I've drunk fizzy lemonade that tasted better.'

'Actually, Bill owns the winery that donated all the champagne for this event,' whispers the younger man on my left, who is sending my gay radar into overdrive.

'What, he made it himself?'

'Sort of,' says Bill, looking embarrassed. 'I own a winery up in the Napa Valley. Ever been up there?'

Gulp. 'No. Is it nice?'

As it turns out, Bill's all right. He's the most charismatic of all the men here. He has an amiable face – too old to be good looking. But he has the rare ability of actually listening to what you have to say. He locks his fingers together, leans forward and actually seems interested. I tell him about my first impressions of LA and how much I like it that everyone's involved in the movies. He asks me what my favourite movie is. I tell him *A Night at the Opera*. He laughs.

I balance a fork on my upper lip, and pretend my knife is a cigar in a bid to do my best Groucho Marx impersonation.

Bill laughs even more.

'Made in 1935. The first one the Marx Brothers made with MGM, after moving from Paramount.'

'Impressive,' he says, studying me hard. 'Second favourite?'

'*Breakfast At Tiffany's* – released in 1961. The high point of George Peppard's career. Directed by Blake Edwards and won an Oscar for best song. But did you know that the film is different from the book, because the movie studio couldn't reveal that Holly Golightly slept with several men?'

'Quite the film buff. Where'd you learn all this shit?'

'I told you I like the movies.'

He tells me I'll fit right on in, in this town, and that this table is made up entirely of people who are in the movie business, but not 'in' the movies themselves.

I want to ask him what he does, besides make champagne, but our conversation peters out as the food arrives and the skeleton next to him diverts his attention. Around the rest of the table the talk is all about the movies too. They're reeling out figures like mathematicians – how many people had been to see which movies, how much the movies cost, how much they had made. But they're being jovial about it. They seem to be cracking jokes at the same time. Of course I don't understand their jokes. I haven't a clue what they're going on about, but I quite like jokes. I happen to have one up my sleeve.

I catch the eye of the loudest of them across the table. 'Have you heard why movie producers become movie producers?' I ask him.

There's silence.

'Because they're all too short and ugly to become actors. Ha, ha, ha . . .'

Silence. I mean, how was I to know they're all bloody movie producers?

I have another glass of wine and pick at some salmon

roulade. I'm grateful for Bill to talk to. After dinner, there's a disco. And I like a good dance. I catch Stephen's eye across the table and ask him if he'll have a twirl with me. Says I've got as much chance of getting him on the dance floor as he has of winning Miss World. I try Bill. He laughs at me. What's wrong with these people? And now they're playing Sister Sledge and I just love that sooo much. And what the hell? Who cares if they don't know how to have a good time? There's always got to be the first one on the dance floor. Bet if I go it alone, they'll all follow.

Nobody does. Last thing I remember is Stephen scooping me up off the floor and stuffing me in his Porsche. And it was the worst hangover in the history of hangovers the next day, but there was light at the end of that tunnel. A bouquet of flowers arrived in the afternoon. The message read: 'For the wine critic, who knows a thing or two, love Bill.'

After the Fosters came the Carpenters. They were a much nicer family. Reminded me a bit of my own – except older. Margery Carpenter was an artist like my dad – better than my dad, actually. She had canvases set up all over the dining room. She'd do still lifes – bowls of fruit and all that. Even did a portrait of me, one day. Douglas Carpenter was in the City. And they had a son, Edward, who was going to university in September.

Edward was the kind of lad Mum and Dad would have approved of. He spoke like I did. He said generous things about his mum's paintings. He'd watch rugby on the telly on Saturday afternoons with his dad, just like my dad did. He'd offer to make me breakfast and then burn the toast. He was calm, patient, good. I hadn't had anyone actually welcome me into their home before. And of course I was horrible to him. Really mean.

His mum was really kind to me too. She bought me clothes, gave me an allowance – money to spend as I wanted. Let me have a room that was my own, said I could watch whatever movies I wanted on the telly, cooked roast beef for Sunday lunch.

But it was as if I'd developed a self-destruct button at the back of my head. All I could do was snarl and yell at them. See, sometimes I was really angry with Mum and Dad. With Dad, really, more than Mum. There were nights when I'd just lie awake and curse and swear and promise revenge. I'd have conversations with Dad in my head, which weren't that pretty. I'm always brave when I'm lying in bed at night. I'd tell him what an arsehole he was to leave me behind. I'd ask him why, if he was going to top himself, didn't he think to take me along too. Unfortunately, there's not too much revenge you can take out on someone who's dead.

Trouble was, after I'd told my dad what for, I'd wake up the next morning feeling guilty. And I'd feel guilty that he killed himself too. I used to think it must have been because I hadn't taken care of him enough after Mum died. Used to think it was all my fault.

And then there I was in the first place where people were kind to me, and I wanted to take it all out on them. I couldn't stop myself. I wanted to burst their happiness bubble. They were all so perfect and content. Resentful? I was Regan from *The Exorcist* – and those were just the good days.

And then one day Edward asked me to go for a drink in the pub with him, and I guess the destructive streak just got the better of me. I loaded myself up with lager, took him back to his room and shagged the living daylights out of him.

Unfortunately, his parents slept in the next-door bedroom. I was back in the social worker's office faster than you could say silly cow.

15

Brett flies back from Canada this afternoon for a filming break. I hadn't been looking forward to his return, but I can see how happy it's making Pearl. She's been though a battalion of beauty appointments all week, and rented a suite in the Chateau Marmont Hotel for a small welcome-home party for him tonight.

There'd been some discussion over whether to make it a surprise party or not, while we ate our sandwiches in our usual spot in the garden, but in the end she decided she'd better tell him, in case he had other plans. I'd argued that any man who'd been away that long would obviously have plans with his girlfriend that night, but Pearl wasn't so sure.

The guest list had then been a big discussion too. 'He wants me to invite a bunch of directors so he can do a bit of networking,' she'd told me with a small sigh. 'I hadn't planned on making it such a big shebang.'

'What about abandoning the party idea altogether, and making it a night with just the two of you?' I'd asked.

'Well, there'll be just the two of us when everybody goes,' she'd said wistfully. 'We'll have the whole suite to ourselves then. Anyway, Brett's really excited about the party.'

In the end, the guest list had reached fifty. Pearl had organised caterers and wine – all at her own expense – bought a new outfit from Fred Siegal, and begged Stephen for the afternoon off so she could meet Brett at the airport. But early in the day there'd been a phone call from his PA, telling her not to meet him. The studio would be sending a limo to the airport, and he'd see her at the party.

Pearl put on a brave face, but I knew she was disappointed. She took the afternoon off anyway to make sure the suite looked perfect, decorating it with lots of tiny Chinese lanterns. It looks beautiful, and by 7.30 p.m. the party is in full swing. Waitresses are weaving through the crowd with little trays of breaded shrimp and sesame-seeded dumplings, there's a help-yourself bar in the corner with vodka jellies, a music system is sending out ambient grooves, and a crowd of beautiful people is gathering on the balcony to watch the traffic speed past along the Sunset Strip beneath. A lot of the girls are Pearl's friends from high school. She introduces me to a couple, and they eye me up suspiciously. Women are competitive in LA. Doesn't bother me. There are plenty of interesting male faces to smile at.

Pearl's good at this – she's a natural hostess. She takes time to welcome every guest, to make sure they feel comfortable and to introduce everyone to each other. She has an ease with people. Sometimes I'm quite envious of that – envious of her certainty in social situations, envious of her confidence. She's the kind of person you'd meet at a party and couldn't help but like immediately – sparky, fun, but all the time kind and caring, maternal almost. She introduces me to a shy man who turns out to be a producer of porn films, but as she does it I can see that her usual composure has turned to perplexity. It's 9 p.m. and Brett still isn't here.

'Have you tried calling him?' I ask, excusing myself from Mr X-rated and taking her aside.

'Three times. He's not picking up,' she whispers. 'Do you think something could have happened to him? This is so embarrassing. A whole party for him and he's not even here.'

'Perhaps he's fallen asleep,' I suggest. 'Would you like me to go round to his place and check?'

'Would you, Bella? God, that would be great. I'd go myself, but—'

She doesn't reach the end of her sentence because Brett is waltzing through the door with a posse trooping in behind him – four girls exposing more wardrobe malfunctions and midriff than Janet Jackson on stage, and his co-star from the movie, Michael Peters. They're high on coke – don't need to work for Customs to see that.

'How ya doin'?' Brett greets a bloke by the door who he must know given the hugs and effusiveness. The girls hover round them – one wraps an arm round Brett and slides her hand into the back pocket of the jeans he's wearing, suggesting a familiarity with him that I'd say doesn't equal fidelity.

Poor Pearl. She's brave, though. I'll give her that. She plants a serene smile on her lips and glides across to the group like the perfect hostess she is.

'Honey, there you are,' Brett says loudly, brushing the other girl away. He looks genuinely pleased to see her, and throws his arms round her in a wild embrace.

He kisses her long and hard on the lips. 'My God, have I been missing you? You look beautiful. Stunning. Boy, am I pleased to be back.'

Pearl smiles happily, apparently oblivious of the other girls.

'And look at this great party. Honey, you're the best. Do you know that? You are the best.' He hugs her tight. 'All this for me? . . . Come on, I want you to meet some of the girls from the film.' He introduces her to the others, and if he had been in trouble before, I can see he's been forgiven now.

The party bangs on past midnight. Brett doesn't have time for me, of course. Not that I want any attention from him. I catch his eye at one point during the evening as he surveys the room, working out his next networking move. But he looks away fast, pretending he hasn't seen me. I think he's surprised I'm still around.

By 1 a.m. the room has begun to clear. The caterers have long since gone. I'm about to leave myself, extricating myself from the porn producer who won't leave my side, when Brett announces to Pearl that he's got another party to go on to.

'But I thought we were going to have our own private party here,' she says to him, looking crushed.

'Not tonight, beautiful. We've got lots of time for that later. But tonight I've got to catch up with Freddy.'

'Freddy? Freddy who?'

'He's a casting agent . . . He says he's got some gig lined up for me. I'll catch you tomorrow.' He makes to leave.

'But Brett. We had this planned.'

'I know, sweetheart. And I'm as disappointed as you.'

His face looks pained, but not enough. 'Look, why don't you get your friend Isabella to stay here with you? You could make it a fun girls' night.' It's the first time he's even acknowledged my presence. He kisses her lightly on the forehead and, before she's had a chance to complain, dashes out of the door.

I don't see much of Pearl or Brett over the next month or so. Pearl and I brush past each other around the Shawes' mansion, but there isn't the time for our long chats or to do anything together because she's so absorbed in the life of Brett Ellis. She's off to PR events with him, or charity dos, and there's the wrap party for his movie. Brett's been round to the house a couple of times, lounged around the sofas as if he owned the place – a move that Stephen seems to welcome, given that he's one of his fastest-rising clients. But I steer well clear – I learned long ago to stay away from trouble. But one afternoon Pearl's in Stephen's office and he's waiting for her in the hallway when I come in after collecting the kids from school.

He looks up from a magazine he's reading, and smiles. 'Hi, Bella.'

'Hi,' I say coolly and walk past him. The children tear past him into the kitchen. I'm in a rush because I've got to get Craig started on his homework.

I feel his eyes following me. 'You're a tough nut, aren't you?' he calls after me.

I turn, not sure of the answer to that. 'Meaning?'

'Meaning . . .' He lets out a sigh, and looks down at his shoes, which I notice are scuffed and dirty. 'Meaning, I'm sorry for what I did.'

Well, blow me. This I had not expected. Pearl must have put him up to it, I realise. But he's doing a good act. His head hangs down and he looks mildly embarrassed. 'Sorry for the lie you told Ashley, or sorry for trying to rape me?' I say dispassionately.

'I wasn't trying to rape you.'

'What were you trying to do then? Fry an egg?'

'Look, I'm sorry. And I know I was wrong. It was very wrong. But do you think we could be friends?' He pauses, and I face him with a stern expression and my arms folded defensively across my chest. If he thinks he's going to get off that easily . . .

'It would mean a lot to Pearl, I think.'

'Ah, so that's why you're doing this?'

'No. Honestly, I'm sorry. I was drunk and I was stupid.' He looks at me and holds out his hand for me to shake. 'Friends?' he asks, and there's a pleading look in his eye which explains why he gets away with so much.

I don't trust him an inch. But I'll do this for Pearl.

'Friends,' I say, and shake his hand.

How is it that with ninety-seven different channels, there's still nothing to watch on TV? You might find something that you know you'd watch if it was on the telly at home because there're usually only five channels to choose from. But because there's so much choice, you keep thinking there might be something better on the next channel, or the next, or the next, and so you keep going, and suddenly it's been an hour and all you've seen is ninety-seven commercials for toilet paper. I'm in my room on a quiet weekday afternoon, cursing the telly, when Pearl knocks on my door. It takes me by surprise. It's ages since she's come up to my room to chat.

'Bella, I've got to tell you my news,' Pearl says, all girlish excitement and zest, bouncing into the room and throwing herself down on my bed. 'Are you ready for this?'

Nothing surprises me any more.

'You're not going to believe what I'm about to tell you.'

'No?'

'You are just never going to believe.'

Oh, for God's sake.

'I'm pregnant.'

'Ah!' Well, that is surprising. 'And you're happy about it?' I say in disbelief. I mean, a child with that jerk? She's out of her mind.

'Oh, Bella, I'm sooooo happy. Brett and I are going to get married in Vegas. He says it's what he always wanted and he's going to be the best dad ever. I think it'll calm him down a lot, make him more responsible . . . I think it's going to be the making of him, don't you?'

'Um . . .' Marriages in Hollywood rarely last the weekend, but this one's unlikely to survive till lunch. 'That's great.'

'And you will come to the wedding, won't you? It's only going to be small. Brett says he doesn't want anything too fancy, just a few friends and family, no big publicity thing . . . You will come, won't you? It's going to be after Christmas.'

'Of course I'll come. Love to.' But I suspect I don't look delighted enough.

'Oh, Bella, you are pleased, aren't you?' she asks,

grabbing my hands and adopting that lost puppy-dog look that you mostly only see in pet shops.

'Of course I am.'

What else could I possibly say?

Stephen is not best pleased about Pearl's news because he's going to have to find a new personal assistant. He complains about it in the evenings when he's chowing down on his cheese nachos. Frankly, I was expecting the heave-ho after making such a fool of myself at the charity dinner. But Stephen seemed to relish the humour of it. 'Next time you have a drink, remember not to bring me with you,' he'd joked the following morning. 'And I think Bill Makepeace would like an early warning too. Heck, never thought I'd see the day when anyone could embarrass him. With a history like his, I'd have thought nothing could embarrass him . . . ha, ha, ha.' He let rip one of his awful laughs. '"Shocking champagne, this,"' he guffawed, doing a bad impersonation of my voice and accent.

Far from giving me the boot, Stephen had actually given me a pay rise a few weeks later, saying how pleased he was because the kids have taken to me so well. On the days when Logan is choking on yet another piece of Lego and Craig is bawling because he's not getting his way, it seems like stretching the point to say they've taken to me, but over all they seem to like it that I can make alligators out of egg cartons, guns out of toilet-roll holders and spaceships out of cardboard boxes. Marcie and Logan cling to me at bedtime – some nights they even find their way into my bed. Craig is still distrustful and sometimes sullen but he doesn't tantrum as much as he used to, and there are times when he'll even come and sit next to me and we'll read books together.

I had one really great day out with him when Marcie was off on a playdate, Logan was with his mother and Craig seemed to be at a loose end. He said he was angry with his mother and didn't want to see her. So I suggested we go and explore the Science Museum together instead. He loves science – all he ever wants to do is make potions in the kitchen, mixing vinegar and bicarbonate of soda and watching it froth all over the place. So we set off early and had a great time, staring into the mechanical insides of machinery, learning about earthquakes and watching baby chicks hatch.

'Thanks, Bella,' he said as we made our way home. 'I liked that.'

'I liked it too,' I said. And I did. After my parents had died, I'd stopped visiting museums.

I was touched by Craig. I never thought I liked children much, but they're less complicated than anyone else. In fact, they're quite simple really. All you have to do is be patient, add water, food and attention, and they slowly open up, like flowers. Craig was desperate to please his dad, but rarely did Stephen pay him enough attention. All the kid wanted was someone to listen to him, I mean, don't we all? I listened to his stories, took the trouble to make a few foaming volcanoes with him in the kitchen, and slowly, ever so slowly, we were becoming mates. I was quite proud, really.

I like living at the Shawes'. The only trouble is I'm no further down the road in my search for a rich man than I was before. Although Stephen never misses a chance to crack a joke about keeping me away from the bottle, he hasn't invited me anywhere else since that party. Dating billionaires is more complicated than you'd expect – especially when you work for them. I found a genius book in a secondhand book shop on one of my afternoons off. It was called *How to Marry the Rich*, by Ginie Sayles, a woman who'd married an oil tycoon. I bought the book and keep it hidden under the mattress in my room – I don't want anyone rumbling me. The author reckons that a gold-digger is the perfect mate for the gold owner because they speak the same language. She says marrying into money is like getting an education, and her advice is to hang out where all the rich people are. Check one. Can't do better than live in LA. Next, get a makeover. Well, thanks to Pearl, I've had one of those. Next, date lots of other rich guys. Okay, maybe that's what I've got to do. Shouldn't be too hard – everyone's a millionaire around here except me.

Adam calls me on the phone. Okay, everyone except me and Adam.

'Bella, I've just heard Pearl's news,' he says. His voice is downhearted and hurt.

'Yeah, kind of disastrous,' I say. 'But what can we do? She's set her heart on marrying him.' I can remember reading an agony aunt offering advice in a magazine column once on what to do when you think a friend of yours is dating the wrong guy. Her advice was to stay quiet because eventually she'll work it out for herself, and by getting involved you risk alienating her. Personally, my flesh crawls every time I think of Brett. But Pearl's a grown woman, able to make her own decisions. If I've learned anything, it's that it's best to not get involved.

'I know,' says Adam, and for a moment I think he's going to blub.

'Wouldn't be so bad if he wasn't such an arrogant pig.' I say soothingly.

'I know ... It's disastrous. He doesn't care for her. You know that, don't you? Bella, you don't think you could talk her out of it?'

'Why would she listen to me?' He's got to be joking, right? No one ever listens to me. I'm just a kid from an orphanage, making my own way.

'She likes you, Bella. I think she'd listen to you. It's worth a shot, isn't it?'

'Yeah, but what's she going to do raising a kid on her own? He might be a pig, but at least he's standing by her.'

There's silence at the other end.

'Adam, are you still there?'

'A kid ... you mean she's pregnant?'

Oh, big mouth, Spires. He didn't know.

Over the next few months, Pearl blossoms. Her hair takes on a glossy sheen, her eyes sparkle and her complexion really blooms in the indescribable way that people say happens to pregnant women. She appears blissfully happy, not least because Brett seems to be stepping up to the role. He went with her to the first baby scan and they shared their first glimpses of their future joyous bundle. They've even been house-hunting together, and he turned up one day at her dad's house with an enormous engagement ring. Everyone seems happy about it, except Adam, whose face is longer than a day at the convent, and me, because I don't much care for tossers.

It's still a few weeks until the wedding but Pearl's dad's on an oldies reunion tour and she's got the place to herself, so she's got ten girlfriends round, and tonight is to be her hen night. The girls are a flurry of overly sweet perfume, giggles and Gucci jeans when they arrive, clutching bottles of champagne which everyone tucks into straight away. Except Pearl, of course, who seems to be, dare I say it, drunk on delusional happiness. Most of the girls went to school with Pearl. They don't talk to me much, reminding me what an exception Pearl is in this town, where beautiful women are suspicious of outsiders. Besides, they're too busy admiring each other's haircuts, telling each other about their latest shopping sprees and checking themselves in the mirror. Boy, do these girls like to check themselves out in the mirror. There's a big one over the mantelpiece in the lounge and they're almost elbowing each other aside to get near it. I've never been invited on a hen night before, but large groups of women – especially these women, who are screeching as if they've been at the helium – hold about as much appeal as a night inside a gas oven.

Anyway, I'm busy pondering how long I've got to suffer this when a middle-aged woman arrives at the door with a suitcase and a sly look on her face. She looks like she might be an air hostess, and I'm just thinking she's surely too old, not to mention the wrong sex, to be the stripper, when she starts settling herself on the sofa and opens her suitcase to produce twelve fully erect, preposterously realistic latex penises – each complete with testicles and a suction cup. 'It's a blow-job party. It's absolutely all the rage,' Pearl whispers in my ear, as she sees me reel in horror.

'Bit late for you, I'd say,' pointing at her stomach. 'You clearly know what to do with one of these.'

Our unlikely MC tells us to each choose our penis and sit it on a plate. Then we are to roll up our sleeves, squelch lubricant on our fingers, and 'Pull up, twist, turn and go down.' The girls are like bees round a honey pot – there's even a small kerfuffle about who gets an oversized black one. But then, as each one of the girls takes her seat, balancing plate and penis on knees or coffee table, the giggles around the room subside to quiet concentration, and the MC begins her lesson, sparing no detail on the nitty-gritty of male arousal.

'I'm going,' I say to Pearl, watching everyone else wrapping their hands round these giant plastic willies, and working on them like it's a pottery class. 'It's too outrageous. Call me a prude, but I can't do this.'

'Come on,' says Pearl. 'Don't tell me there's nothing you can't learn here. And anyway, no one's going to know.'

I reach for my handbag to leave, but somehow it's impossible to walk away. It's like watching a car crash in slow motion: fascination conquers distaste. Pearl offers me a penis on a plate, like a tempting piece of chocolate cake, and smiles. 'No one's going to know,' she repeats with a giggle.

It's 1 a.m. before I make it back to the Shawes' but the lights are still on. I expected everyone to be in bed by now. But I meet Jamie in the hallway, where he's perusing the mail on an antique table. I knew he'd be coming round tonight, and I'd hoped to see him before I left for the evening, but he'd been late turning up for dinner with his dad. I've bumped into him a few times since Marcie's party, but it's mostly been brief – either I've been on my way out of the door with the children, or he's been racing in on his way to catch his dad. We'd barely had time to do more than wave at each other.

'You're out late,' he says, looking up with a wide, but ever so slightly crooked, smile. He really *is* handsome. But more than that, there's something super-gentle and tender about him. He's the kind of man you know would rescue spiders from the bath, walk old ladies across the street, and give money to homeless people.

'Heard any good pickup lines recently?' he says flirtatiously, holding a bunch of junk mail in his hands.

'Oh, hundreds. Men are always trying to pick me up,' I say, trying to look as adorable as I can, because there's something about him that makes me melt when I'm in his company.

He's been coming round to the house a lot recently because he's working on a documentary about the Los Angeles gangs. His dad is finding the funds to finance it. He'd told me about it a few weeks ago, on the one occasion when we weren't both flying in different directions. I'd come across him in the garden on my way back from the sandpit with Logan, and he'd walked back into the house with us and watched me attempt to feed real food to a boy who only likes to eat choking hazards and dirt. I'd asked him about himself – not meaning to pry, but just being chatty. I was curious about how he fitted into the family.

His mother lives back in Idaho. She was Stephen's Shawe's first love, his high school sweetheart. Stephen was the footballer and she was the cheerleader, except he was too fat to be a good footballer and she was too bright to be dancing around on football pitches – she was on course for Harvard. They'd been in love once. 'Probably for no more than a week,' Jamie told me. But then she got pregnant. Stephen did the right thing and married her, but he wasn't about to give up on his Hollywood dreams so she had to come too. And she'd faithfully stuck around for the first fourteen years of his career, supporting him through the difficult times, putting up with the tiny, squalid apartment in Los Feliz which was all they could afford when they first moved here. It was Jamie's mother who would advise Stephen on which actors to woo as clients, how to expand his business, how to do the books. And she'd quietly watch him canoodle with starlets and waltz off to Hollywood premieres, leaving her at home with Jamie. Then one day he came home and said he wanted a divorce. Told her she didn't fit his Hollywood image. She was too homespun. And Jamie's mum gave in without a fight, moved into an apartment nearby so that she was around to raise Jamie, and then fled back to Idaho as soon as her son was old enough to go to university. She had never remarried.

Jamie grew up negotiating between both parents. He knew about diplomacy and tiptoeing around hurt feelings. He had bedrooms in two homes and lives in both places. His mother taught him about kindness, the importance of education and not being taken in by the superficiality of Hollywood. His father taught him about the movie business.

Looking at him standing there in his ripped and faded jeans, I wonder briefly if he counts as another rich date. Would he ever ask me out anyway? Bound to have a girlfriend. But he's never mentioned one. So I'm about to brush up the wit and sparkle – which isn't easy at this time of night, especially when you've still got the screeching of a hen night ringing in your ears – when I suddenly remember I'm carrying a plastic bag in my hand which has the words 'Man Handling' written all over it. It was a going-home prize from Pearl, and it's filled with condoms, saucy knickers and a vibrator. I hadn't wanted it, but Pearl was insistent.

I try to hide it discreetly behind my back, but unfortunately he notices the gesture and I feel like a two year old trying to keep forbidden sweeties out of sight. So then I think I'll just shove it in my handbag and have done with it. But I realise, too late, that it's too big for my bag and suddenly there's a psychedelic pink vibrator rolling around on the black and white tiled floor.

'Been doing some late-night shopping then?' he says, picking it up and examining it before handing it back to me with a smirk.

'It was a gift,' I blurt. If my cheeks get any redder, I might burn up.

'Of course.'

'No, it was. It was a going-home prize from Pearl's blow-job party.' Oh, shit.

'A blow-job party.'

Sod him, he's sounding like an academic on the verge of an intellectual breakthrough.

'Yes, a blow-job party.' I grab the wretched thing and march up the stairs to my room. This is too awful for words.

16

It's a known fact that an average foster child tangled up in the 'care' system for more than four years is likely to live in forty-seven different homes. My life was not so much a journey as a series of commutes from one family to another. It was like permanently living on board a tour bus. There were the Beadales where I learned to play truant, the Lovells where I learned to inhale, the Joneses where I learned to play computer games, and the Hills where I learned to play with myself. Then there were the Winklers where I learned that sex is a useful tool to get what you want, the Formans where I learned to drive a car – lessons were paid for by playing with Mr Forman himself – and the Fitches where I realised I was going nowhere.

Here are some other facts about foster children. Seven out of ten foster kids are homeless by the time they've left the care system, that is, once they've turned eighteen. Six out of ten of them will end up at Her Majesty's pleasure. Only one out of ten of them will go to college, and of those only one out of a hundred will actually finish the course and get a diploma. How about those for odds? And here's another fact: girls who lose their mothers young usually end up being promiscuous.

I was in Marks & Spencer when I had my Scarlett O'Hara moment. You know, the fabulous scene when Scarlett returns to Tara and she walks through the ruins of Twelve Oaks and finds a turnip in the ground, and then she rises from the dirt, still looking incredibly beautiful in spite of the mud on her face, surveys the ruined land and vows defiantly that she'll never go hungry again. Well, there was no dramatic sunset behind me – only the knickers section, three pairs for £7.99. No violin strings either, just a small child throwing a tantrum in a pushchair. And it wasn't as if I was that hungry – I'd only just had breakfast. But there amongst the frilly undies I realised how much I hated being stony broke, how much I loathed my life, how it was time to turn things around. There was a bra I wanted, a nice lacy one. Only £10.99 for crying out loud. And I hadn't got the money. And I wanted it. Why shouldn't I have it, I thought to myself? Other people bought bras without having to shag their foster father for his small change. I'd never got as far as nicking stuff before, but it crossed my mind then.

And I'd found myself wondering where I was going with my life. I was seventeen years old, shagged anything that moved, and was about as aimless as a drunk pissing into a toilet. Mum and Dad would have been appalled.

Dad had left a letter for me. A suicide note, I suppose you'd call it. I'd only read it once and then stuck it away. It had made me too angry. But the night before I'd unhooked the clasps of the picture frame which held Mum and Dad's wedding photo and pulled out the letter from the back.

Darling Isabella,

Things you need to know: there are a few share certificates in a brown envelope in the desk, don't think they're worth much, but you must have them. There's also a life insurance policy that should ensure you have a comfortable future – I'm sorry to say I'm worth more to you dead than alive.

Don't let the cortisone cream run out, and don't forget to brush your teeth. Aunty Suzy says she will take care of you, and I'm sure she'll do a better job than me. She's promised she will.

I'm sorry that I'm not going to be there myself. But know that you were loved. Know that when you were a baby, chasing cats, chewing through electric cables and opening the fridge door before you could even walk, you made my heart sing. Know how proud I was when you won school running races and beat me at Scrabble. You're a clever girl, I know you'll go far. Know how much I loved holding you close, wrapping my arms round you on the sofa as we read stories together, and how often I watched you sleeping at night with your golden face blissful on the pillow. Please know that if I thought there was another way, I'd take it. Please forgive me.

Be strong. Make me proud.

I'll be watching over you, always, Daddy.

I'd been offered a place at a convent by the social worker that week. It made my stomach twist at the thought of all those nuns in their spooky outfits. But I'd get some really good teaching – there was a school attached that had a good academic record. And I wouldn't have to keep moving on. Foster kids don't get much choice about where we end up, but sometimes there are options. I'd already told the social worker I wasn't interested in dormitories and religion – all that salvation and saintliness. I'd long ago decided God must exist, because somebody was out there, wreaking havoc in my subsection. As a result I didn't much care for all that love that went on for him. And as for Catholicism? Who'd want to put faith in a religion which, as the saying goes, makes a sin out of sex, and a sacred act out of drinking alcohol? But there, amongst the Marks & Sparks undies, I found myself thinking again. There was an opportunity to get myself out of this hole. If I could just turn off the self-destruct button, I might succeed at something, I thought to myself. I wasn't sure at what. But I wouldn't be dirt poor any more. I'd decided, then, to do what it took to get ahead. I'd put up with Jesus and his God squad, for a chance at getting myself sorted out.

And that's how I ended up at St Michael's Academy. And for nearly two years I was as good as gold. No sex and enough church time to guarantee me a place in heaven. It was during that time that I came up with the idea of marrying someone rich. I like to think it was God himself who put the idea in my head, but really it was a Marilyn Monroe film.

17

Christmas arrives in LA with a rash of oversized plastic Christmas trees, sprayed with genuine spruce essence. And I'm just planning a trip to take the kids shopping for their own Christmas tree because no one else seems to be bothering to get one for them when Stephen phones me on my mobile phone from New York, where he's away on business. 'Tell the kids we're going to have Christmas at the condo in Aspen,' he barks.

'Condo? What condo?'

'And I'd like you to come too,' he says, all business-like. 'You'd be paid double time. Can you come?'

'I'd love to.'

'Great. Pearl will tell you the details.' He hangs up.

Pearl is going to have Christmas with Brett in LA. They've found an apartment in Beverly Hills, and they'll be decorating it and having some quiet time together before the wedding, which is to be on New Year's Eve. The minute I get back to LA from Aspen, I've got to leap on a plane to Vegas. Talk about jet-setting it. I can't believe my own life sometimes.

'Are we going to be taking the jet?' Craig asks when I tell him his Christmas plans. Turns out he's never flown on a commercial flight, not even once. He's never known what it's like to wait in a crowded departure lounge.

'Yes,' I tell him. 'But you've got to be good. No tantrums.'

'Goody, goody, goody,' Marcie sings, dancing round her bedroom. 'We're going to Aspen, we're going to Aspen.'

'Goody, goody, goody,' echoes Logan, caught up in the excitement.

Getting the kids ready for a skiing holiday is an uphill struggle, without any chair lifts for help. I've got to buy Marcie new salopettes, Craig needs new ski boots, Logan needs new everything. And there's still heaps of Christmas shopping to do. What the hell do you buy the family who already has everything? And to make matters really interesting, Stephen has asked me to potty train Logan, which means so far just about everything has been covered in poo.

Fortunately, I've stopped getting lost every time I get behind the wheel of the car. 'Bella, why are we on the 405 passing signs for San Diego?' Marcie used to quiz me from the back seat as we were nipping to the shops. Only in LA can getting lost mean a two-hundred-mile diversion.

For a place that prides itself on tinsel, Tinseltown's sparkle becomes pretty lacklustre, I'd say, in the run-up to Christmas. While out Christmas shopping, with the temperature soaring into the eighties, the kids and I pop into a hotel for a lemonade, and come across twenty men dressed in fake beards and red jumpsuits, standing around a swimming pool yelling 'Ho, ho, ho' to each other. Fortunately, the worldly-wise children at my side seem to require no explanation. They tell me soothingly, as if it might be me who is disappointed, 'It's okay, Bella, those are just the fake Santas.' And they're right. Turns out the men are graduates of a Santa Training Institute.

Then there's the queue of people we find at our local shopping mall waiting to meet a bare-chested muscular hunk, hanging around outside Gap, wearing nothing but a suntan, tight trousers, and a furry Santa hat balanced over his long flowing locks. He isn't famous – just muscular. And for five dollars we could have our photo taken with him, instead of Santa in his grotto a few steps away. Many women, as well as several men, are. But the kids aren't interested on the grounds that he isn't giving away any toys.

Bing Crosby's 'White Christmas' gets piped into every sunshine-drenched corner, images of snowflakes and snowmen fill the shop windows, and all the houses get covered in Christmas lights. The competition in some streets is so fierce, I'm surprised aircraft don't mistake them for runways.

But really, it's not like Christmas at home. I think people are more festive back in Britain. Walk into any pub and it will be packed with rosy faces wishing goodwill to everyone. Go to the shops, and there will be a feeling of generosity that I don't believe anyone at the Beverly Center can know anything about. Just take a walk down the street on Christmas Day. Even if it's raining, strangers will be wishing Happy Christmas to each other. Bonhomie is what the Brits do well . . . and I must be feeling homesick or something because this nostalgia has got to stop. I didn't go to all this trouble to make a new life only to get misty-eyed about dreary old Britain.

Mind you, it would help if I'd got just a little bit further in my plan to marry a millionaire. Finding alternative millionaires to go on dates with hasn't been exactly easy, as prescribed by the book under my bed. In fact, number of dates so far? Zero. Number of potential dates: zero. The author doesn't explain quite how to collar Bill Gates while hanging out at Toddler Time with a two year old. Or how to flirt successfully with movie moguls while waiting at school gates with a load of overdressed mums. The only interested movie mogul I've met so far has been Stephen and you could scarcely call the charity ball fiasco a successful date. After the incident with the vibrator, it's too embarrassing to even look Jamie in the eye either. I hope to God he's not coming to Aspen too.

But I'm not ready to give up yet. Aspen is going to be full of prospective rich husbands. It's where movie moguls merge with oil magnates, who brush shoulders with publishing tycoons, who mingle with bankers, who talk business with internet barons. It's where the crème de la crème come to party and I'm going to be a doll in the fur-lined ski jacket that Pearl's promised to loan me.

By the time we all pile into the Gulfstream IV on Christmas Eve, I'm so exhausted after getting the kids packed up that I'm very nearly achieving that emaciated look that's so fashionable. Stephen's cheerful as he sinks into one of the leather chairs and takes the beer offered to him by our own personal air hostess. 'Ever been on one of these?' he asks jovially, as we all climb aboard.

'All the time,' I tell him and he laughs raucously.

Maria is coming with us to cook the turkey. She clambers into a back seat with me. And at the last minute, dishevelled as always, Jamie climbs on board.

'Hey, Jamie,' cry Marcie and Craig together, rushing to hug him and forgetting their argument over who sat where. 'I thought you weren't coming?' says Craig. 'I thought you always had Christmas with your mum.'

'I wanted to have Christmas with you instead,' he says affectionately.

'Did you bring me a Christmas present?' asks Marcie, fixing him hard with puppy-dog eyes.

'Lots,' says Jamie.

'What?'

'Not telling.'

Then he notices me at the back of the plane. His face breaks into a broad grin. 'Hi, Bella. You had any interesting gifts lately?'

'Oh yes, plenty,' I say, feeling the colour rising in my cheeks. 'I have everything a girl ever needs.'

Flying in a private jet is everything you would imagine it is. It's like a private party at thirty thousand feet. There's space and luxury such as you could never imagine from an economy-class seat on British Airways. You can put your feet up and lounge around. You can do pirouettes, and gymnastics, you can stand on your head if you feel like it. And Marcie does. Craig goes into the cockpit to watch the pilot. And Logan falls asleep on my lap.

Aspen is beautiful. There's thick snow everywhere and craggy mountain peaks all around cutting you off from the rest of the world. I feel like I'm walking into a Christmas card and keep expecting to meet Santa or an elf or two. Except that mostly what you meet in Aspen are the people who wear the latest in ski fashions and those silly yeti boots with fur on the outside that just get wet.

The Shawes' condo is on the edge of town overlooking a creek and the mountains beyond. In the understatement of the year, Stephen had described it as a modest holiday home. All I can say is there was a bedroom for each of us, with enough left over for a passing coach of tourists.

I have my work cut out unpacking the children's clothes as they cavort around the open-plan living room putting out stockings for Santa over an enormous fireplace. Pearl has organised a floral decorator to come in to dress a ten-foot Christmas tree which towers in one corner. Other decorations abound in a way that only Hollywood achieves – over-the-top wreaths, table decorations, and tasteful, if enormous, flower arrangements. Boxes of food and wine are stacked up in the kitchen. Christmas, it seems, has been delivered. Stephen disappears to talk business with a neighbour, and Jamie stays to help me put the kids to bed.

There's something super-attractive about seeing a man take time with children. That caring side is so much sexier than muscles. He mock-wrestles with Craig, discusses the merits of tutu fashion with Marcie with all the earnestness of a fashionista and produces water pistols for everyone at bathtime so that we all get completely soaked. Then he reads them stories and listens to their jokes, and by the time he's tucking them into their beds I'm totally in love with him.

I'd found myself watching him as he threw himself into the children's games. I liked the way he pushed back the tendrils of untidy hair from his face, the way he rolled his shirt sleeves up to reveal a mass of dark masculine hairs, the way he held back his strength and allowed the children to pummel him. I'd caught his gaze several times, and felt an unexpected stab of joy that he should look my way. I'd realised then how much I was enjoying this, and how much I was yearning for him to look my way again. I'd felt the warmth of his hand too, as he'd insisted we all link hands for a game he'd devised. I'd held on willingly and breathed in his scent as we all danced absurdly in a circle round the room. But then the children let go and abandoned the game, leaving Jamie and me holding hands still. He'd held on, refused to let me go, and for a second he stared at me, long enough for my insides to melt, long enough to suggest a connection between us. I'd yearned suddenly to lean in to him and have him hold me close. Could he be interested in me, I'd wondered? But there were children who wanted his attention, and the moment passed.

And anyway, I don't do falling in love. Love is for those who can afford it. Love is emotional involvement that only leads to tears when it all goes horribly wrong. What makes a girl secure is diamonds on her fingers and six figures in her bank account, not kisses and cuddles followed by a broken heart. Just look at Pearl for starters.

We're all up early the following morning. The children have opened their stockings before I've even woken up. Logan comes bouncing into my room to show me a

Thomas the Tank Engine. 'Choo, choo,' he says, sending it on a course up my bed. By the time I'm dressed, Stephen is bounding around the living room in that mauve tracksuit – somehow it seems to have come with us – delivering presents.

Not being part of the family, I'm keen to let them have their space. Anyway, I need tea. I go to find Maria in the kitchen. But Stephen stops me en route and presents me with a small box. It's a Cartier watch. What is it with rich men and watches? There's an envelope attached. In it is five hundred dollars.

'A small thank you for all the hard work you have put in with the children. It's appreciated.'

Blimey. This is turning into a good Christmas. And I haven't even had breakfast yet.

'Thank you,' I say and give him a peck on the cheek. He smiles benignly. Then Marcie comes running over and puts her little arm round my neck. She presses her rosy cheek against mine. 'Did you get me a present?' she whispers.

Actually, I was rather pleased with the presents I'd got the kids. I'd tried to be ingenious rather than extravagant, since extravagance is all they know. Logan got Play-doh. Cost me four dollars and got way more attention than the $300 pedal firetruck his dad had bought for him. Craig got a build-your-own-rocket kit that runs on baking soda, and Marcie a book about fairies that came with collapsible fairy wings made out of netting and a wand that you had to decorate yourself.

'Shall we make the wand now?' she demands and leads me to a table where she scatters glitter everywhere.

I wasn't sure whether I was meant to get Stephen a present. Wasn't sure what the form was. Maria said she never bothered. Said they were richer than her, and they already had everything. Seemed about right to me, but now I felt perhaps I should have.

After breakfast, Stephen and Jamie disappear to ski together. I am to take Craig and Marcie to ski school, and Logan, who has never been in the snow before, is to try out the nursery slopes. Easy enough, surely? Except that Logan, being the Californian child he is – I have a life and death struggle with him every morning just to put on a T-shirt – is not happy at the prospect of clothes. I'm three disputes down before even an undergarment has gone over his head, let alone salopettes, gloves, hats, boots, sweater, ski jacket and – least likely of all – ski goggles.

By 10 a.m. all Christmas goodwill towards men is over. Logan is prostrate on his bedroom floor banging his fists into the carpet yelling, 'Damn, damn, damn.' Marcie is angry because I haven't packed the pink polo neck sweater which matches her new pink salopettes and Craig, who is attempting to dress himself, has his sweater on inside out, salopettes on back to front, and is tearful because he can't find his goggles.

Craig and Marcie's lesson is booked for 11 a.m. And it will take fifteen minutes – ten if I race – to get there in the SUV which has been left for me. Did I mention that we also have to call in at the ski rental shop to be outfitted for skis? Did I also mention that Aspen is at 7,900 feet, and just climbing out of bed brings on the same degree of breathlessness as an hour at the gym?

The central heating doesn't help either. By

10.30 a.m., what with all the layers I'm wearing, I'm ready to pass out from heat exhaustion. But at least the children are dressed. Well, almost. Logan won't wear the jacket, but he's got everything else on. Now it's just me I have to organise. Money: check. Sunglasses. Camera (Stephen was insistent on pictures). Juice boxes. Snacks. Check. I billet them inside the pockets of my jacket, giving me a strange lumpy look, but at this stage who cares.

'Okay, kids, let's get in the car,' I plead. We may still do it if they're fast at the ski rental place. But now Logan has had an accident in his trousers and needs changing. Quick, back inside, to remove all the clothes I'd fought so hard to put on. Ten minutes later we're back at the car, but Marcie's boot has fallen off and she's got a wet sock. No matter, we'll buy her a new one at the rental shop.

We drive to the rental shop, but there's a queue of at least twenty people. Climbing Everest in slippers must surely be easier than this. I find the manager and wave one of the hundred-dollar bills Stephen had given me to buy the kids lunch with under his nose, explaining how desperate I am for us to be kitted out at once. It's amazing what money will do. Marcie and Craig are only ten minutes late for their lesson. Now I only have Logan to deal with.

Skiing at Aspen is like one giant outdoor cocktail party. Everyone seems to know each other. And at the bottom of Exhibition chairlift where the steeper slopes lose pace and ease up enough to make a gentler nursery slope, it looks as if Hollywood society has simply transplanted itself here. I get a good chance to ogle it because Logan, who refuses to let me attach the skis to his boots, just wants to play in the snow. We're there all morning, pottering around, throwing snowballs, breathing in the gloriously fresh air and sizing up the ski wear. It's not a bad way to spend Christmas at all. And it gives me the space to muse on the touch of Jamie Shawe. Just the thought of him holding my hand last night gives me goosebumps. Could there have been something between us, or was I just imagining it? Was I letting myself get carried away? I'm just thinking to myself how wonderful it might be to allow oneself the luxury of falling in love, safe in the knowledge that the object of your desire happens to be rich, and how amazing it would be to snag a man like Jamie, when, out of the corner of my eye, I catch sight of Stephen and Jamie in the crowd lining up for the chairlift.

Their faces are rosy and there's a line of white snow down the side of Jamie's ski suit where he must have fallen over. And I'm about to call out to them, when I spy a blonde curling her fur-lined arms round Jamie. She's wearing a fuchsia-pink ski suit with matching earmuffs and lipstick. He's clearly dazzled – and not just by the ski suit. They talk for some time. He laughs, she laughs. They kiss each other on the lips in the way that people who are very familiar with each other do. The last I see is the pair of them on a chairlift together laughing all the way to the top.

There, I must have been imagining it after all.

18

Jamie would be easier to impress if I could ski. I mean, it looks easy enough. Fake it till you make it, has always been my mantra. 'Of course I can ski,' I'd told him on what we'd call Boxing Day morning back at home but no one here calls anything, except the day after Christmas Day. After a pancake breakfast it had been decided that Maria was going to look after Logan, who was showing the first signs of a cold after refusing to wear his jacket yesterday. Stephen was displaying a rare moment of paternal interest in Marcie and Craig and wanted to ski with them, and Jamie had asked why didn't I come along too. And even though there had been a lot of huffing and puffing to get myself from the ski rental shop on to the chairlift with these wretched things strapped to my feet, I'd made it. But now I was looking down Northstar, which is one of the hardest runs you can do – a long vertical drop, down which skiers were throwing themselves without a care in the world, like kids on a playground slide.

'Oh, shit,' I say, leaning on my poles, which I've got wedged into the snow – the only things that are stopping me from sliding over the edge to certain death.

'Come on, Bella,' Stephen yells from way down

below. Marcie and Craig are even further ahead – small black dots in a sea of white.

'Oh, shit,' I say again, as I try to move backwards, but find my skis are crossed over each other. And the poles are in the way. And I can't move forward or back. And now I'm on my arse, clinging to a small shelf of flat snow. Jamie, fortunately or unfortunately – I'm not sure which – has yet to throw himself over the edge of the run. He leans over and offers me his ski pole to pull myself up on. I take it and I'm up. I'm looking good. But only for a second.

'Confession time?' he says with that crooked smile, looking down at me in the snow and offering his pole once more.

I stare at him defiantly. 'I don't know what you mean.'

'Don't you? Come on then, I'll race you down the mountain.'

'Okay. Okay. I confess. I don't know how to ski. Are you going to help me or just stand there and smirk?'

Jamie throws back his head and laughs. I throw a snowball at him and it gets him in the face.

'Now do you want my help or not?' he says, wiping snow off stubbled cheeks that I suddenly feel an overwhelming urge to touch. 'Come on.'

It takes the best part of the morning to get me off that slope. Jamie skis backwards, holding my hands, and guides my skis into a V-shape between his legs. We bend and turn, bend and turn, leaving the trail of a wiggling serpent in the snow. We're so close I can feel the warmth of his breath against the cold. I fall a lot and he laughs mercilessly every time and tells me to get off my 'sorry ass'. And eventually we make it down, and I might not have been the coolest skier on the slope, but I was the one that got all the personal attention, and I loved every minute.

We meet Stephen and the kids in a bustling self-service cafeteria at the bottom of the hill. They are on their desserts by the time I rest my sorry ass down on a bench.

'Where were you?' Stephen says, licking his lips over a giant ice-cream sundae. 'I thought you said you could ski.'

'She can now,' says Jamie with a grin, resting down a tray with a plate of chips for us to share.

The children laugh and we're all enjoying the joke when Miss Fuchsia arrives at our table.

'Mind if I join you?' she trills, putting down her tray and making a big deal of swooshing back her long blond hair.

'Jennifer, sweetie, of course,' says Jamie, leaping to his feet, kissing her hard on the lips and settling her in a chair next to him.

'How ya doin', Jen?' says Stephen. 'Happy holidays.'

'Jennifer, this is Bella, our nanny. Bella, this is Jennifer,' says Jamie.

'Bit old for a nanny, aren't you, darlin'?' Jennifer coos at Jamie without even looking at me, and running manicured fingertips along his arm. He catches her hand and gives it a squeeze.

Jamie tries to include me in the conversation. She's an old school friend of his and works in documentaries too, he explains. I say, 'How nice' and look interested, but she's not interested in me. And nor is he any more. I feel the crush of disappointment.

Meanwhile, the kids are itching to get back on the slope, and now that Stephen's finished scraping the bottom of his ice-cream bowl, he wants to get back out there too. Jamie stuffs as many chips in his mouth as he can and gets up to leave, collecting together his gloves and goggles.

'Well, Bella, are you up for another run?' he asks.

'Think I'll give it a miss,' I say. I'm not sure my legs will ever walk again, let alone ski.

'Come on, Jen. You're up for it, aren't you?' he demands.

'Of course I am, honey. Which side of the mountain are we going?'

Stiff doesn't even begin to describe what my legs are feeling. And boy am I glad to get out of those ski boots. It feels like I'm walking on air when they're off. I hang around the bottom of the ski runs, where all the skiers finally descend and load their skis on to car roofs. It's a pretty afternoon – crisp and clear. The atmosphere in these mountains reminds me of champagne, all bubbly and sparkling. I can see why people go on about it. I find a seat at an outdoor café where I can sit and soak up some sun. I'd buy a mug of hot chocolate, but it's ten dollars a cup and if they think I'm paying those kinds of prices, they're out of their minds. But no one seems to object to my sitting here.

And I'm busy watching how those who can afford a ten-dollar cup of hot chocolate without wincing live, when I see a small figure come careering down the slope. He's going very fast, clearly out of control. He just misses one skier and then, crash, hits another. There's an explosion of snow, skis, poles and flying limbs. And even then they still continue to slide down the hill. Eventually they come to a stop, only a few hundred yards from where I'm sitting. But the bodies don't move. Then a boyish voice begins to wail – a deep, bone-chilling cry of pain – and suddenly I'm aware that it's a familiar voice.

'Craig,' I yell and start to run up the mountain. 'Craig, are you all right?'

Other skiers are by his side by the time I reach him, but they don't seem to be doing anything but gawping. There's a vivid red pool of blood growing larger in the snow around his face and his leg is contorted into an unnatural position that makes me flinch. I don't need a doctor's certificate to know it's broken.

'Quickly, someone, call an ambulance,' I shout back down the mountain to the café below. 'Craig, sweetheart.' He looks so grateful that I'm there. And I'm surprised at how intensely I feel for him. He's not just a snotty kid any more, I realise suddenly – he's someone I care about. I stroke his tiny, frozen hand, but I'm frightened to try to move him. He's still wailing and looking scared. I cradle his head in my lap, wiping away the snot and blood that is gushing from his nose.

'You're going to be okay,' I tell him. 'Breathe deep. We're going to get a doctor.'

The other skier seems unharmed, apart from a long gash on his cheek where Craig's ski pole must have struck. He leans over and asks Craig if he can move his other leg. But he's crying so hard now, he's not listening. And it seems like for ever till the ambulance arrives. Meanwhile, the crowd around us is getting bigger all the time.

'Let me through.' I hear Stephen's voice in the throng. He shoves his way in with Jamie, Marcie and Jennifer behind him. He'd heard Craig and recognised his cry too.

'Craig? Oh my God.' He kneels down beside him.

'Oh, God, there's blood,' squeals Jennifer, and throws her head into Jamie's shoulder. 'Oh, I can't take blood. Oh, oh, oh.' She's screeching and squirming like a bad actress. And the performance is ... well, it's a performance. 'Jamie, darling, get me away from here. I can't do blood.'

Jamie tells her calmly to go on down the hill. He'll meet her later. But he stays to hold Craig's other hand.

'What happened, Bella?' he whispers. 'Did you see?'

Eventually the ambulance arrives and parks outside the café. A crew races up the snow with a stretcher and gently transfers Craig's bent little body on to it. 'Bella, don't leave me,' he cries pitifully. 'Please stay with me.'

'Course I will, sweetheart,' I say.

There's only room for one extra in the ambulance, the crew tells us. And Stephen is still in his skis. Not to mention looking pretty clueless for someone so powerful.

'Stephen, get out of your ski boots and drive the car round to the hospital,' I bark at him. But he's doing his stunned mullet impersonation again. 'We'll meet you there,' I yell. He doesn't move. 'Jamie,' I order. 'Get your father out of his ski boots and drive him and Marcie round to the hospital. Now.'

By the evening Craig is heavily sedated in a hospital bed in his own private room overlooking a snowy car park.

His leg is in plaster and there is a whole sunset of colours stretching over his nose from underneath his eye – pinks, blues and purples. He finally looks peaceful. I'd sent Stephen home in the end, with Marcie. All he could do was pace up and down shouting at the doctors, threatening to sue if they didn't do it right. He was a man who liked to be in control of everything, and this played in to all his worst fears, because he was helpless. Marcie hadn't helped either because she'd got hysterical, convincing herself that Craig was going to die.

'Stephen, why don't you take Marcie back to the condo?' I'd suggested eventually, once we'd heard the verdict and knew that Craig was going to be fine. 'I'll stay with him, so he's got someone here when he wakes up.'

Stephen looked uncertain.

'Go on. Everything's going to be fine,' I said, sounding just like my mother used to when I scraped a knee. 'He'll be laughing about this tomorrow and bugging us to sign his plaster. Go on, off with you. I'll phone you if there's any news.'

'Promise?' said Stephen, looking heartily relieved.

'Promise.'

Jamie decided that he would stay to keep me company, and then disappeared to find us some coffee, leaving me to watch over my charge. Craig is laid out carefully in the centre of the bed, arms tucked neatly by his side, head suitably positioned on the pillow. I pull a blanket up to his chin and his shoulders twitch in protest. Even when he's asleep, there's something sad about him. There's still an air of disappointment on his face.

Jamie arrives back in the room carrying two styrofoam cups from a vending machine. 'Looks cherubic, doesn't he?' he says quietly, handing me one of them. I nod. 'I broke my arm when I was eight. Fell off a horse. All I can remember now is my skin itching like hell under the plaster. What about you, you ever broken anything?'

With my kind of history, it's easier to just say no. The stories get too long and complicated. It's peaceful in the hospital. Out in the corridor, there's the occasional sound of footsteps or squeak of a wheelchair being pushed along, but otherwise it has the same air of serenity as a church. I lean back in the armchair by Craig's bed and put my feet up on a coffee table on which some journals have been arranged like a fan. Jamie takes the other chair and chooses a yachting magazine to flick through.

'Thanks for all your help out there,' he says earnestly. 'How'd you learn to be so calm in a crisis?'

I hadn't given it much thought really. I guess I'd been taught the hard way over the years. I've always hated drama queens anyway. Mum had an old school friend, my aunty Bev, who was a fearful drama queen back in Guildford. Her children never had colds, it was always flu or pneumonia. If she had a problem, it was never just one, it was always compounded by several – her car breaking down, her house falling apart and the dog vomiting on the carpet. And she'd deliver it all in one martyred, breathless tirade that said, 'Aren't I wonderful for putting up with it all?' And I remember my mum patiently listening to her stream of crises and always soothing her in some way. She'd say it was just

Aunty Bev needing some attention, because she'd never had any when she was young. She told me it was good to be forgiving. She was always soothing people, my mum.

'Think I must get it from my mum,' I say quietly, and wonder what happened to Aunty Bev. All my parents' friends just seemed to disappear into the woodwork after their deaths.

'You must miss her a lot,' Jamie murmurs.

'I do,' I say, realising that Stephen must have told him she was dead. I'd told Stephen eventually one evening when we were watching some movie or other. He hadn't reacted, just nodded and grunted, and I'd been grateful.

'Must be hard growing up without any parents.' He fixes his deep brown eyes on me and adopts the usual expression.

'Nah, piece of cake,' I say, doing my usual joke. 'None of your parents' baggage to carry with you.'

But he doesn't laugh. Instead, he says: 'I think you're great. I mean, you seem so together. So ... so ...' he pauses to consider the word carefully before eventually spitting it out, 'so ... undamaged.'

'Ah, but you haven't seen the mean, cruel and twisted side of me yet,' I say, grimacing. 'I'm a monster after dark.'

He still doesn't laugh. 'How did they die?'

It's a funny thing but people don't normally ask me that. They might be curious to know, but they're usually too frightened of what they might unleash by asking. Sometimes I let people off the hook and simply tell the basic facts, just to let them know I'm not some crazy girl who's going to mess up their shirts with tears. I tell them deadpan about the aneurism, the car crash, the debts, the foster homes. But I don't usually lavish the story with details and heartache because what's the point? What can anyone do about it now? But something compels me this time to tell Jamie something closer to the truth than the bullshit I usually churn out.

Jamie listens quietly, leaning forward in the chair, hands hanging between his knees. Another wheelchair squeaks past in the corridor outside, echoing in the silence. Then suddenly I feel an overwhelming urge to cry. I don't know why. I never cry.

'The hardest thing is wondering what my life might have been like if they'd stuck around,' I blurt out. 'It's all the what ifs. What if I'd gone to college, then I might have got a decent job and not been so fucking poor. What if I'd grown up in one place instead of twenty billion, then maybe I could fucking sleep at night. What if I'd had someone to take care of me, then maybe I wouldn't have to be so bloody brave all the time. Maybe I wouldn't be so compelled to turn everything into a bloody joke.'

I'm surprised at how angry I sound. I mean, I often sound angry inside my head, but I don't usually unleash it on people. Jamie reaches over to touch my arm, but I pull it away and escape to the window, staring into my own reflection because it's dark outside now. The girl staring back at me frightens me, she looks so indignant. Her eyes are spilling over with tears. It's not the me I'm used to.

I take a deep breath. 'Sorry,' I sniff. 'I told you I turn into a monster after dark.'

'Don't think anything of it,' he says and puts his hands on my shoulders and massages them.

'It's just . . . it's just . . . sometimes I wonder who I really am. God, that sounds so Californian. I mean, sometimes I just wonder if I might have been someone else if I hadn't been me.' I laugh, knowing it sounds ridiculous.

Jamie laughs too. 'Well, I happen to like who you are, whoever that might be.'

I turn to face him and he brushes away the tears with his hand.

'Sorry,' I say again and stare down at my shoes. I'm feeling heartily ashamed of the outburst. But he stoops down to kiss a wet patch of cheek, and cradles my face in his two hands. He kisses me tenderly at first, and then long and hard with a passion that I've never experienced before.

I spend the rest of the week eating hospital food, playing Junior Scrabble with Craig, and watching the clock for Jamie to visit. A camp bed is set up in the room so I can sleep with Craig, and pretty soon we fall into something of a daily routine. He is dosed up with painkillers, but buoyant about how brave he is and what kudos he'll get back at school with a leg in plaster. Stephen comes and goes – between ski runs and parties – and Jamie does indeed visit, every day.

He always arrives with gifts for Craig – Lego, art kits, table football – and we sit and play with them on the bed together, while I get to know that he studied documentary film at Berkeley, that he thinks he must be the only straight man on the planet who loves disco music, that he prefers organic food to McDonald's, that opera ought to be for everyone young and old, that he's a champion Lego spaceship builder and that there are a hundred and one different things you can build out of styrofoam coffee cups.

I long for him to hold me close again – it had felt so deliciously soothing and warm, like brandy on a cold day but without the kick in your belly, but I don't want the kids knowing what's going on, and certainly not

Stephen. I don't want my employer knowing my personal business. And anyway, there's one thing I need to clear up before we go any further.

'How's the love of my life,' he whispers in my ear at the hospital coffee vending machine one afternoon while Craig is sleeping.

'I don't know. How is she?' I ask.

'You,' he says emphatically. 'You.'

'Sure it's not your friend in the pink?' I say somewhat boldly. 'She looked like a love in your life.' All right, it's a bit brazen. But I want to know. If Jamie is going to consume my every waking thought, then I need to be aware where the potholes are on the runway.

'Oh, she's just an old friend,' he says, looking somewhat crestfallen.

'Looked like more than that to me.' I give him a flirtatious smile, because I don't want him to think I'm a nag before we've even started.

'Okay, confession time,' he sighs.

My heart sinks. Damn it. I knew there was more.

'She's an old girlfriend. We dated way, way back. And I didn't know I was going to bump into her here, and I think maybe she'd like to rekindle things. And she's very flirty and kinda fun. But the truth is, I fell for you the minute I saw you wiping jelly through your hair and wearing Coco Pops on your shirt. I don't know whether you've noticed, but girls tend not to do that around here.' He smiles deliciously. 'And I loved that you looked so ridiculous in your Cinderella costume—'

'Ugly sister, actually.'

'And the truth is you've made such a difference to our wildly dysfunctional and crazy family. You were the reason I came along on this trip. I'd normally have Christmas with my mum, but ... I know this sounds crazy, but I wanted to see if I stood a chance.'

If there's a loud clanging noise to be heard, it's my heart crashing to the floor in shock. Could this be my very own happy ever after? Could I have actually fallen for someone who loves me back? This kind of stuff doesn't happen to me. 'Surely some mistake,' I hear a voice inside my head. But it's too late to pinch myself to see if it's a dream because he's wrapped his big, warm arms round me again and I'm falling hook, line and sinker.

He takes me out to dinner at a French bistro that night. We go straight from the hospital. It's a casual kind of place anyway, and I like that. I feel more comfortable when I don't feel out of my league.

'*Une bouteille du Beaujolais Villages, s'il vouz plaît,*' he asks the waitress as we get seated.

'Show-off,' I say, and he laughs.

'So tell me everything about you. I want to know everything,' he says, leaning forward. I feel flattered that he's interested, but after my meltdown I'd rather not be in the spotlight.

'Like what? What do you want to know?'

'Um, let's see.' He holds his stubbly chin and thinks hard. 'I want to know all the things we're going to disagree on ... It's good to know these things ahead of time.'

'Like what?'

'Like . . .' He pauses to think. 'Do you think that it's right to put oranges in a green salad?'

'Don't be daft.'

'I'm serious. I want to know. Do you like fruit in salad? Some people do, you know.'

'Actually, no. Fruit should be in fruit salad only. Only lettuce and cucumber in a green salad.'

'Thank God. There, see, no arguments in the kitchen then.' He makes a face and I laugh. But he's on to his next question. 'Who's the greatest R'n'B singer of all time?'

Everyone knows that. 'Marvin Gaye.'

'Ah ha!' Jamie is pleased with this answer. 'My thoughts precisely.' He pauses to think of another question. 'For or against gay marriage?'

I hadn't really thought about it before. I hesitate. 'For it, I suppose.'

'Sure about that?'

'Think so. Doesn't hurt anyone, so I don't see it's anyone else's business.'

'There, see. A true liberal.'

'I am?'

'Sure you are. See, I knew we'd get on. Do you get up early or late?'

'Early.'

'So do I. Do you think Navratilova's going to win Wimbledon next year?'

'I thought she'd retired.'

'Good, trick question. Who's going to win the NFL this year?'

'I don't bloody know.'

'Neither do I. See, there's nothing we disagree on.'

Jamie overwhelms me. He's funny, charming, knowledgeable. There's not a single topic he hasn't got an opinion on. But he wants to know what I think too. I feel so underqualified to talk about a lot of what he's interested in. Do I think there ought to be a female president? What do I think about the oil situation? What do I think is the solution in the Middle East? What should America be doing to stop global warming? It's not that I'm not aware of these issues, and I do my best, but I'm not exactly up on it all. So as our steak frites arrive, I try to steer the subject on to something I know more about.

'Tell me about your movie,' I say. 'When will it be out?'

He laughs. 'I haven't even started filming it yet.'

'But you told me you were making one.'

'I am. Well, I hope I will. But it takes ages for a film to be green-lit. There are hundreds – probably millions – of films "being made".' He raises his fingers to make air quotes. 'But no one gets the camera out until the money's in the bank.' He sighs. 'It's a frustratingly slow process. First you've got to come up with a proposal and a script, then you've got to put it to the money people, then maybe you try and find some actors, or maybe you try to get a big name attached, then maybe you're more likely to get the money . . .'

'But yours is a documentary. You don't need actors.'

'But I still need money to make it. It all takes time.'

I like his readiness to explain. I find it fascinating and I tell him as much. 'Well, you're a good listener. I like telling you things. Did you know you frown when you concentrate and it makes you more beautiful than ever?'

'And your chin juts out when you flirt.'

He smiles. 'The girl who squirms at compliments.'

*

The relief on Craig's face is conspicuous when we get home. At the end of the week, they'd decided he was fit to travel back in the jet, and it had been a horrendous day for me. I'd had to get him out of bed and dressed for the first time since the accident, and also pack up all the children's gear including three juggernauts' worth of Christmas presents.

'Thanks for staying with me,' he says as I tuck him and the other children into bed.

'It's nice to be home, isn't it?' And I realise this monstrous house feels like home to me now. 'All safe in your own little bed. Now, you know I'm going to be gone tomorrow, don't you? I'm going to Pearl's wedding. Your mum's coming to collect you in the morning and you're going to stay with her.'

Craig sighs unhappily.

'Oh, come on. Your mum loves you, and I know you love her,' I say cheerily.

'But she left us,' he says crossly. 'She left us behind. Why would she do that, if she loved us?' He juts out his jaw defiantly. 'Well, I don't love her any more.'

Ah. A tricky one. 'Sometimes grown-ups are forced into situations that they can't control,' I say gently. 'It's not your mum's fault she's not here. Really it isn't. When you grow up you'll understand. I know she loves you desperately.' I give him a kiss on his bruised little cheek.

Downstairs Jamie is watching the St Louis Rams hammer the Cincinnati Bengals in a game of football that looks closer to open war than anything I think of as football. I know he's waiting for me. He'd been shooting me glances all the way home; so many, I was convinced

Stephen would notice. So I'd refused to look back, staring out of the window instead, and reading stories to the children.

'So,' he says, as I deliberately choose to sit on the sofa opposite him, not next to him.

'So,' I say back with a grin. I can hear Stephen bustling about in his office at the other end of the house.

'So what's next? More dinners? More pickup lines?'

'Don't tell me you've got more,' I say with a sigh.

There's something fabulously tantalising about flirting with someone you haven't had sex with yet. Once you have sex, it all changes. Every woman knows that. It's like the itch has been scratched. There's no need for flirtation any more. No need to play coy, no need to tease. Just a simple touch along the arm before sex can send electrifying tingles everywhere. But after sex, that same touch means something else – the electrifying sizzle is gone. There's nothing daring about it at all.

And the timing of when to have sex is important too. You don't have to read *Cosmo* to know that. Men like to feel they've made a conquest, and if you were as easy to catch as a venereal disease, then it's all over. To give the impression you've been on more laps than a lapdog is tantamount to disaster. But you can't leave it too long either. If they think you're the iceberg that brought down the *Titanic* and you're never going to crack, they usually get bored and find someone else. You've got to waft sex at them, lure them in with the promise of it, rather like bakeries wafting yummy smells at you in supermarkets to get you to buy the bread.

The truth is I'm a little unnerved by how Jamie makes me feel. I always promised myself that I would never let infatuation blow my intentions away. I came here to marry for money, to put a line between me and the past. I've got to stick to that resolution. Jamie could be the billion-dollar prize – gorgeous, good, and gives me goosebumps every time he looks at me. But I must remember that those qualities are just bonuses. It's the fact that he's rich that makes him really worth hanging on to. Life in the convent is ingrained on my memory deeply enough to tell me that I don't ever, ever want to go back there.

In my *How to Marry the Rich* book, it says sex is an absolute no-no until you've got them down the aisle. Being a rich man's girlfriend isn't any use to you. It might yield a few fancy gifts, but you've got to marry them if you want to set your bank account up for the future. The problem is, it also says quite categorically that you're not to fall for them either. You've got to maintain a cool disinterest if you want to hook them.

I look across at Jamie on the sofa and a zap of lust shoots through my body. It's taking every inch of resolve not to throw myself at him now. But Stephen's only down the corridor and I'm off to Las Vegas early tomorrow, so it's going to have to wait. He walks over to sit next to me, and takes my hand. There's a serious expression on his face that I suspect means he cares. 'I want to know everything about you. I want to know what would make you happy,' he says tenderly. 'Tell me what you dream of.' There must be a million women in the world longing for a man to ask them that. Unfortunately I'm not sure I'm one of them. I've never been good at long, meaningful conversations – it's too reminiscent of counselling.

The only dream I can remember having after Dad died was him coming to rescue me, and apologising for having been away so long and wasn't it an awful thing that I was told he was dead when he wasn't. And I'd forgive him and then we'd drive off in his car, and go to the seaside maybe and eat ice creams and chat about Mum. And now I realise how stupid that must sound. So I grab the first thought that comes into my head.

'Oh, you know, a happy ever after, roses round the door, children in the backyard . . . big wad of money, all the usual stuff,' I say cheerfully, as if it's a joke, although it's not that far from the truth if I'm really honest.

Jamie doesn't say anything. The sports crowd roars with delight on the TV as the Rams score again. His gaze returns to the screen for a few minutes. Then the adverts pop up. 'So what are you doing tomorrow?' he asks.

'Vegas, dummy. I told you I was going to Vegas for Pearl's wedding.'

'Oh, yeah. That's right.' He pauses. 'Want company?'

'Sorry?'

'Got a date to take to the wedding with you? I like weddings.'

The author of *How to Marry the Rich* is very clear in her book about the rules you must follow in order to catch your rich mate. Having ensnared a potential husband, you've got to set certain tests to find out how rich he is. When he takes you out to dinner, you've got to pick out really expensive champagne, whether you like it or not, to see whether he flinches. You've got to research his job, and see how much he makes. You've got to find out where he lives and check out if he owns it.

I didn't have to work on any of that with Jamie because I already knew. His dad had set him up just fine. Not to mention that making documentaries isn't exactly waiting tables. And talk about flash with his cash – not only did he upgrade my airline seat to first class so that we could be together when we flew out to Vegas, but he reserved us a whole suite at the Wynn Hotel, where Pearl is staying, with two bedrooms and a living room in it, so that propriety could be observed. 'That way, you can choose where you want to sleep,' he'd said with a smirk as we checked in. I'd appreciated the gesture. The thing I really like about Jamie is he isn't pushy like other blokes. He's dead calm, dead patient. But Pearl had also reserved me a room, and, well, I was torn. But treat 'em mean keeps 'em keen, so I tell Jamie that I'll be using the room Pearl's booked, but I'll come and visit him in his suite. 'Whatever,' he says as I say goodbye to him in the lift, promising to meet him later.

Las Vegas is extraordinary. Of course it's only polite to hold one's tongue when talking about taste. Just because my idea of a romantic holiday destination is not Wizard of Oz themed carpeting, and a bed that turns into a faux Camelot castle, it doesn't mean I don't understand it could be someone else's. Still, it seems unbelievable to me that the over-amped fantasy town is America's top holiday destination. I mean, how can anyone think the labyrinth of casino tables, plastic façades and neon-lit streets are as beautiful as, say, a gently lapping seashore or an autumnal forest? And to get married here, amongst the clanging of change from all the fruit machines? Among the weary sighs of people losing money as they gamble? They've probably never seen a quiet little church in the English countryside, I tell myself. If ever I get as far as the altar, please God don't let it be a plastic one right here in Vegas.

Pearl seems happy with it regardless. I meet her in her suite, which is on the top floor. She throws her arms round me as the door flies open. It's an astonishing room with wall-to-wall windows overlooking the whole city and the brown shimmering desert beyond. I get vertigo just looking out. And inside there're fancy pillows and soft sofas and chocolates and more TVs than you could ever watch. Meanwhile, Pearl is on to the nitty-gritty of which shoes should she wear and should she wear her hair like this or like that? And don't I just adore the dress, which is splayed out across the king-sized bed like a dead swan? It's a Vera Wang, custom fitted to disguise her bump which is now hard to ignore. And which way should she wear her veil, and isn't this fun? She's alone in the suite. Brett is downstairs gambling with Adam, her dad and Ashley.

Ah, Ashley. Better spill the beans.

'Pearl, I hope you don't mind but I've brought a date with me,' I say with just a tad of trepidation in my voice. I don't want to appear rude. It isn't as if Jamie was invited.

'You have?' she says cautiously, looking at me standing behind her in the mirror where she's attempting to pin a flowery headdress on to her short straight hair, which isn't working.

'Yeah.'

'Who?'

'It's Jamie.' Silence. 'Look, you don't have to have him at the wedding if you don't want to. But he wanted to come.'

Pearl closes her eyes to consider for a second, as if concentrating hard on what she should say.

'It's a good match,' she pronounces, like some aged aunt whose opinion is desired in an arranged marriage. 'But what about Stephen?'

'He doesn't know. And besides, Jamie's just a date for tonight,' I find myself saying, although I hope it isn't true. 'He said he was at a loose end.'

'Not a bad-looking date though.' Pearl grins.

'Ashley's not going to be offended if I bring him along, is he?' I ask. 'I don't want to hurt his feelings.'

'No, he'll be fine. Just as long as there's lobster for dinner afterwards, he won't care.'

Two manicurists arrive and Pearl and I retreat to the giant sofa overlooking the view, where our feet are immersed in buckets of warm soapy water. 'Tell me about Jamie. How did he get to be a date?' Pearl demands. 'I always had him down as a workaholic. In fact, I can't ever remember him with a girlfriend.'

Pearl is such a hopeless romantic. All she ever wants for anyone is a happy ever after, and she might be irritatingly girly, and almost annoyingly naive in thinking that love and dates are the only things that matter, but she's loyal to those she loves, and she cares. I tell her about my Christmas with its various sideline attractions and she breathes it all in like oxygen, loving every detail. And then she tells me about hers – how Brett had to do some filming reshoots so their Christmas together was cancelled, and how she could have joined her dad in Mexico or her mum in Hawaii if he'd only told her about it before, but he hadn't and so she'd had Christmas at their new apartment all on her own. But she says Brett's promising to make it up to her on their honeymoon, when they get round to it after the baby's born. And anyway, as she brushes his bad treatment of her under the carpet as usual, Vegas is such fun and she's dying to meet his parents who are flying in from Ohio tonight ready for the wedding tomorrow.

Later in the evening, Adam and Ashley are leaning against an oak-panelled bar, cocktails in hand, in a restaurant where we are all to meet. They greet me with kisses on both cheeks and shake Jamie's hand heartily as we join them. Pearl arrives soon after us. I had thought it might be awkward to see Ashley again, but I can tell there's no hard feelings. And anyway, he's buzzing with the news that Adam has finally sold his script.

'But that's great, Adam,' I say, hugging him. 'That's really great.'

He beams from ear to ear. Jamie high-fives him and offers congratulations. 'Can you tell us what it's about? Or is it a secret?' he asks.

'It was actually an idea of Pearl's,' Adam says and nods in her direction. Pearl, who is ordering a Martini, dismisses the notion immediately.

'It was,' Adam repeats. 'Credit where credit's due. Pearl's such a creative person. She was the one who thought it all out with me.'

'Don't be silly,' she says.

'No. I think you deserve a share in the royalties.'

'Which should be fairly sizeable,' Ashley interjects. 'I know. I drew up the contracts. Adam stands to make a fair chunk of change if the movie does well.'

'Well, who knows,' says Adam modestly. 'At least it's being made. That's the main thing.'

'But what's it about?' I ask. 'Come on, tell us.'

'It's a romantic comedy about a penniless bus driver who falls for an heiress. It's all about how he struggles to find the money to romance her in the way she's accustomed to.'

'How exhausting,' I say, as a joke.

'It's kind of an updated version of *The Merchant of Venice*.'

'That's fantastic,' says Jamie enthusiastically. 'Who's the director? Have they found a lead yet?'

I never get to hear the answer because Pearl's dad

and Heather join us, shortly followed by Pearl's mum, who's flown in from Hawaii where she lives with her new boyfriend. Bonnie looks exactly like Pearl, except a bit older – very petite, a short bob of dark hair, and so much mascara, I'm surprised she can lift her eyelids. Her boyfriend is a personal trainer from Mexico, who barely speaks English, but grins a lot and has some spectacular muscles. He must be half her age. Brett is the last to arrive. He greets everyone effusively – even me – and when everyone's got a drink, we move towards our table.

It's nice to have friends. I've always led such a solitary existence, I've never really had a chance to make friendships last. I was forever being moved on to the next family, the next home, the next set of circumstances. Now I look round the table and it feels so great just to be part of a crowd. I suppose just to be invited along.

For me, it's a fabulous evening. Jamie is attentive and funny and keeps a hand firmly on my knee under the table. I've never seen him wear a suit before, and he looks so dapper, so statuesque, so manly, it's all I can do to hang on to my knickers. He tells me that this is what Americans call the Rehearsal Dinner. I've no idea what we call it in Britain because I can't remember a single wedding I've ever been to, except Aunty Bev's, when I was five. I was a bridesmaid, and all I can recall of that was refusing to wear my headdress, which was itchy and covered in daisies.

But whatever it's called, it's awful for Pearl. It's about as tense as Tom Cruise at a Prozac convention. Pearl's brokenhearted because the groom's parents haven't shown up. Brett starts making excuses for them, saying that some relative or other is ill and couldn't be left, and what a shame it is, but it doesn't matter because it was only ever going to be a small wedding anyway. And then Pearl snaps at him because she thinks he's being dismissive of the whole thing, and it might be a small wedding but it's important to her. I can see she's holding back tears. And she's doing well, but then her mum and dad start on at each other. Gavin's favourite joke is 'If you want a good divorce lawyer, use my ex-wife's' – and he's never forgiven Bonnie for walking away with so much of his dosh.

'How much you paying him to be here?' he jeers, nodding dismissively at Manuel, he of the youthful rippling chest.

Of course, Manuel doesn't understand a word and just keeps on beaming. But Bonnie's not the sort of woman to put up with that kind of remark.

'Not jealous of him, are you, Gavin? Not jealous of a man who knows how to treat a woman properly?'

'Don't be crazy,' Gavin barks back, voice and hackles rising. 'I looked after you. I looked after you good.'

'Like hell,' she shouts.

They're embarrassingly loud. Everyone round the table is uncomfortable, except Manuel who is still beaming. Pearl's furious.

'Stop it,' she shouts. 'This is my wedding, not a divorce court. Can't you two even be civil to each other for one night? Can't you ever do something for someone other than yourselves?' She storms out of the restaurant in tears.

*

For all the kitsch plastic flowers, fake Roman columns and laughable dove decorations, the wedding the next day is actually lovely. It's New Year's Eve and the ceremony's at 7.30 p.m. in one of the wedding chapels along the strip, where Bruce and Demi once said their vows. There aren't many guests – about twenty or so – mostly Pearl's girlfriends from school, and their dates, who have flown in during the day. There'd been talk of her sister coming too, but she'd phoned to say she couldn't make it. Brett doesn't seem to have any friends with him, and Ashley is his best man. But Pearl is more beautiful than I've ever seen her before. Her eyes sparkle like the huge diamond choker that's wrapped round her neck. She'd decided against the wedding veil in the end, opting for just a circle of crystals in her hair, and the layers of chiffon float behind her as she walks, making her look like some kind of celestial angel. Brett is uncharacteristically loving. They've made up their own vows, promising to love each other 'through good times and bad, whether happy or sad'. And they say them with such feeling that I'm almost convinced they mean them – and as they kiss, I find myself praying that this will work out for Pearl.

When I arrived in LA, I never imagined I'd get so caught up in someone else's life that I'd find myself rooting for them. Never thought I'd be longing for someone else's happiness, and hoping for the best for them. I'd always been too absorbed in my own life to care for anyone else before. But then I'd never found a friendship like this before – a friendship that seems to be unconditional. Pearl has shown nothing but kindness and affection to me. She's good in a way that I wish I could be. She deserves some happiness – I hope she gets the romance she wants.

After the nuptials, Pearl's mum and dad, carefully seated at opposite ends of the table, behave themselves at a banquet dinner and then we all retreat to Lure, a super-hip nightclub within the Wynn. There, we knock back bottles of champagne that cost three hundred dollars a pop and grin stupidly at each other because the music is too loud to do anything else. By midnight the place is heaving, and a DJ announces that the New Year has arrived. We all kiss, and drink more champagne.

'They seem happy,' Jamie hollers in my ear above the noise of the music, as we watch Brett and Pearl take to the dance floor from our party's private table.

'Yeah,' I holler back. 'I wonder how long it'll last.'

'Sceptic,' he bellows.

'Realist,' I say, and lead him on to the dance floor.

Dancing isn't really his thing. I can see that. He might like listening to disco music, but he sure as hell doesn't know how to dance to it. He jerks about uncomfortably, looking miserable and uninterested as the crowd bounces around him. I catch his eye, and lean forward to hug him. But he's not up for it. Instead, he grabs my hand with a surprising amount of force and pulls me through the crowd.

'Where are we going?' I shout, but he can't hear.

We squeeze into a packed elevator which takes us to the casino. The trill of the fruit machines hits us. It's another world down here – a world where no one cares what time it is, whether it's New Year's Day or half past Sunday. We pass rows of old women with buckets of change, sitting on bar stools, pouring money into the machines like drones. Then come the tables – craps, blackjack, roulette and a whole host of other games I'd never heard of, all with crowds of people poring over the green felt surfaces.

'Here,' says Jamie, handing me a stack of hundred-dollar chips. 'Let's have some fun.'

'But I don't know how to play,' I say rather pathetically.

'Easy,' he says and pushes his way to the front of a roulette table, where he casually throws a thousand dollars' worth of chips on to the table. A thousand dollars!

As a croupier throws a small ball on to the spinning roulette wheel, Jamie patiently explains the game to me. How much you can win depends on how you place your chips. His confidence is overwhelmingly sexy, but I'm too much in shock at the thought of losing a thousand dollars at the toss of a small ball to care. The ball lands on twenty-two – not one of Jamie's chips was even close. He's lost the lot.

'No matter,' he says cavalierly, and retrieves another stack of chips from his suit pocket, and places them on the table. He loses them too – and then more. It's excruciating to watch. In the space of less than an hour, he's lost thousands. I'm not sure if I'm meant to be impressed by the amount of money he's just throwing away, or if he's genuinely enjoying himself. But there's a glint in his eye, as he does it, that suggests he can't stop.

'Come on,' I say, pulling him away. 'This isn't fun at all. I can't bear to see money go to waste. It's crazy.'

'But you haven't used your chips yet. Let's see you play.'

I'd rather just cash them in and keep the change. There must be a thousand bucks in my hand right there – that's more than a week's wages, and why would I want to lose that much? But Jamie's insistent.

I decide to be brave and place them all on one number. Either I win a lot or I lose it all and we can get out of this place *tout de suite* because throwing money away is hurting my sense of decency. But what number? I choose seventeen, the date of Mum's birthday.

The wheel spins, the ball bounces, I close my eyes, and then suddenly Jamie's clapping me on the back.

'You won,' he whoops. 'You won.'

Three thousand five hundred dollars – that's how much I won. That's more money than I've ever owned at one time, ever. Can you believe it?

'Come on, let's get out of here,' I say to Jamie, gathering up all the chips and the bottle of champagne that he'd had a waitress bring to us. 'Let's quit while we're ahead.'

He urges me to play on, tells me I'm on a winning streak. I can see that glint in his eye that's making it hard for him to walk away. But I'm firm. We escape to the pool area, which is mostly deserted because it's chilly – a reminder that Las Vegas is slap bang in the middle of the desert. Overhead the night sky is fabulously clear and thick with stars. The redundant sun loungers look absurd in the moonlight but we grab a couple and lie out in them as if we're sunning ourselves at midday. Jamie offers me his suit jacket – just like George Peppard does for Audrey Hepburn in *Breakfast at Tiffany's*, a move that is not lost on me because everyone knows that Holly Golightly was doing no more than I am – looking for a comfortable, rich man to take care of her. Her mistake was falling in love with the poor guy.

'Do you know how beautiful you are?' he asks me, as we stretch ourselves out on the loungers.

'Don't be daft,' I say. He's right, compliments do always make me feel awkward.

'You don't even realise it, do you? That's the really astonishing thing about you. You're that beautiful and so totally unaware.'

'Do you want your money back?' I offer casually, changing the subject, and playing with one of the chips in my hand. I know he won't, but it seems polite to offer. 'It was your stake money, after all.'

'Your winnings. You keep them,' he says, letting out a sigh and stretching out on the lounger. 'I like it when people win.'

'Do you often win?' I ask. 'Assuming, of course, that you must sometimes do better than your pitiful performance this evening.'

Jamie laughs. 'I'm not much of a gambler really. Not compared to some people.'

'Could have fooled me.'

'We're in Vegas. It's what people do here. They drink, they gamble, they get married.'

He reaches over and pours champagne into both our glasses and then leans back again in the lounger, clutching his glass to his chest. 'Anyway, let's not talk about gambling. Let's just say you can now cross two of the Vegas must-dos off your list.'

'Three,' I say. 'We did the wedding thing, remember?'

'Ah, but we didn't do it ourselves,' he says. 'So it doesn't count.'

Silence.

'Care to try out the third?' he asks, as casual as if he's asking me to pass the bread rolls.

'Sorry?' I say, sitting up and looking over at him. His gaze is firmly placed on the stars.

'Care to get married in Vegas?'

'Are you actually asking me to marry you?' I say, sounding a lot more incredulous than I would have liked.

'Yes,' he says confidently, and turns to face me. 'I am.'

American women are very big on romance. The idea of it, rather than anything else. It's as if the concept was taken over in a joint bid by Hallmark cards, Interflora and Nora Ephron and then resold as a 'must have' package to the unsuspecting, blinding them in a cloud of pink tissue paper and netting. In order to have a real romance, you must have flowers delivered to your door, you must be wooed over dinner, you must be sent a stupid cuddly teddy bear and you absolutely must wear Victoria's Secret underwear. It doesn't matter how much a man has in his bank account – and some women don't even bother to check – because as long as he's presenting you with some microfibre foam-filled cuddly toy clutching a silky red heart that's made in China, then it must be love and therefore a lifetime's worth of happiness. It's amazing how many women fall for it. Vegas, being the 'Romance Capital' of the US, is naturally full of this crap. There are shops bursting at the seams with teddy bears and roses – and the worst places of all are the wedding chapels, which are so thick in kitscherama they must surely define the term.

Vegas is the last place I'd ever have thought I'd get married. It's more like my idea of a diabolic underworld than the fantasy it's billed as. There isn't time to buy a wedding gown – barely even to put on some lipstick – but when you have a rich man offering to marry you right then and there, propriety, not to mention common sense, dictates that you don't hang about. This is a man, I think to myself, who deserves a good wife – and, as Groucho Marx once said, it seems only right to marry him before he finds one.

I feel a little guilty, mind you. Jamie is so good natured, so romantic. You'd never think someone from LA could be that naive. I mean, he really thinks I'm the sweet, innocent abroad who's here because she loves kids. He thinks that's the real me. It's almost too easy. He'd be shocked to know I'm here to marry someone rich. But then, I do really like him as well. Who says life can't be convenient sometimes?

The marriage licence office is open twenty-four hours in Vegas on holidays. It takes a matter of minutes to fill in the forms to get the licence, and then it's a cab ride to find a wedding chapel that's open with an official to do the necessaries. There are hundreds of wedding chapels in Vegas – millions, it seems. We pass the Little Chapel of the Flowers, the Little White Wedding Chapel, Cupid's Wedding Chapel, the Sweethearts' Wedding Chapel, the Little Chapel on the Corner, the Chapel of Dreams, and perhaps most hilarious of all, given that the ocean is nearly a thousand miles west of us, the Chapel by the Bay. All have their bright lights blinking, advertising wedding packages from as little as $129 including free limousine and photographs. Jamie wanted to go for a Drive Thru wedding. I told him I'm not getting married in a car. The least he can do is stand up. So we settle for The Garden Wedding Chapel, which has some green carpeting outside surrounded by a white plastic picket fence – possibly someone's idea of a garden. It's the only one that doesn't have a queue outside and we turn down an Elvis lookalike who offers to walk me down the aisle – all three steps of it – for an extra fifty dollars. It takes all of five minutes. There, beneath an arbour of pink candyfloss netting, with the most cheerless rendition of 'Here Comes the Bride' I've ever heard blaring through hissing speakers, and a minister who makes us both giggle because there isn't a single tooth in his mouth, I become Mrs Shawe. We're not even drunk.

In fact there's nothing so sobering as a marriage proposal. Once I'd said 'yes', Jamie was on his feet, dragging me out of the hotel, whisking me into a jeweller's for a wedding ring and telling me that spontaneity is the calling card of life. Had he thought it through? I don't know. I didn't care.

All I know is that I have allowed myself to fall for him, and the emotion almost frightens me. The impulsiveness, the sharp, desperate hunger, the ache and longing suddenly make me feel that the ground beneath my feet is no longer there. I feel dazed and suddenly terrified of the violent feelings it's stirred up in me. I want to be with Jamie more than anything in the whole world. And it's a different kind of feeling from anything I've ever felt before.

And so is making love to him. After our matter-of-fact, no frills wedding in a chapel that smelt of damp and chemical air freshener, where Jamie said 'I do' so seriously that I couldn't help but laugh, we make a beeline for his hotel suite.

'You know what this means, don't you?' Jamie had whispered in my ear, while I was signing the register.

'What?'

'This means you get to come to my suite after all.'

Jamie is sensual, kind and eager to please. His touch alone takes my breath away. If it was a quicky love story, it's no quicky in bed. I'm stunned by how he makes me feel. Sex with him makes me realise for the first time what all the fuss is about. It's like a new world has opened up for me. I feel relaxed, calm – and for the first time, comfortable in someone else's company.

I lie awake in the enormous king-sized bed covered by an even more enormous duvet after we've consummated our marriage. Dawn is breaking outside. Through the gap in the curtains, a garish sun is emerging, lighting up the sky with a violent arrangement of pinks and orange. I'm exhausted – we've been up all night, but somehow I can't sleep. I stare at the ceiling, stomach unsettled, eyes wide.

Jamie lets out a rasping snore. I can't resist reaching over to touch him, but as my fingers make contact with the warmth of his back, his breathing stops and he turns.

'Not asleep, Mrs Shawe?' he demands blearily and pulls me deep into his chest where his voice booms from within. 'Not having regrets, are you?'

'No, course not.'

'You sure? I'd be heartbroken, but there are ways out of this if you're having second thoughts.'

'No. No second thoughts ...' I say, rubbing my cheek against his chest hair.

'What then?'

'It's just a strange sensation.'

'What is?'
'I think to be in love.'

For two full days, I'm not so much walking on air as dancing the fandango from cloud to cloud. I don't need to go to the top of the Stratosphere, the highest observation tower in the US, where you can climb on board a roller coaster at 1149 feet – I'm already on top of the world. I don't have to be at work until the end of the week, and Pearl certainly isn't going to want company, so we stay on in our Las Vegas suite, blithe and smug in the secret that's ours. I find myself going over and over our wedding night in my mind. If I'm not smiling on the outside, I know I am on the inside. Was it wise to get married so quickly? Mum always said to trust your instincts, that you know when something's right. A wealthy husband, who also happens to be in love with me – well, that's got to be right, hasn't it? There was also the added bonus of becoming legal in America by marrying an American. The holiday visa in my passport had already expired.

'So isn't there anyone you want to call back home?' Jamie asks me on the plane back to LA, looking up from a copy of *Newsweek*, while I'm peering out of the window watching Vegas become a tiny Legoland city on the arid landscape.

'I've got an aunt somewhere but I don't suppose she'd care,' I tell him. 'What about you? You going to tell your mum and dad?'

'I've already told my mum,' he says. He unwraps a packet of sweetener, pours it into a cup of coffee and stirs.

'Already!' I feel strangely betrayed.

'Well, I haven't exactly told her we're married. I told her that there was a girl I wanted to ask . . .'

'When did you tell her you were going to ask me?'

'Oh, before we left.'

'You mean you had it all planned?' I turn and stare at him in surprise.

'Of course,' he says, smiling complacently, putting down his magazine and sipping his coffee.

'And how did you know I'd say yes?'

'I didn't.'

All I can find to throw at him is a packet of peanuts and I fake outrage, but really it's flattering to know that he acted from intent rather than impulsiveness. This is turning out to be better than I could ever have imagined. I return my gaze out of the window. There is a long single track forging its way through the desert beneath us that goes on for miles and must lead somewhere. I wonder briefly where it goes.

'Anything else you've got planned that I should know about?' I ask him.

'Um, let's see . . .' he says nonchalantly, not looking up from his magazine again. ' "A happy ever after, roses round the door, children in the backyard", wasn't that it?'

'Something like that,' I say, smiling cautiously, and grab his hand as some turbulence sends the plane bouncing around the sky like a leaf in autumn. 'Anyway, what about your dad? You haven't told him yet, I take it.'

'No, we'll tell him when we're ready.'

'Better tell him soon. He's not going to be pleased about losing a nanny.'

'What? You're going to quit?' he says, looking up from his magazine. He looks quite stunned.

Jamie is aghast at the idea that I'd stop working and leave Craig, Marcie and Logan. It shocks him that I don't want to work any more. I mean, blimey, what does he think I did the job for? The love of it? But I can see he's heartbroken at the thought of our romance destroying the balance in his siblings' lives, so when he begs me to wait I agree, because I can't bear to see him so upset. And because, now I come to think of it, I suppose there is a part of me that does do the job for the love of it too. And I guess Craig, Marcie and Logan are family now.

That night I stay at his apartment in Beverly Hills. It's big, airy and modern, and overlooks lush private gardens with the condo's own pool and gym, but it's decidedly short of home furnishings. There are clothes, CDs and guitars strewn across the polished wooden floor. There's a pool table, TV of course, shelves groaning under the weight of books, and a desk absolutely overwhelmed by paperwork and a computer, but not much else.

'I'm afraid it's not very tidy,' says Jamie, walking into the bedroom and scooping up the clothes off the floor and putting them in a washing basket. 'I thought the maid would have been in to clean, but she doesn't seem to have. Sorry it's such a mess. Should have done a bit more planning, perhaps . . .'

I reach up to kiss him. I love the way he smells. I love the way his wardrobe is full of beautiful clothes, but he only ever wears jeans. I love the way he's confident in so many ways, but suddenly apologetic about himself. I love the way he knows about everything, but has the humility to never show off. And I love that he clearly hasn't had another woman in here or she'd have put a few feminine touches about the place.

'I'm not worried,' I assure him and I'm not – I'm already planning on how I'm going to change a few things. Curtains and sofas, some dinnerware from Bloomingdales . . . I'm sure he won't mind. And besides, we'll be wanting to buy our own proper house soon anyway.

In the morning, we drive up to the Shawe mansion together early to break the news to Stephen before I start work. As long as we stress to Stephen that he won't be losing his nanny, Jamie's convinced he'll be pleased for us. Briefly, I find myself wondering on the way what kinds of wedding presents rich dads give their sons and heirs. Houses? Cars? Antiques? Money? I know that sounds mercenary, but it's honest. It's what most women think all the time. But I should have saved myself the headspace.

Watching Stephen's face twist into rage and fury was like watching a typhoon break over an open landscape. Angry? He was like a wrestler on speed, pacing up and down the ring, fists clenched, teeth bared and expletives erupting.

'You did what?' he bellows at Jamie, picking up a pile of papers off his desk in his office and hurling them on the floor. 'You got married? To her?'

Jamie looks pale and shifts uneasily from foot to foot. 'Don't take it like that, Dad. I thought you'd be pleased. She's a great girl, you said so yourself.'

'Yeah, but I didn't mean you to go out and marry her, for Christ's sake . . .' He stops to draw breath, and glares at us. There's a terrifying silence while we contemplate what he's going to do next. In the office next door, a temp is sitting at Pearl's desk. She stops click-clacking on her computer. Upstairs I can hear the distant hum of Maria vacuuming. The French windows into the garden are open and outside someone is clicking shears.

'But Dad, she says she's happy to stay working as a nanny for the kids. It won't be as if you'll lose her. This way we get to keep her in the family for ever . . .'

'For ever?' The idea of this seems to upset him more than anything. 'This whore in the family? For ever? This piece of white trash?'

'Don't speak about her like that. If you've got a problem about this, call me names, but not her.' It's the first time I've ever heard Jamie sound stern. 'She's done nothing wrong.'

'Wrong? You don't know anything about her,' storms Stephen. 'You barely know her. She's a two-timing waste of space. I won't have her near my children,' he yells, spitting as he speaks, and now marching up to me so that his face is inches from mine. 'You come near my children again, young lady . . .' He's roaring at me now, pointing a finger in my face. 'You come near my children and I'll have the sheriffs on to you. You've got ten minutes to get your things and get out of this house. Ten minutes, you hear?'

He storms out of the French windows into the garden, leaving us in silence.

Jamie lets out a long sigh. His face is filled with hurt and confusion. 'He'll come round,' he says eventually, looking anything but confident that he will.

'Jamie, I'm sorry,' I say and reach out to touch his

hand, but he's too absorbed in his own thoughts to notice.

'Better get your things,' he says and leads the way up to my room to help me pack.

On the stairs, we meet Marcie, who throws her tiny arms round Jamie, and then me. There couldn't have been anyone in the house who hadn't heard Stephen's outburst.

'Don't leave us,' she says, fixing her big blue eyes on me with a beseeching look. 'We love you.'

'Don't worry, Marcie,' says Jamie, 'we'll be back. Dad's a bit angry just now but he'll calm down.' He kisses her on her cheek. 'Come on, Bella. We better get your things before Vesuvius blows again.'

'But I must say goodbye to Craig. I want to see how his leg is.'

Jamie hesitates and looks back into the garden where Stephen is still pacing.

'Better be quick. I wouldn't want to push our luck. There's no knowing what he'll do when he's this angry. He's got a gun in his desk drawer and I've seen him pull it out before.'

I race to Craig's room and quickly tell him what's happening. He's looking forlorn in his bed with his leg still in plaster. 'Don't worry, it'll all work out in the end,' I say. 'The good news is we're related now. Bound together for ever, so we're always going to be friends.'

It takes only minutes to throw my scant possessions into a suitcase, and then I tell Jamie to go down and start the car so I can retrieve the two gold Cartier watches which I've got hidden under the mattress along with the cash I've managed to save and Ginie Sayles' book. There's no time to feel sad. And anyway, it's bound to blow over, isn't it?

22

It's a mistake to imagine that there are no seasons in Los Angeles. It almost seems like there aren't any because it's nearly always sunny and the palm trees never change. But they're there if you look closely. It never gets cold enough in winter for the bulb flowers like daffodils and tulips to survive here. They need cold in order to emerge in spring, the way they do at home. But some trees do lose their leaves in the autumn, and some trees blossom beautifully in the spring, like the jacarandas which suddenly explode into purple, sending down a thick carpet of flowers on to the pavements. It's important to look for the changing seasons here, because otherwise it's as if time stops. There's nothing to mark its passing.

The jacaranda trees are about the only things that are beautiful about the street where I found us a one-bedroom apartment. It's in Koreatown, an area that is not noted for its salubrious accommodations, but rather its cheap rents. We've got one window that looks out on to the street below, and when the jacarandas are not in flower the tangle of city living is clear, stretching way out beneath us – vacant lots, boarded buildings, empty bottles, broken glass, homeless people. The most prosperous building on the street is an acting school, notable because occasionally we hear people arguing and swearing at each other outside its doors. You'd think someone had been murdered for all the noise they make, and several times I thought to call the police, but it turns out the actors like to rehearse their lines on the street. And what makes the spectacle all the more surreal is that most of them are Korean and they're swearing at each other in broad Korean accents.

The apartment isn't very big. It's on the third floor, reached by dark stairs that often smell of wee. I fear dreadfully how it would crumble in an earthquake. The front door opens into the living room, off which is the bedroom and a cramped shower room (it would be an exaggeration to call it a bathroom). And there's a teeny kitchen – just two work surfaces, a small electric hob with an oven beneath and a fridge.

The good thing about the place is that the bus stops right outside our building's entranceway, which is useful because it gets me all the way to Beverly Hills in less than an hour. I've got a job at Barney's, a department store that prides itself on its celebrity clientele, where I work in the make-up department, selling overpriced cosmetics to women who need them. It's not so awful, although the perfumed air makes me sneeze, but it's ten dollars an hour, plus commission.

I'm in a rush this morning because I've got an audition at a modelling agency after work and I want to look good for it. I pile on the free make-up from work, and choose one of the jackets Pearl gave me all those months ago. Killer shoes, killer handbag – or purse as they say here – jewellery, bare legs. They could use a bit of a tan, I think to myself. Jamie doesn't stir as I bustle around him. He's breathing deeply and regularly in the bed. He sleeps a lot. Mr Wilberforce, the stray kitten that we found one night in the gutter outside our apartment, is curled up next to him. I kiss Jamie goodbye, but he doesn't wake, so I grab a protein bar from our bare little kitchen and head out for the bus.

The bus is where I do my mourning. I mourn for the marriage I had envisioned. So much for the dinnerware from Bloomingdales. It has been nearly five months since we were married and not so much as a side plate. Neither Jamie nor I could have predicted how devastating Stephen's ire would be. At first, Jamie was convinced his dad would come round to the idea of our marriage. Stephen was never good at having new ideas sprung on him, but once he'd grown accustomed to the notion he was sure to like the concept of a daughter-in-law. Jamie had tried calling him several times, but his calls were not returned. He'd tried turning up at the house, but the security code at the gates had been changed once again and Jamie was turned away. Then Stephen cut the funding for Jamie's documentary. Then he stopped paying the rent on Jamie's apartment, and cancelled the repayments on his car. Jamie's strangulation was slow and painful. He approached other producers to fund his documentary, but no one wanted to get involved with the errant son of Stephen Shawe. He tried to get other directing jobs, but without an agent he was cut off.

Our relationship had grown and deepened at first. It bloomed in the face of an unreasonable enemy and we found comfort in each other. Jamie took me for walks in the hills. I'd never been into 'hiking' as he called it, but the big outdoors was empowering.

On our first hike, we'd left his car at the bottom of Franklyn Canyon, beneath sycamore trees offering shade. Then Jamie had started to stride out along a footpath, telling me to hurry up. The air had been dry, but fresh and unpolluted up there. Fennel plants had lined the overgrown rocky path, filling the air with their aniseedy scent.

'Come on, Bella,' Jamie had called from ahead. He was fit, and had left me breathlessly trying to catch up.

The path had slowly climbed the hill, twisting and turning and revealing more and more of the city beneath. The traffic had roared below, but up there it had been quiet, peaceful enough to hear the bees. A kestrel or hawk of some kind, had circled over us. I was red-faced by the time we had reached the top and looked out over the reservoir to the billion-dollar mansions which clung to the hillside on the other side of the canyon.

'Phew, I'm going to be stiff tomorrow,' I'd said.

'But it's worth it. Isn't it beautiful up here?' he'd demanded to know. A bead of sweat had made its way down the side of his face. 'The hills are the best part of this city, I always think.' He'd looked at me, seeking my approval, and I'd agreed with him, reaching for his hand to hold.

'You know everything's going to work out fine,' he'd said. 'Dad's going to come round, and I'll make my movie and then I'm going to take you to see the world. I want to show you Mexico and Hawaii and the Caribbean. We're going to have a great, great life together. You know that, don't you?'

I'd nodded and kissed him. I'd hoped it was true, and up there, with the sun beating down, a cloudless sky overhead and the familiar gridded streets of the city below, it all seemed possible. From up there, anything seemed possible.

I was always certain Stephen would change his mind, and initially it was an adventure to explore our partnership and get to know each other. By day, we'd laze around his apartment, idly watching movies, swimming in the pool. Jamie would study his newspapers and current affairs magazines and make changes to his documentary plans, and I'd work on my tan. Life was agreeable. There really seemed little over which we disagreed and I soaked up every small quirk and facet of Jamie's character – he seemed so intelligent, so impressive. I marvelled at his knowledge. And at night, passion was unleashed between us in a way I know I will never forget.

Jamie was everything I'd ever hoped a husband would be. Supportive, encouraging, entertaining. He made me feel like a prized and precious jewel. We made plans for trips round the world, and he promised to buy me a proper engagement ring once things had calmed down. I felt safe, secure. I felt I'd finally found a platform from which I could build a life that wasn't overshadowed by fear.

But as time went on, Jamie's mood darkened. It was as if the sun went in. He became quicker-tempered, shorter with me. It wasn't like him. He began to disappear in the evenings, leaving me alone. After a month or so of hearing nothing from his father, he became consumed with wanting to know why his dad had reacted so violently. He said he couldn't understand why he was being punished so harshly, why his dad hadn't come round to the idea. He didn't understand.

Then one day, while poring over bounced cheques and bank statements at his desk, he asked me: 'What did Dad mean when he said you were a two-timer?'

It hadn't even registered with me that he had. I'd closed my ears to most of the tirade, and tried to blank it from my mind. 'I've no idea,' I said idly from the sofa, where I'd been watching *E.T.* on the telly. And I hadn't. But then it got me thinking. E.T. was about to make all the children's bicycles fly – the bit that always made me tear up – but my mind suddenly focused. It seemed unlikely, but could Stephen have actually seen our evening at the Beverly Wilshire as a proper date? Was it possible that he really did have me in mind as a romance? He hadn't been exactly forthcoming if he had. There had only been that one date, and that was months ago. And even then, I was sure I had never been more than just a useful fill-in. Not to mention the fact that the evening hadn't exactly gone swimmingly. But could there have been more to it? Was it possible that he'd had plans for me and I'd missed the signs?

I told Jamie and suddenly his face didn't seem to belong the same person I'd known only seconds before. I'd never seen him so angry. 'Why didn't you tell me you'd been on a date with him?' he shouted at me, now on his feet.

'You didn't ask,' I said defensively. 'Besides, it wasn't a real date. He only invited me because he didn't have anyone else to go with him. He said so himself.'

'But that's just Dad's style. Don't you see that's why

he's so mad?' Jamie yelled, throwing up his arms in exasperation. 'It explains everything. Don't you see?' I gaped at him blankly. 'Don't you see? He's jealous. He wanted you for himself.'

Well, you could have knocked me over with a feather. Had I been so stupid that I'd misread the signs from an ardent billionaire? And not just any old billionaire, only one of the most powerful men in Hollywood? I reached for the remote control to turn *E.T.* off. Clearly I had. There he'd been, the billionaire prize ready for the snatching, and I'd missed my opportunity. The realisation left me shell-shocked. I felt faintly sick. Despite all the best-laid plans, I'd blown the big chance, and scuppered my prospects with Jamie too. Fuck, fuck, fuck.

To make matters worse, we got an eviction notice the next day. We had a week to get out of Jamie's beautiful flat in Beverly Hills. Turns out Jamie didn't have anything in his bank account after all – nothing, once his allowance had gone. Any money he'd made from his films went to pay off credit cards and debts, racked up by I don't know what. He wouldn't say. Even worse, he hadn't a clue what to do. He was like a helpless child without his security blanket. It was as if all his confidence disappeared with his money.

It was a harsh week. Both of us were unsure how to deal with the other. Jamie became clingy. I suddenly felt suffocated. 'Well, at least we have each other,' he'd had the nerve to say on our last night in the apartment, after I'd sold his guitars in order to find the deposit for the hole in Koreatown. 'You know I still love you,' he'd whispered in my ear, reaching for me in the dark. Yeah, but love don't pay the rent, I'd thought to myself and turned away.

Initially I'd wanted to punish him. Punish him for so savagely taking me off my course. I'd got so close to the finish line, and now here I was virtually penniless again. Worse off, because now I didn't have a job and I had a hopeless passenger to carry too. I was angry with him. Angry that he could have been so starry-eyed and impractical. Angry that he was nothing without his father's money. Furious that he couldn't stand up on his own. Hadn't he thought about what we'd live on when he asked me to marry him? And he was pathetic about what to do next. I thought about leaving him.

But sometimes feelings aren't black and white – they are a million different shades of grey. Over the months I wavered between every monochrome extreme. For as many days as I was angry, there were as many when I couldn't bear to be away from him. One day we even caught the bus to the beach – it had been Jamie's idea as a way to cheer us up, and we'd laughed all the way. And on the morning of the last day in the flat in Beverly Hills, I'd looked at Jamie in the bed next to me, surrounded by packing boxes, so serene and tranquil, so totally clueless about money, and realised I couldn't abandon him. I'd grasped the edge of the bed sheet, feeling its smoothness in my fists. Somehow, in my days of fury, I'd forgotten how sweet-tempered and kind he was, how funny and compassionate. And he would bounce back, wouldn't he? A man this clever, this brilliant, this good, couldn't be down for long. With a bit of strategic planning, we'd be back to a life of mansions before we knew it. I'd help him.

The trouble is, money does strange things to relationships. It's all right when men have more of it than women in a marriage. But things fall apart when a woman's got the power. Look at all the rich and powerful female movie stars who struggle to keep a man who's not their equal – Sharon Stone, Britney Spears, Jennifer Lopez. Is it that they cease to respect a man who doesn't match them in status, or is it that the men can't hack the humiliation of earning less than a woman?

Jamie struggles with my going to work every day and paying the bills. I earn just enough to cover us if we aren't extravagant, but he doesn't like it. I try to make it easy for him, leaving cash on his desk so he doesn't have to ask, but the money's always gone and he's moody when I get home. He stays at home every day to work on his computer, sending out CVs and emails to anyone who might take any interest in his movie project. I'm always optimistic. I tell him he had a track record in Hollywood – he's not a nobody starting out. Something will give. But he's not so sure. Love is so much sweeter when you've got oodles of cash.

But we can't stay living in this hole for ever. So now I'm doing the Hollywood thing I promised I'd never do. A talent scout had come into Barney's last week and asked if I was interested in modelling. Told me the money was good – all I had to do was call in at her agency and meet her boss.

Well, let me tell you, when you're clock-watching at Barney's and the most exciting part of your day is recognising which plastic surgeon worked on which of your customers (sometimes it's possible to tell – you just need to know their trademark looks), you don't ignore an offer like that.

The offices are on Sunset – the expensive section in West Hollywood. And they're posh. Black and white faces of girls stare out of picture frames on the walls in reception. There's a labyrinth of small booths where office workers are plugged into telephones. But I'm led into the boss's office – vast, with tinted windows keeping out the sun, and a small Yorkshire terrier curled up in a basket in the corner.

Jean Harvey is old. Intimidatingly so. She must be in her seventies, but she's still beautiful, with her mane of silver-white hair cut short into a sophisticated and meticulously coiffed style. She dresses like a power-house – black and white checked suit, silk blouse, and pink silk scarf tied round her neck, held in place by a giant diamond pin. There are half-moon glasses halfway down her nose and a stern expression that scares the living daylights.

'Isabella Shawe, how nice to meet you,' she says, looking up from the application form I'd filled in in the waiting room and the photos her assistant had taken of me. She sounds almost British, an accent that might have faded after a lifetime away. She holds out a hand with long manicured talons across her desk and signs for me to sit down on the chair in front of her. 'You're British, I see. Where are you from?'

'Guildford,' I say, doing my posh royalty accent. 'It's sort of south of London.'

'Yes, I know where it is,' she snaps abruptly and returns her gaze to my application. 'Twenty years old.'

'Yes.'

'Well, let's see,' she says, peering over her spectacles. 'Stand up and turn.'

'Sorry?'

'Stand up and turn,' she barks, looking at me like I'm some kind of idiot. 'So I can see your profile.'

Tummy in, chin up, bosom out.

'Hmm . . .' she muses. 'Walk,' she barks.

I walk the length of her office, conscious that her critical eyes are scrutinising me.

'You need to lose ten pounds,' she pronounces. 'Thank you, Miss Shawe. Have a good day.'

That's it? All this way for that? An insult? I look confused.

'Thank you, Miss Shawe. My assistant will show you out,' she repeats, and bellows for her assistant who comes running to lead the way.

At the bus stop, I contemplate grapefruit diets and stomach stapling. My jeans are only a size eight yet I feel I must be bigger than Tracy Tumblad from *Hairspray*. No wonder every other woman in Hollywood looks like a walking skeleton. I call Pearl on my mobile.

'How'd it go?' she trills.

'Disastrous.' And I fill her in on all the details which she always likes to hear. It's one of Pearl's most irritating habits – she's a stickler for details.

'Why don't you swing by?' she offers. 'Come and have some vodka and sympathy. You can hold the baby, and we'll order in a takeout.'

I worry about Pearl. She doesn't go anywhere any more. Refuses to leave her apartment. Sometimes she won't even pick up the phone. And whenever I go round there, she's never wearing anything but pyjamas. That's never been her style. It's as if she's given up. I told her to see the doctor for anti-depressants.

She had the baby at Cedars-Sinai in Beverly Hills – a whopping ten pounder called Thackeray (don't ask me why. Said the name came to her in a dream). I went with her, because Brett had already abandoned her by then. She didn't seem to have anyone else to hold her hand. Ashley offered, but it's not the kind of occasion you take your brother along to. I'd been chuffed to go. I'd never seen a birth before and I was surprised at how emotional it was. That little baby was so defenceless and needy, so innocent and pure. He couldn't help it that he was Brett Ellis's son.

Pearl had always ignored all the stories in the press about Brett. Over the two years that they had been dating, there had been a battery of pictures of him caught out with different women – and in one gloriously clichéd moment, there was one of him snogging a masseuse in a nightclub. But Pearl was always absurdly indifferent, insisting the tabloids were always trying to set him up and she wasn't interested.

Far harder for her was the harsh reality of having her husband kissing another woman on screen. And it didn't help that Brett was sent to Hawaii to film his next movie almost as soon as they'd left Vegas. In the closed-in, hothouse atmosphere of a location film set sizzling with beautiful people and exposed nerve endings, Pearl knew better than any that the sexual heat always rises. And she became far more concerned when the pictures of Brett with an array of different women were replaced by pictures of him with only one – the lead actress in the movie. Eventually even she couldn't ignore the photos of him liplocked with Conzuela Martin that were plastered across the front of the *National Enquirer*. Only a few weeks before her due date, she flew to Hawaii – lying to the airline about how far along the pregnancy she was so that they'd let her on – and confronted him. She should have saved herself the airfare. Now that Brett was set on his career trajectory, all thanks to her, she was as useful to him as a broken phone. He told her he was in love with Conzuela. Said he was sorry things hadn't worked out between them.

I call in on her as often as I can after work. She always seems totally alone and the arrival of the baby has done as much to lighten her mood as a night in with *Schindler's List*. She's in her pyjamas now as she answers the door – white flannel with pink sheep, and matching fuzzy slippers. There are dark rings under her eyes and her face is deathly pale. We air-kiss on the doorstep of the apartment she and Brett chose together. It's a nice place – a tiled fountain tinkling in the lobby, terracotta floors and a balcony with lots of leafy plants.

'Here, these are for Thackeray,' I say, handing her a Barney's bag containing a few bibs and booties. They'd been on sale and with my staff discount they'd cost me almost nothing. Thought they might brighten her up.

'Thanks,' says Pearl, and puts the bag down on a table, unopened.

'Where's the baby?'

'Asleep,' she says, sinking into the sofa and curling her feet under her. Jerry Springer is on the TV. Two girls are attempting to tear each other's eyes out. Cockfighting and bearbaiting are illegal. But somehow human baiting is legal on Jerry Springer.

I peep into the room Pearl's turned into a nursery. Thackeray is an alarming mini-version of Brett – the sharp nose, the high forehead. It's as if Pearl had nothing to do with his creation. He looks saintly, sleeping in his cot.

'How's it going?' I ask Pearl, sliding on to the sofa next to her, and pulling off my heels. My feet are hurting.

'Oh, fine . . . you know. Same old same old,' she says in a faraway voice. There's a brochure for Melodie May, Psychic to the Stars, sitting on the coffee table in front of us, alongside Pearl's regular stack of fashion mags and romance novels. I pick it up.

'She's good,' says Pearl, nodding at the brochure. 'You should go, Bella.'

Load of old Californian crap. 'Really?' I say. 'What'd she tell you?'

'Says Brett's going to come back to me.'

Hmm. Delusional as well as depressed. 'Got anywhere with the lawyers?' I ask brightly.

'They say it'll take months,' she says, fixing her stare on the TV. 'Ouch, that must have hurt.' Two men are now tearing each other apart.

'But what are you meant to live on until then?' I ask.

'Oh, I dunno,' she says hopelessly. 'It'll be okay. Dad'll help me out if I really need it. I think he's been paying money into my bank account anyway.'

After much chivvying from me, Pearl is supposed to be serving divorce papers on Brett, but the lawyers are pitifully slow, not to mention expensive. And I suspect she's not pushing that hard at all, mostly because she's convinced Brett is going to come running back to her and the sun is going to set on a happy ever after. Meantime, Brett's not paying her anything to support her or the baby. And in a move that's just too despicable for words, he's denying the baby's his. Of course he knows it's his. It's just a delaying tactic. And once the legal work is sorted, there'll be no wriggling out of it for him – Californian law is good for women. But until then Pearl's living off thin air alone. Not that it seems to be bothering her – one of the great advantages of having a rich family for a safety net, I suppose.

'Have you asked the lawyer if there's anything he can do to hurry things up?' I ask her sternly. 'You know you've got to stay on their case.'

She waves a dismissive hand at me and refuses to take her eyes off the telly.

'You really need to sort this out, Pearl. He's been a bastard to you. He needs to be taking care of you.'

Pearl shrugs. It annoys me that she doesn't seem to be angry at all. All the fight seems to have gone out of her. Jerry Springer reaches its conclusion – audience hysteria – and she switches it off.

'What shall we have – Indian? Chinese? Thai?' she says, changing the subject breezily. She gets off the sofa and pulls out a wad of takeaway menus from a cupboard in the kitchen.

'Thai,' I say. She shuffles back in her slippers, bringing the menu and a tumbler for each of us filled with vodka, orange juice and large chunks of ice.

'Anyway, tell me about Jamie. How's real romance?' She curls back into her seat, her big eyes guileless beneath her fringe. The nitty-gritty of my life holds a fascination for Pearl. When I told her that Jamie and I had got married spontaneously, she'd almost wept with joy. It was as if all her fairy-tale visions of romance had come in at once. I was her living proof that love conquers all. The fact that we were living in a slum, I was working my arse off in a department store and my husband was totally penniless didn't matter at all. It just made the story all the more romantic as far as she was concerned.

I try to fill her in with the reality of my life: 'I think Jamie's depressed,' I say earnestly. 'It's killing him having no work. It makes him very morose.'

'Oh, he'll find work and then he'll be fine,' she says breezily. 'He's Jamie Shawe. Everyone rates him.'

'Yeah, but no one's giving him any work.'

'Sure they will,' she says dismissively. 'Anyway, it must be nice having someone there when you come home from work. Does he buy you gifts?' she asks, as if this is the definition of a happy marriage.

'Well, he does sometimes,' I say. But it's hard to explain to someone who has never been deprived of material possessions that there's nothing romantic about an extravagant birthday present bought with money from a joint bank account that had been set aside to pay for next month's rent.

'It's not quite the bed of roses it ought to be,' I tell her.

'Yes, but does he tell you he loves you?' she demands.

'Well, yes, he does,' I say with a sigh. But too often, to be honest. Sometimes it drives me crazy. Every five seconds, it's 'I love you, honey'. We wake up in the morning and it's 'I love you, honey'. I go to work and it's

'I love you, honey'. I speak to him on the phone and it's always 'I love you, honey'. I go to the bloody loo and it's 'I love you, honey'. I mean, 'goodbye' would be fine. Mum and Dad never used to have to fill every silence with 'love you's', and they loved each other more than anyone else I've ever known. Seems like a drastic devaluation of the currency to me. Why can't Americans love someone without drowning them in sap?

'Well, there you are then,' says Pearl, satisfied, picking up the phone and dialling the number of the takeaway restaurant. 'Nothing to worry about.'

It's nearly midnight and our apartment is dark shadows when I get home, carefully returning the self-defence spray mace that I carry in my hand when I'm on the bus at night into my handbag. Mr Wilberforce rouses himself from the couch to brush past my legs by way of greeting me and tell me it's Whiskas time. I don't turn on the lights in case Jamie is asleep. But the small green light that signals that Jamie's computer is still on is illuminating the living room and bedroom doorway, enough to enable me to see there's no one in the bed, so I switch on the overhead light.

Jamie often goes out in the evenings. He tells me he goes to see friends and he needs to network, so I'm not bothered. In fact, sometimes it's a relief to be here alone. I kick off my shoes, unzip my skirt and reach over the desk to switch off the computer. Normally I don't go near Jamie's desk; it's his world and I leave him to it. But it's unusual that he's left the computer on and there's a credit card bill half hidden under the keyboard. I wouldn't have thought twice about it, except that the way it's folded away there makes it look like an attempt had been made to conceal it. I flip it open idly. Casinochecklist.com – $25,000. Alljackpots.com – $3,000. Intercasino.com – $10,000. Pokerstars.com – $5,000. Blackjackmasters.com – $7,000 . . . What the heck is this?

I read it again. Surely this can't be right? There are debts here of over fifty thousand dollars. Not to mention the interest. I check the name on the bill. Jamie Shawe. I didn't think credit cards could go up this high.

My heart pounds with fury. Since we moved into this hole, Jamie has run up over fifty thousand dollars' worth of debt by gambling online with his credit card. But that's just on this card. I know he has others.

I don't like confrontation. Hate arguments. People always say things they don't mean and I'm always nervous of the consequences. So I didn't immediately confront Jamie about his gambling debts. I was angry, of course, and something had to be said. But what? What could be done? What do you do with addicts? I'd seen enough of them in foster care to know addiction is a disease, same as cancer. I wanted time to think things through before I dived in with accusations. So I kept quiet for several days. I wanted to find his other credit card bills too. And I wanted to make sure it wasn't all a big mistake. The optimist in me had imagined briefly that perhaps the bill wasn't real, a prop from a movie maybe. Stupid. Of course it wasn't. The other bills I found in his desk told a sorry tale and for the first time since arriving in LA, I felt the kind of despair that I'd been so familiar with in England. Even if I worked at Barney's for the rest of my life, we'd still be paying these debts off. The future suddenly looked like a very dark place. Why hadn't I realised that he had a gambling problem when we were in Vegas? The writing was on the wall then. I was stupid not to see it. Stupid, stupid, stupid.

I'm still mulling over what to do about it at work a few days later when a tall, older gentleman turns up at the Clarins counter. He looks absurdly out of place. If men come into this section of Barney's, they're either gay or passing through to the restaurant on the fifth floor. Over six foot tall, broad shoulders like an American football player's, a big physique, salt and pepper beard straddling a round, affable face, quite bald on top, and dressed in a long Australian Drizabone coat because it's raining outside. He's reading the packets of face creams, and I'm wondering why he looks familiar when I remember. It's Bill Makepeace, the guy I met at the charity dinner.

One of the other girls is about to open her mouth to give him the hard sell, but I've already clocked him, and swiftly elbow her aside.

'It's Bill, isn't it?' I say, nudging her over some more with sheer body pressure, and smile sweetly.

'Yes.' He looks up and his expression is momentarily puzzled. I can see him searching the archives of his mind for a clue to who I am. Then a triumphant smile breaks. 'Ah yes, I remember you,' he says jubilantly. 'The champagne expert!' He pauses for a second and beams some more. 'Been to any good wine tastings recently?'

'Oh, sure,' I say chirpily, grateful that he's got a sense of humour. 'People all over the world want my opinion on wine. There isn't a vineyard I haven't visited.'

'Haven't visited mine,' he says, in an accent that I know is from the south, all long vowels and a gentle drawl that almost has a musical quality to it. He rests his hands on the counter top.

'Haven't been invited,' I say pertly.

'Well, we'd better change that then. And let's hope I get a better review than the last time.' He chuckles to himself and begins to fumble in his coat pockets. 'Now, maybe you can help me here,' he says, looking all businesslike. 'I need an expert on face creams. I don't supposed your field of expertise stretches into that area too, does it?'

'Actually, yes.'

'Good,' he says, now searching in his trouser pockets. 'Where's the damn list?' And he eventually produces a crumpled piece of paper, unfolds it, puts on his glasses majestically and reads: 'Extra-Firming Neck Cream, Line Prevention Multi-Active Day Lotion, Line Prevention Multi-Active Night Lotion, Super Restoration Redefining Body Lotion, Extra-Firming Eye Contour Cream, and Moisture Quenching Hydra-Care Lotion.'

He looks up at me, I think for confirmation that he's read the list correctly.

'They're for my mother,' he says emphatically. 'She's ninety.'

We both laugh.

'She's not given up the good fight then?' I say.

'She's got more wrinkles than a Shar Pei,' he chortles. 'And God knows how much she's spent fighting time. But longevity runs in our family and she's not going anywhere soon. Do any of these things actually work?'

'I've no idea,' I say, reaching under the counter for everything on his list. 'I don't make them. I'm just trying to earn a crust selling them.'

'How very truthful of you,' he says, watching me stuff all the boxes into a carrier bag. 'What are you doing here anyway?'

'Long story.'

He reaches in his pocket for his wallet. 'Want to tell it to me over dinner some time?' And hands me his business card along with his credit card. 'Call me.'

If it weren't that we were so broke, and facing a lifetime paying back credit cards, marriage would be a breeze. It's a nice feeling to have a partner to go through life with. It's way more fun than doing it on your own. And, even though our apartment is tiny and it's not quite the existence I envisioned, our daily life has a routine to it that I like. I've taught Jamie how to make a decent cup of tea – well, passable, anyway. There's a shop in Santa Monica which sells Tetley tea bags and so we make the trek there sometimes on the bus and I stock up on frozen kippers and Marmite. (Jamie tells me that you have to be raised on these things in order to appreciate their special qualities.) Jamie brings me tea every morning in bed, and we plan our weekends – which almost always include a hike, as well as trips to the movies and Trader Joe's, our local supermarket. We buy chickens for roasting and vegetables to turn into curries. Those are Jamie's two dishes. And then we eat them at night with cheap wine at our tiny dining table.

I remember evenings when Mum and Dad were at home together. Dad would put Nat King Cole on the record player and they'd wrap their arms round each other and sway in our living room to 'Let's Fall in Love', and he'd be whispering into her ear, and she'd be giggling, and I'd think to myself, that's what love is all about. And there are times when Jamie lives up to that standard. Of course, he's not the tidiest person in the world to live with – what is it with men and their inability to find either the washing basket or the kitchen sink? It's not like they're hidden. But he's attentive and loving and he treasures me.

He'd been the one who found Mr Wilberforce. We were on our way home from the movies one night when Jamie spotted the bedraggled furball – we'd have stepped over it, assuming it to be a piece of rubbish, except that it had mewed at us. Jamie had brought it in, cleaned it up and let it lap milk from a saucer.

'I think we'll call him Mr Wilberforce,' he'd said, making it comfortable among some cushions on the sofa. We'd watched *Amazing Grace*, the movie about the anti-slave trade campaigner, that evening. The furball purred as if happy with the name. It had beautiful brown and black markings, and ears that had tufts of fur sprouting from them, like an exotic wild cat.

'How do you know it's a boy?'

'Looks like a boy to me.'

'Which will be fine until it has kittens. Better take it to the vet to have it neutered,' I'd said, hating the practicality in my own voice.

The symmetry of our relationship has shifted since we've been married. I've become the practical one, and – all right, I'll admit it – I'm quite bossy sometimes. Jamie is compliant . . . passive. We have our ups and downs, the most serious down being that Jamie gets hopelessly depressed. It's like living with Eeyore on the day that everyone forgot his birthday. And I'm about as helpful as Piglet offering him a burst balloon to make him feel better. Jamie tells me he's a failure. I tell him he's not, he tells me he is, and on it goes and hell, sometimes he's so convincing I think well maybe you are a failure. You're bloody moody to live with, that's for sure.

I appreciate being broke is much harder for him. I've always been this way, so it's kind of business as usual for me. It must be a much grimmer reality when you've gone from having so much to having so little. I realise it's a huge ajustment to make. Perhaps it explains the credit cards. I try to be understanding.

In a moment of desperation I'd even called Candice, Stephen's ex. Not for camaraderie among social outcasts, but because it had upset Jamie so much not to see Craig, Marcie and Logan. I'd missed them too, but it had really troubled Jamie. I'd begged Candice to let us come and see the kids one afternoon at her house and she'd agreed.

'Jamie!' The kids had come bursting out of the front door to hug him. They'd grown.

'And what about me? Don't I get a hug too?' I'd asked, and been gratified that they hadn't forgotten me.

'Did you bring us any gifts?' Marcie asked, setting her big round eyes into their usual plead mode.

'Actually, we did,' Jamie had said with a wide smile, and produced balsa wood gliders we could build ourselves and then throw around the garden. We'd spent way more than we should have done at Toys 'Я' Us, but it had been worth it to see Jamie so happy again. Candice told us we could come round any time, and discovering that this particular door was not closed off to us was strangely comforting. But the next day Jamie had been back to his old miserable self.

We don't tend to row – in fact there are rarely ever

cross words between us at all – we just sort of get on, which is one of the things I love most about living with him. It's almost as if we think the same way sometimes. How hard must it be to live with a religious zealot who insists on church every Sunday, for example? Much easier to live with a man who waves his hand skyward casually and says, 'Well, if he's up there, I'm sure he loves me as much at home as he does at church.' I'd always thought the same. And how difficult must it be to live with a man who doesn't want any kids, or a man who insists on hundreds of them. Jamie just says a family might be nice one day, when we're ready. And I think, yes, one day. We even like the same radio station – he introduced me to KCRW and that's the one we always have on the small radio in the kitchen. It's so much easier not to argue. Which makes it all the worse when I finally tackle him about his gambling debts. I'd found all the other bills, and the figures were enough to make anyone pale. The conversation had to happen. It was our first ever big fight.

'Jamie, I need to talk to you about something,' I start, perching myself next to him on the sofa, where he is sprawled out watching a news special on Israel and the Palestinians on the telly. Mr Wilberforce is purring in his arms. I am hoping to do this as tactfully as possible.

'What is it, honey?' he asks, not taking his eyes off the screen, but putting an arm out to stroke my back. 'How was your day?' A bomb goes off on the TV screen and the camera cuts to a small wailing child who has lost its parent.

'I found this credit card bill,' I say, as gently as I can, pulling it out of my bag.

'Jamie says nothing.

'I thought you said you weren't a big gambler.'

'I'm not,' he lies.

'Well, what's this? Fifty thousand dollars isn't big gambling?' I feel the anger rising in my voice, and try to control it. I don't want to be angry. I want him to stop and address this.

'What are you, a spy?' he says defiantly.

'I wasn't spying. You left it lying around.'

'Well, no one asked you to look,' he says, like a petulant schoolboy who's been caught out. He stares at the TV set. I stare at the bill and there's a long, awkward silence while the Middle East falls apart.

'Is this what you do all day? Gamble?' I ask eventually, trying to keep my voice even. I don't want an argument, I just want him to stop.

'And what if I do?' He clicks off the TV, and storms over to the window. Mr Wilberforce jumps to the floor looking most put out.

'What if you do?' Now I *am* angry. 'While I'm slogging my guts out at some vile department store to pay the rent, you're sitting here playing games. I'm busting a gut every day and you're lounging around playing poker?' I pause a second to draw breath.

'Fucking hell, Bella, what am I supposed to do?' he shouts. 'I'm not playing games. I'm trying to make some cash for us. Can't you see that?'

'Are you out of your mind? By gambling? You're nuts. You think this is going to get us out of debt?'

'It might.'

'It might if you won, but you don't, do you? How the fuck do you think you're ever going to pay these off?'

I'm so frustrated, I storm out and find myself walking for hours, down past the Wilshire/Western subway entrance with its blast of hot air, past the homeless people sleeping outside St James's church, past the restaurants offering kim chee and sushi, past Korean libraries and signs that I don't understand. It's cold outside in the night air and I haven't remembered a coat. Finally the temperature drives me home.

Jamie is sitting on the couch with his head in his hands, his broad shoulders hunched over. 'I'm sorry,' he says straight away, and looks up. His eyes are red and he's twisting a paper napkin in his hands. 'You must be wondering why you ever married me.'

You can say that again. I go to the kitchen and put on the kettle for some tea, before settling myself next to him on the sofa.

'Are you addicted to gambling?' I ask gently.

'No,' he says emphatically, and blows his nose into the napkin. 'Yes. I don't know. I was trying to win us some cash. Really, that's the truth. I feel so bad that you're the one going out to work every day. I want to surprise you with the engagement ring you never got. I want to take you travelling like I promised. I want you to live in a palace, not this dump . . .' He stops and tears well up in his eyes again.

'I feel so powerless, Bella,' he says. 'I just don't know what to do with myself.'

'But gambling isn't going to help, sweetheart. It really isn't,' I say soothingly. He nods silently. 'It's just going to make things worse. You know that.' He nods again. 'You're a clever guy, things are going to pick up. They really are. You've got to have faith in your own ability.' I pause a second. 'I do.'

Eventually we hug and promise ourselves a brighter future. He agrees to go to Gamblers Anonymous, and I jokingly offer him ten to one odds that he won't. Then we fall into bed and make love as if we haven't a care in the world.

But we have got cares. More than fifty thousand dollars' worth of them. And within a month we've drifted back into the same old routine. Jamie promised me that night that he'd get a job – any job – to start paying off the bills. But he hasn't. There was a job as a doorman going at Barney's that I told him about, but I could see that he felt it was beneath him. He said he had other irons in the fire, and he had something lined up on a new movie that's being made, but the job hasn't materialised.

Resentment grows inside me. I try to fight it off, but it gnaws away at me, especially on the days when our mailbox is stuffed full of bills. And I distrust Jamie's easy promise to abandon gambling, as if it's as straight forward as promising to give up chocolate for Lent. An addiction is never as easy to forgo as a simple promise. So one night I find myself searching through his belongings for other credit card bills. I don't find any, but I find bookies' receipts instead. While I am working overtime just to pay the rent, he's blowing my wages on horses, football matches, tennis games – if it moves, Jamie's betting on it.

Anger seethes. Bill Makepeace's business card, hidden at the bottom of my handbag, beckons. I've tried to ignore it, but now I think maybe it's a lifeline. Would a drowning man ignore a raft? Surely this is the time for action? Underneath Bill's name, in bold type on his card, it says Producer, and I've been in this town long enough to know that's not just any old position. It's a position with money and influence. Maybe he could come up with the funding for Jamie's movie and get us out this mess. More important, maybe he'll be able to help me. Just like Tony Montana in *Scarface*, who didn't come to America to break his back working, I didn't come here to live in a squalid apartment in Koreatown and work in a department store. I could have done that at home. I came here to find money. That hasn't changed and nor have I, I tell myself. So the next day, I call during my lunch break and his secretary puts me through straight away, as if she's expecting me.

'It's your wine expert here,' I tell him.

'Oh, good,' he says keenly. 'I've got some wine that needs tasting. I'll pick you up at seven.'

'What, tonight?' I hadn't expected him to be so harefooted.

'Why ever not?'

Because I've got a husband who'll probably wonder where I am, I think quietly to myself. But when opportunities come knocking . . . Mum always used to tell me that you've got to make your own luck. If your boat doesn't come in, you've got to swim out to it. So I'm swimming. I'm on to plan B. Everyone's got a plan B, right? Bill Makepeace is my plan B. I call Jamie to tell him I'm working late for stocktaking. He says, 'Whatever,' like he doesn't care anyway. Depression makes people moody. Bill picks me up from Barney's in a big, silver, straight-out-of the-showroom fancy car. Don't ask me what sort – I don't know about cars. All I know is it reeks of aftershave, leather upholstery and wealth.

Bill is so well known at Spago he has his own special table there. It's in the courtyard where smokers are allowed. Bill knows everyone. It takes us ten minutes to reach his table because he has to say hi to all of them on his route through. Finally we're looking at a crisp white tablecloth laden with shiny silverware and an array of highly polished glasses.

'Care for a cocktail, madam?' asks the waiter.

I hesitate, wondering what's appropriate. But Bill's poring over the menu and not giving me any leads.

'I'll have a Cosmopolitan,' I say, like I drink them all the time.

'I'll have my usual,' says Bill and looks up to smile benignly at me. Little bit older and he could be Father Christmas.

'So how are your mother's wrinkles?' I ask him, as I quickly scan the restaurant for famous faces. Spago is well known as a celebrity spotter's paradise. But there's no one I recognise. 'Bet you got brownie points for getting all the right things.'

'Oh, I did,' he says and opens his menu. 'Now all I've got to do is pick up her plastic surgeon's bill.' He plays with his beard as he surveys the entrées listed on the giant sheets of paper. He's clearly relishing the choice. 'So, you got married, I hear?'

'Word spreads fast,' I say, somewhat taken aback. I'd actually taken my wedding ring off, because I wasn't sure if he knew.

'Oh, word spreads very fast around here,' he cautions, lighting a small cigar and exhaling a puff of smoke into the air. 'Hollywood's a very small town indeed when it comes to gossip.'

The drinks arrive and the waiter takes our order – broiled black cod with a sesame-miso glaze, house-smoked salmon and two roasted racks of Sonoma lamb. We clink glasses. The sweetness of the Cosmopolitan claws at my teeth.

'And how are you finding married life?' he asks with the kind of look that says everything about cynicism. I rather suspect he knows more about me than I'd care for him to.

'Oh, it has its moments,' I say coyly, stroking a fingernail which I'm pleased I'd given a manicure to over the weekend.

'Bet it does.' He smiles, and after a long study of the wine list orders something red and French. 'Jamie's not doing much at the moment, so I hear?'

'Is that what you hear?'

'That can't be easy for you,' he says with just a touch of sympathy in his voice and looks me straight in the eye.

I stare back with the best orphan expression I can muster. 'Well, it hasn't exactly been a bundle of laughs,' I say dolefully. If I'm going to play this game, I might as well do it right. When a man of Bill Makepeace's age and social standing invites out a twenty-year-old girl he's happened to meet over a make-up counter, chances are he's not asking her out for her intellectual prowess. I know that and he knows I know that. It's a game of cat and mouse. I've got what he wants – youth, sex and beauty. And there's the status thing, I realise now. I'm what Stephen Shawe didn't get. The question is, what can I spin this out for?

I'd done my homework before I'd called him, of course. All it had taken was a quick Google search on Jamie's computer to find out that Bill Makepeace has been the major bankroll behind several blockbusters. He's sixty-two but still the perennial bachelor and socialite. There isn't a society magazine that hasn't carried a picture of him at a party with a blonde in one hand, a drink in the other and a wry smile all over his face. He's a man who is never without a date for long. Going way, way back, there was once a brief marriage; also rumours that he'd once had a rather close friendship with Ely Goldstein, the gay owner of Prevalent Pictures, one of the big movie studios, but those rumours were never confirmed.

'Of course, you were playing something of a dangerous game there, weren't you?' he says, with a mock guffaw that I suspect means he's enjoying knowing my circumstances. 'I mean, if you will play dangerous games, you're bound to get your fingers burnt. Can't date the dad and then run off with the son.' He laughs at the preposterousness of it.

The food arrives, and he surveys the pretty arrangement on the plate that looks more like art than food.

'Do you like playing with fire?' he asks.

' "Experience is the name everyone gives to their mistakes," ' I say, tucking into the salmon. 'Here, would you like to try a little of this?' I suggest, keen to change the subject. I offer him a forkful, which he leans forward to eat. 'Oscar Wilde.'

'Ah, so you read.'

'Sometimes,' I say. 'Mostly I watch movies.'

'And you remember quotations?'

'Other people usually say things better than I do. I like to remember them.'

'And your favourite movie is *A Night at the Opera*. Isn't that right?'

'Yes!' He'd actually remembered our conversation at the charity ball. I'm chuffed.

'Of course. You're the walking film guide, aren't you? So tell me, what did you think of *The History of Pendennis*?'

'Good plot line. Beautiful cinematography. Wasn't sure about some of the acting, but I liked it.' It was a safe answer – I'd been smart enough to look up some of Bill's films beforehand and watch them. This was his latest, a modern-day version of a William Thackeray novel. I wasn't going to be caught out again.

'You really liked it.' Bill seems genuinely pleased.

I ask him about the new movies he's currently involved with. And he tells me all about them, entrusting me with information that I know must be secret. I'd be lying if I said I wasn't enjoying the evening. Perhaps I do like to live dangerously. I never thought I did, but there is a frisson to this occasion. The thrill of a clandestine meeting, the suspense of a new chapter, the promise of effectiveness, the intoxication of power. I enjoy talking about the movies Bill's making, and hearing the mechanics of his work. He seems to relish my opinion, too. Wants to know what I think of different actors, and that makes me feel important. It's strangely seductive – more flattering than being told I'm beautiful.

There's a boyish enthusiasm and charisma about Bill that I wasn't expecting. He seems to be less the dirty old man I'd anticipated and more the convivial party die-hard. And I was wrong about his being too old to be good looking, too. He is still a handsome man.

'How do you find the wine?' he asks, trying to hold back a smirk.

'Hmm . . .' I breathe in the aroma before sipping. 'A complex character, but approachable, good depth, a slightly earthy finish. Full bodied, and . . .' I hold the glass up the way you're meant to. 'And great legs. Definitely great legs.'

Bill laughs heartily at my performance. 'Interesting,' he says, after we order a second bottle and share a chocolate souffle, which I eat most of. 'You like to eat food.'

'Aren't I meant to?'

'Most women here don't.'

'Ah, but I'm on the seafood diet. I see food and eat it,' I tell him, and then remember that I'm meant to be shedding ten pounds. I tell Bill about my fruitless attempt at a modelling career.

'Why didn't you tell me? I know Jean Harvey very well. I'll give her a call,' he says casually. 'You see, I can do things for you. A cute face can go far in this town, but . . .' he leans forward to stroke my cheek and push a loose strand of hair that has fallen across my eyes, 'it goes further with some help.'

'Well, I could sure use some help,' I say with big eyes and kiss him lightly on the lips. It wasn't a serious kiss, just a gesture of encouragement.

'How about we continue at my place,' he whispers in

my ear. The offer is more tempting than I imagined it would be. He's quite charming really. Would he be looking for a wife? The thought flashes up in my mind. Divorces are easy to get around here and I could still achieve what I came to America for. I look at him as he smiles back and consider how he could give me everything I want. This could work, I tell myself.

'Oh, I'll need to review a few more wines before we get to the premier cru,' I tell him, pulling back and straightening my hair. Everyone knows a quick shag will get a girl nowhere.

Jamie's more Eeyorish than ever this morning. I wonder briefly if he has somehow, by osmosis perhaps, picked up on the previous night's deception. The trouble with sensitive sorts is they can read people's thoughts. I'm feeling guilty that I lied. It's a new sensation to me, and takes me a little by surprise. Telling fibs to get what I want has never bothered me before.

It had actually been a really fun evening out – fabulous food and wine, and the luxury of conversation with someone who didn't grumble once. Bill had even paid for a cab home. But now I feel bad about lying. It was a mistake to have gone. It was stupid. What was I thinking? And how could I have thought to abandon Jamie? Grouchy or not, he's still my Jamie. I reach over to hug him before I leave for work. He smells so familiar, so comforting. 'I love you,' I whisper in his ear. But he's reading a magazine and doesn't respond. He's like that sometimes when he's down.

'Have a good day,' I say.

'Doubt it,' he says moodily.

'Sure you will. Have you checked your email for any news?'

'Yup. Five rejections and three advertisements for penis enlargement.' He sighs. I don't know anyone else who takes junk mail so personally.

'Well, you've just got to keep trying. Something's sure to turn up.'

'Will it? I'm glad you're so certain.' He pauses, and then adds with a surprisingly venomous snarl, 'Easy for you to be so confident.'

'Don't be like that.'

'Like what?' he bites back.

I don't need this aggravation. I close the door and disappear to work.

At work, it's the quietest morning on record. Only three facelifts – sorry, I mean customers – and one of them wants to bring something back.

'I'm sorry, we can't exchange opened goods,' I say politely.

'But you must. This cream doesn't work,' says the Joan Rivers lookalike, who admittedly has even more shopping bags under her eyes than in her hands.

'It will if you keep using it,' I say tactfully.

'But I want my money back.'

'I'm afraid it's the store's policy not to refund on opened goods.'

'I want to speak to the supervisor.'

Thank God for my morning break. There are four voice messages on my mobile. The first is from the modelling agency, telling me they've got a job for me and can I call them back immediately. The second is from a personal stylist called Cindy whom Mr

Makepeace has asked to call. What? Me? I replay the messages again to make sure I've heard it correctly. The third message is from Pearl, just checking in with me. She wonders if I'd like to go round to hers tonight. It sounds as if the anti-depressants are working. The fourth is from Bill inviting me to a party – also tonight.

First things first. I only get fifteen minutes' break and we can't make any calls on the shop floor. I call the modelling agency. An advertising agency liked the look of the snaps Jean Harvey's assistant took of me. They want to meet me tomorrow to consider my face for a new ad campaign. Wow. Bill moved fast. I'll have to chuck a sickie off work.

Next up is Cindy. 'Mr Makepeace asked me to take you shopping this afternoon,' snaps a squeaky voice, reminiscent of Minnie Mouse herself. 'Where's convenient to meet?'

Heck. Is this really for real? Could Bill really make this happen? And who's going to pay for this? I express my concern to Cindy. But she's quite clear. Bill has commissioned her, and Bill will be paying. Well, blow me. What kind of mug would turn down an opportunity like this? I promise to meet her at the Coffee Bean and Tea Leaf on Robertson, the heart of celebrity shopsville.

Next up is Bill. 'Well, you've been busy,' I say in a chastising voice.

'I told you I could do things for you,' he says calmly. 'So what about it?'

'About what?'

'The party tonight.'

There's the sparkle of excitement and the prospect of fun in his voice. I remember Jamie used to have it once too. I feel the wrench of remorse. What happened to the Jamie I knew? He's so difficult now. Why shouldn't I go, when Jamie offers me nothing but neediness one minute and misery the next? Why shouldn't I have just a few laughs? And anyway, it's just a party. It's just one night out.

'I'd love to come,' I tell Bill.

'Great. I'll pick you up from Cindy's.'

'From where?'

'From your stylist's.'

I call Jamie to tell him I'll be late again tonight. He doesn't seem bothered at all. He says he'll be out tonight anyway – he doesn't say where, but I have come to suspect that these nights out are usually poker games. There isn't time to call Pearl back. Besides, I know she won't approve of my evening's plans, and she of all people is impossible to lie to.

It's a performance worthy of an Oscar that I put on for the make-up department supervisor. By the time I've asked to sit down feigning sickness and dizziness, I could almost believe it myself.

Cindy is sitting at an outside table poring over a fashion magazine. Dressed in a floral floaty top with string straps and jeans, she's another girl my mother would have wanted to feed a good meat and potato dinner to. Her arms are so thin, they barely look strong enough to lift up the rows of bangles on her wrists and the cigarette she's frantically puffing on. Speaking a million words a minute, she starts by telling me how busy she is, and, in case I was not aware, that she is the stylist to the stars. All the A-list come to her. But she likes new projects, and she's worked with many of Bill's clients before. 'The important thing is,' she pauses to inhale sharply on her cigarette, 'that we get your look right right from the start.'

'Right from the start of what?' I ask her, somewhat bemused. She pulls out a notepad and starts writing down my hair colour.

'Your new career,' she says, now looking confused herself. She runs her hands through her long, straight sandy hair and pushes it behind her ears, which are weighed down by some large hoop earrings. She looks like a Nicole Ritchie clone – probably one of her clients. 'Bill said to set you up.'

'As what?' I ask her.

'As the next It girl, of course.' She leans forward, grabs my chin and holds it in order to study my face. 'Need to get those eyebrows done . . . My job is to make sure you've got the right wardrobe. Cute accent, by the way.'

'Wait a second. What do you mean, an It girl?'

'An It girl. You know, Paris Hilton. Kate Moss. Sienna Miller.' There's an impatience to her voice.

I must look like the village idiot.

Cindy sighs. 'You have heard of Paris Hilton, haven't you?'

'Yes, of course.'

'So. Bill plans on giving you a public persona. You'll do some modelling, go to a few of the right parties. You'll be a micro-celeb . . . Maybe you'll even make it into the big league, but for starters he wants you to become a celebutante.'

My jaw must be on the floor again, because Cindy is

inhaling sharply on another cigarette and looking at me as if I'm stupid.

'Look, celebutantes don't just happen magically,' she says, deciding that the situation needs spelling out. 'It's not like they're just cute girls who happen to fall into the spotlight. It's the mistake all the wannabes make. They think if they look cute enough and spend hours at the gym, they stand a chance. But celebrities are created. Behind every one of them is a team of publicists, PRs, agents, stylists. They plan out how much exposure is needed, which parties you need to be seen at, what image you ought to have, what boyfriend you ought to have . . .' She drops her half-smoked cigarette on to the pavement, stubs it out with her pointed leather boot and then rifles though her bag to find another.

'It takes more strategic planning and politics to create a star than it does to draw up war plans. Hell, it's the biggest misconception of all, that talent has anything to do with any of it. If Bill Makepeace has set his mind to make you something in this town, if you've got his backing and he thinks you've got what it takes, you'll do it. Because . . .' she fumbles with her lighter, 'you've already got what it takes. Him.'

What surprises me most is that Cindy talks as if my future as a celebutante is a given. As though someone might choose one day to be an It girl, just as they might choose to be a bank teller or a bus driver. All you do is decide on what you want to be, buy the wardrobe and suddenly you're it. I tell her I can't believe that I stand a hope in hell. But Cindy brushes any concerns aside like a dry cleaner confident of getting out a stain.

'But I've already told you. If you've got Bill

Makepeace's backing, you're in. There are all kinds of games played by people in power here. Hollywood is all about swapping favours. It's a big old game of snakes and ladders. Bill is your ladder up. Watch out for the snakes, though.'

My mind is still racing. But Cindy's searching through her pad, filled with impressive doodles and sketches of women in high-fashion outfits (she's quite an artist), and finds some notes she must have written down whilst being instructed by Bill.

'What size are you?'

'Size eight English.'

'That's a size six here. Good. Some people would like you to be thinner. But I like that you have some curves. And good boobs, I can see that. Fake or real, by the way?'

'Real, of course,' I say with just a small huff. This is so personal.

'How tall?'

'Five foot eight.'

'You sure? I thought you looked taller than that to me.' She writes all my details down. 'I wouldn't say you were typical model material. They're usually taller and skinnier than you. But I can see why they went for you . . .' She pauses and checks me over. 'You do stand out. And besides, curves are making a comeback.

'Now, I suggest we start out at Kitson, where Paris Hilton gets her T-shirts, then Lisa Kline where Nicole Kidman gets her jeans, Agnes B for dresses, Diavolina for shoes, and we'll pop into Adriano Goldschmied – they've got some really cute tops in there. You're welcome to tell me what you like, but I find it much

easier if my clients just leave the choices to me. You'll
find it works best that way.' She sounds so officious.
Pearl's makeover was much more fun than this.

'You'll get lots of freebies once you're out there. All
the designers come begging you to wear their clothes
the minute your face starts showing up in magazines.
Paris Hilton never needs to buy a thing. But initially we
need to invest.'

'Could we get a dress for tonight?' I ask cautiously.
'Only I'm going to a party.'

'Honey, you're going to have dresses up the yin-
yang.' She looks up from her notes and starts playing
rather roughly with my hair. 'When was the last time
you had your hair coloured?'

'Never. It's naturally blond,' I say, unsure whether to
be affronted or not.

'Wow. A real blonde.' She seems pleased with this.
'You could use a few highlights though – make it look
just a touch warmer, brighten it up a bit – and a good
cut. I'm going to see if Lorri can squeeze you in this
afternoon. She takes care of Jennifer Aniston and Meg
Ryan.' She's on her phone before I can even say starry-
eyed, and asking my shoe size while she's on hold.

'I think the look we're going to go for is glam rock.
You're young enough to make it really work—' She
breaks off to talk into her phone. 'Yes, hello. Sweetie,
can you squeeze a client of mine in this afternoon?'
There's a pause while she whispers to me, 'We'll do
clingy dresses by night and boho chic by day . . . Yes,
two o'clock. Super. Can you do some eyebrows too?
Thank you, darling. Kissy kissy. I owe you . . . What was
I saying? Yes, we'll do boho chic by day. Lots of

jewellery. Lots of accessories. I want you to have a subtle sexiness . . . Get rid of this.' She looks down at the leopard-print low-cut top I was wearing – one of Pearl's giveaways.

'What were you going for here? The British barmaid look? From now on I don't want to ever see you in tight-fitted low-cut tops, sweatsuits, sneakers, baseball caps or anything in leopard print. Keep the killer instinct for your plans, not your wardrobe . . .' She pauses and plays with her earrings.

'You can wear jeans, but only the ones I'm going to buy for you. You can wear low-cut tops, but they've got to be subtle, floaty. I never want you out without sun-glasses and I want you to imagine you're Paris Hilton. You never, ever see her looking drab. Think of yourself as the most glamorous movie star ever, hold yourself that way, and you'll soon see the transformation.'

By the end of the day, Cindy is clutching carrier bags with thousands of dollars' worth of clothes in them. My hair has been coloured, cut, glossed and ruthlessly straightened. A make-up artist was at work on my face while the hair was being blow-dried and my fingernails are painted in fluorescent orange. We retreat to Cindy's apartment, not far away, for a lesson on which clothes to wear, when and how and with what items of jewellery. You'd think any idiot could work this out and at first I thought she was just having a laugh. But now, as she matches this colour with that bag and the other style with those shoes, I can see there's a lot to this fashionista business. She puts together outfits that I never would have thought to create myself. Cindy lives for clothes – it's all she thinks about – and by the time all the different variations are explained to me, I've realised why she earns a thousand dollars a day to do this. Those girls you see on the gossip pages don't just throw something on at the last minute – there's serious thought and painstaking planning behind the looks.

For tonight, Cindy dresses me in a black, above-the-knee Marc Jacobs dress that hugs every curve and leaves plenty of skin exposed, some knee-high black suede boots, and a green silk handbag that barely holds a handkerchief. Then she loans me her own hoop earrings because she thinks they're essential to complete the look, and we hadn't bought any.

Not many people know this, but the term It girl came from a Hollywood silent film called *It*, made in 1927. The term was used to describe the actress Clara Bow, who appeared in the film. 'It' became synonymous with sex appeal and Bow was 'It'. She became wildly famous. Frankly, in this outfit, I'm a million light years from Clara Bow in her flapper dresses, but I'm feeling the 'It' factor with bells on.

I stare at myself in the full-length mirror in Cindy's bedroom. I scarcely recognise me. It's been nearly two years since I got off that plane from Heathrow with my suit from Marks & Spencer. I realise that the cocky little girl who thought extravagance was a handbag from Top Shop had long since disappeared. If I thought Pearl had given me a makeover, it was just a preliminary rehearsal to this. Now I look like something I could only have marvelled at in magazines at home. I stare hard, and for the first time I see why Bill had seen potential in me. I was beautiful. Not just attractive. Not just a sophisticated face and a slender, curvy figure. I was striking. But there was something else – beyond the Marc Jacobs dress, highlights and artfully applied kohl. There was a harshness, a dead look in my eyes that shocked me a little. I hadn't seen it there for a long time, not since before I married Jamie.

I hadn't come to LA to be famous. That was never my plan. Little girls in America seem to dream of nothing other than getting their faces on the movie screen. Celebrity culture here is bigger than football back home. But I've never seen the attraction of public scrutiny. All I knew when I left England was that there was money to be found in Los Angeles, and money equals security and that was my mission. And I'd been right. There's bloody tons of it. I've never met so many people who think that lunch at the tennis club is roughing it. Los Angeles is a town that has more millionaires per acre than it does street lamps. Only trouble is, somehow I've managed to balls everything up. Somehow, in a town filled with people who never need to ask the price of anything, I've ended up with the guy whose credit card bills are so big, they actually come with a fanfare. I need to rectify big time. I'm doing the right thing.

Bill doesn't speak as I emerge from the lift into the lobby of Cindy's apartment, where he's waiting for me. I can see he's taken aback.

'You're stunning,' he eventually says, his eyes checking me over with a look of wonder.

'You're staring. Don't you know it's rude to stare?'

He laughs heartily.

'Thanks for the clothes, by the way,' I say as casually

as I can, as we climb into the car. No point going over the top.

In foster homes, the social workers tell you to keep your head down, but when it comes to Hollywood parties the exact opposite holds true. Keep your head up or risk missing seeing a celebrity walk by. Keep your head up or miss being seen yourself. You can even get neck strain from watching everyone else peer over other people's shoulders to see if there's someone more important nearby. Cindy, I think, had taken pity on me in the end, and given me her four rules for Hollywood schmoozing whilst I was getting ready. Rule one: Have a drink to fortify yourself for a long night on those heels. Rule two: Stake out a good position, one that enables you to watch the stars. Rule three: Chat up the 'below the line' types because they're the ones that really make things happen. Rule four: Don't forget to hang out in the bathrooms – no place is as effective an equaliser or a better breeding ground for female solidarity.

The party is at Hyde, an oh-so-exclusive nightclub on Sunset. It is to launch a new type of phone gadget that sends emails, photos, text messages, the larger animals of LA Zoo, extraneous household items, and just about everything except a fresh cup of tea. Bill seems to be impressed by it, and tries to explain what it does, but technology leaves me about as excited as a plate of soggy chips. He gives me one to take home, and I promise I'll use it, knowing I never will. Far more mesmerising is the sight of all the stars struggling to understand theirs. There's nothing quite so gratifying as seeing celebrities struggle like the rest of us. Then there's Lindsay Lohan sweeping through the crowd, Ashlee Simpson tucking into finger food, Avril Lavigne standing at the bar. And outside the fans are shouting out names: Rachel! Heather! I feel like I'm living out a Fellini movie.

Bill leads me to the bar and explains that an evening like this is all about symbiotic publicity. The phone gadget manufacturers want everyone to think their product is so cool that all the stars are using them. So they throw a lavish party like this, making sure there are plenty of photographers on hand, and give lots of their phones away. The stars come because they have an image to maintain and need to be seen out at the hip parties, and no matter how much they complain about the paparazzi, they need to get column inches to stay in the public eye.

What's a man like Bill doing here, who needs neither a new phone nor publicity? It quickly becomes apparent that he just likes to pretend he's forty years younger than he is and can't miss a good party. He introduces me to everyone – casting agents, party promoters, photo-graphers, producers, actresses – he knows lots of actresses! But he doesn't just make standard introduc-tions. He's funny. 'May I introduce you to my assistant,' he says, and suddenly pretends to be a magician. 'Here, hold this,' he says, handing me his glass, and then produces coins from behind my ear. He transforms dollar bills into handkerchiefs and back again. He can make watches magically disappear from one wrist and appear on another, and he always laughs at the triumph of it.

He can jump on tables too. Several Rusty Nails down, with feet firmly fixed together, he bends low and then masterfully springs at least five feet into the air like a giant kangaroo to land on table tops, sending drinks, candles and napkins flying. It's an impressive sight, especially since he must weigh over fourteen stone. He's rarely serious. 'What state are you from,' I hear a girl ask him during some polite chit-chat at the bar. 'Denial,' he says with a guffaw.

He makes a big deal of never leaving me on my own, always ensuring we're at the centre of the party, always seeing my glass is filled. And I'm grateful. Parties can be rather stressful: the fear of standing all alone like a loser, the pressure to say the right thing, the risk of drinking too much . . . oh, yes, I knew that route. But Bill is lovely. He also makes sure I'm photographed at the door and he keeps me for a long time with a reporter from the *Los Angeles Magazine* who writes the society pages, introducing me as a new up and coming model. Up and coming is an expression that's used a lot in Los Angeles, and I confess I rather like the sound of it when it's used in relation to me. It's a nice feeling to be cosseted and protected by a man like Bill. This was what I came to LA for in the first place, wasn't it? For protection, wealth, insulation from the real world?

There isn't a single moment when we're not surrounded by a crowd of people, until at 2 a.m., when it's time to leave, he leads me outside into the cool night air. A troupe of Hispanic valets in matching red waistcoats are running to find people their cars. I ask one of them to call me a cab.

'Can't I persuade you back to my place?' says Bill, curling an arm round my shoulder to keep me warm, because it's suddenly very chilly. I lean in to him. His warmth is tempting. He smells of expensive aftershave –

it's a manly smell, a virile smell – the smell of masculine protection. He's old enough to be my father, possibly even my grandfather, but that's strangely attractive to me. It holds the advantage of wisdom, the promise of guidance. I could so use it sometimes. Why is power such a turn-on? I contemplate returning to his house. It will be big and luxurious and I'd be the guest, not the servant, as I was at Stephen's.

'I've got the biggest bed this side of the Atlantic,' Bill boasts.

'And is that what impresses all the girls?' I ask cheekily.

'It's not *all* that impresses them,' he drawls. 'Wanna come back and find out?'

Bill would be a good lover and take care of me. I knew that. But for how long? Until the next plaything presented herself to him? There's no quicker route to losing a man's interest than giving in too soon. This has to be played carefully, I tell myself.

'I can't. Not tonight.' I kiss him lightly on the cheek, feeling his beard scrape against my skin. 'It wouldn't be right,' I say, and make a dash for the cab.

24

It's hard to believe it's Christmas again. It's like the season comes up and slaps you unexpectedly in the face here. There's no warm-up to it, like there is at home with the onset of chilly days. You'll simply be walking through a shopping mall one day wondering how it's possible for shops to be selling winter boots and flip-flops at the same time, and suddenly a familiar smell will greet you. And you'll look up and it's a pine tree, shipped in from Oregon, smelling of Christmas, and you wouldn't have known otherwise. It's been a year since Stephen whisked us off to Aspen. Nearly a year since Jamie and I were married.

Do I really want to sleep with Bill? Jamie hadn't been at home when I'd come back after the party at Hyde. I could have gone back with Bill to his house and Jamie would never have even noticed. He had come in at 4 a.m., reeking of whisky. He hadn't touched me in bed. Just crawled in beside me, and snored like an old man. In the morning he was sullen – a sign I took to mean that he'd lost at poker.

'How was the game?' I'd ventured, calling him on it. He'd told me he'd given it up, but we both knew no one was fooled. Jamie didn't even bother to speak. He just stared at me, with a pathetic, hounded look in his eyes.

'How much did you lose?'

'I don't want to say,' he'd sighed.

I'd left it at that. There was no point in arguing.

At what point in a marriage are you justified in looking for a replacement? Is there ever a justification for being unfaithful? My mum would have said there never was. She wasn't religious, but morality mattered to her. I'm sure she was pure and virginal when she married Dad. But what if your husband turned out to be a moody old bastard who gambled too much, and you never had any money? Wouldn't that be a good enough excuse? I could hear myself arguing with Mum inside my head.

'Nothing is plain sailing,' she'd tell me. 'You loved him once. You'll love him again. Work it out.'

'But that's easy for you to say, when you had everything you ever wanted,' I argue back.

'Marriage is for keeps,' she'd reply. 'Love doesn't just disappear at the first hurdle. Don't throw away something that's right. This is just a hiccup. Jamie's a good man. Do you really want to lose him? Do you really think marrying your way into someone else's fortune is going to make you happy?'

Of course it is, I tell her. Of course it bloody is.

'Do you think you could really be fulfilled?' I hear her asking me. 'Do you really think money's going to satisfy you?'

Of course it will. And look, I'm all alone here, without you, Mum. I've got to make my own decisions now. You don't know what this feels like. And I'm so sick of being poor. You never knew what it was like to be really poor, Mum. Sometimes you have to make sacrifices to stay afloat. You wouldn't understand.

I switch Mum off inside my head.

And anyway, why is there always such a fuss about sex? Perhaps I'll just be Bill's mistress. He'll turn me into an It girl and in return I'll be his regular sleepover guest. Maybe that will be my route. Sex isn't such a big deal if you think about it – it's even smaller if you don't think about it. It barely takes up any time, doesn't require a commute on a bus and does more things for career advancement than an employment agency. Sex is no more than a means to an end. Would it even mean I was being unfaithful? Body entanglement is different from mental entanglement. Everyone knows that.

Bill has to go back to the East Coast for the Christmas holidays so the decision is postponed anyway. Meantime, from the minute I turn up for my second interview at the modelling agency, my life becomes a regeneration project. Heck, it gets such a facelift that even I have trouble recognising me sometimes. Turns out the ad agency likes me. They spend three days photographing me. I smile so much, I get cheek ache. I'm to be the face of a new watch campaign for Rolex. It's going to be huge – magazines, newspapers, bill-boards. Fancy that. My beaming face staring out from billboards across America. Jamie says he always knew I was a star. I'll say this for him – he's always supportive.

And there's a snowball effect too. No sooner is it announced that I'm on the campaign than the modelling agency is calling me with all kinds of other jobs too – clothing catalogues, fashion magazines . . . I'm not tall enough for the catwalk, but they say there will be plenty of photographic work. And then the *Los Angeles Magazine* comes out with a picture of me at the party at Hyde, and suddenly I'm on the PR list too. Now, I'm someone to invite to parties.

'I always knew you'd go places,' says Pearl, offering to come to a few events with me. She's pushing Thackeray's stroller back and forth with her Prada-clad boot while we sit at a table outside the Kraft Services van on the set for Adam's movie. It's finally being shot and he's invited us both down to watch.

Adam and I had started to become really good friends after he'd called me one day, not long after Pearl's wedding, to ask me to an industry screening of a new film. He'd often taken Pearl to events like these before, but after she got married she'd become hell-bent on transforming herself into a good housewife – not to mention being too large and uncomfortable to sit through a movie. I'd willingly been second choice and Jamie had encouraged it. Told me I needed to have a life that was beyond just him and me. Said it was healthy in a relationship. He'd really cared about me back then.

That first night with Adam was hysterical. After the movie was a Meet and Greet with the director who'd made it. Problem was, the film was awful. A stinker. 'Shouldn't have been released, not even on parole,' as Stephen used to say. And then I get introduced to the director. Well, what are you meant to do?

Adam goes for the safe option. 'Great film,' he says. 'Well done.'

I say, 'Nice costumes.'

'You didn't like it then,' the director says to me.

'I didn't say that,' I protest.

'Might as well have,' he snaps.

'Well, I might have done it slightly differently,' I try, and before I know it the man is yelling at me, and Adam and I have to leave.

Adam thinks it's funny. Which it is. From then on, he always asks me to screenings, and we discuss character development and plausible plot lines. We diss the bad acting and applaud anything that makes us laugh. But then they start to make his movie, and new scripts come in all the time for him to work on. It's a rare thing for me to see him at all these days. He's really a big name in screen writing now.

I just wish Pearl would open up her eyes and see how perfect he is for her. He does have an annoying stutter, but he's got a great sense of humour and his constancy is touching. Even when she'd only just married Brett, he'd ask after her. 'H-h-how's Pearl doing?' he'd asked me. 'D-d-d-do you think she's happy?' Of course we both knew the answer and I'd been careful not to give him false hope. But when Brett had abandoned her, and she'd gone into hospital to have her baby without him, it had been Adam who'd appeared first with flowers and gifts of baby clothes. He's gentle, kind, has integrity and patience; and most important, is besotted with her. He's even driving a BMW these days, now that he's in the money. He's perfect for her in every way. But sadly he's not a bastard, and that, it seems, is Pearl's prerequisite in a man. He's also not Brett, who she is so convinced is going to come running back to her one of these days that it's getting beyond boring.

Rather disappointingly, watching Adam's movie being made is also pretty boring. I'd been dead excited at the thought of seeing a real film set in action, but it's about as exciting as reading the *LA Times* (and let me tell you, that's dull). At first it's intriguing to see all the lights and cameras, and people buzzing round with walkie-talkie headsets, talking into them importantly. It's impressive just how many people are involved. But then it takes a whole morning to shoot a few lines – the actors repeat them over and over, while the camera moves from this position to that to the other. Blimey, even the make-up counter at Barney's is livelier than this – not to mention that you see more movie stars.

So we retreat to the catering area for lunch. 'But what I don't understand is why the modelling agency did such a U-turn,' says Pearl, after we've picked at salads and she's droned on with her false hopes about Brett's return. Adam has disappeared gratefully into a meeting with the director. Pearl looks better than she has done in ages. Her hair has been recently cut, and she's masked the dark rings of tiredness under her eyes with make-up. 'I thought they told you to get lost.'

'Ah, but then I found a benefactor, who twisted their arm,' I say joyfully, picking out an apple from the fruit bowl on the table. By now all the rest of the cast and crew are back on set and we're by ourselves.

'Who?' she says, looking up from tucking a blanket around Thackeray, who's chirruping adorably and looking curiously around him, trying to make sense of some pink plastic elephants set up in a row on a string in front of him.

'Bill Makepeace came into Barney's and offered to help me.'

'What?' says Pearl, rather incredulously.

'Well, it didn't happen just like that. I'd met him before at the charity thing Stephen took me to. And when he saw me at Barney's, he invited me out to lunch, and I told him about the agency, and he said he knew the owner and he could help me . . .' I'm about to go on, but Pearl interrupts me.

'Please don't tell me you're sleeping with him,' she says, her newly plucked eyebrows knotting in genuine concern.

'No, I'm not,' I say defensively. 'He's just helping me with a new career. Says I've got the makings of an It girl.'

'Oh, Bella, please,' she gasps. 'Please don't sleep with him.'

'But I haven't slept with him,' I say firmly.

'But men don't do that kind of stuff out of the kindness of their heart. And what about Jamie? What about your marriage? I thought you said you were in love.'

'I am . . . I was . . . Look, I haven't slept with Bill Makepeace.'

'I never thought you were like this, Bella. This is crazy.' She is jiggling poor Thackeray in his stroller like his life depended on it.

'For the last time, I haven't slept with him. But Pearl, you've got to understand. I don't have a family to fall back on. I don't have anyone to put money into a bank account for me when the cupboard's bare. I have no security. There's no one looking after me, except me.

And along comes a rich guy who offers to help me. What am I supposed to do? Turn him down?'

'Let me think about that. Be with a man who makes me happy, or a man who makes me rich.' She spells it out slowly like it's a no-brainer. Like everyone knows the answer is obvious.

I stare at her in disbelief. How could she not understand?

'What about Jamie?' she repeats. 'Is he just a piece of furniture now? Money won't make you happy, you know.'

I'm surprised at how angry she is. It was a mistake to tell her about Bill, clearly. Somehow I thought she had an understanding of how Hollywood works. Everybody shags everybody here to get ahead, and no one even blinks at it. I didn't imagine it would be such a big deal.

'Jamie's about as useful as a sofa which has lost its springs just now. He's got a massive gambling problem and I don't know what to do about it, if you really want to know,' I say sternly. 'Romance is never perfect . . . as you should well know.' This is unfair. But some resentful streak in me wants to burst Pearl's bubble. 'I mean, look at you. When are you going to come to terms with the fact that Brett's never coming back to you? What romantic ideal are you holding out for? You think keeping a flame burning for a man who's used you like toilet paper is romantic? Sometimes life isn't romantic.'

Pearl's eyes fill up with tears. And just to make me feel really bad, Thackeray starts to howl, so she picks him up and rocks him back and forth in her chair, hugging him to her chest. Now I feel awful.

'I'm sorry. I didn't mean to be mean,' I sigh. 'I'm

really sorry.' Pearl's searching in her vast Prada bag for a tissue. 'But it's true. Even if Brett were to come back to you, it could never work now. You don't need him. You don't.'

'I know,' she sobs. 'I know you're right.'

I lean forward to hug her, which isn't easy with a baby jam-sandwiched between us. I can't believe I just made her cry.

'It's just that it's so hard to find real love. I don't think I'll ever find it. And look, you've found it. Don't throw it away.' She looks up at me pleadingly. 'Please, Bella. Please.'

I don't hear from Bill until the end of January, when he calls me on my mobile. I'm having my make-up done for a photoshoot by Jay-jay, who had better be gay or that's a serious waste of Lycra. 'How's my little wine taster?' Bill asks, all brightness and fun in his voice.

'All the better for hearing your voice,' I say, a trifle cheesily. But it was the truth. Pearl's admonishment had stopped me in my tracks awhile and I'd hesitated about whether I'd done the right thing to go out with Bill. But what did Pearl know about having no money? Bill had been fun to flirt with; he'd made me feel good. Our night out had been the most excitement I'd had in a month of Sundays. I'd also been frightened that I'd blown it by not sleeping with him. The cheques from the first couple of modelling jobs had come in – and I'd had to sit down I was so surprised at the size of them. I could see light at the end of the tunnel, earning this kind of cash. I'd even felt confident enough to quit working at Barney's. But would the modelling jobs dry up without Bill's patronage? He was in a position to take it all away from me if he wanted to.

So when he calls me from Manhattan where he's been held up, I'm thrilled. He's backing a movie which is in production there, and they've run into some technical problems that're going to cost an extra two or three million.

'Oh, that's small change to you, isn't it?' I say. He likes me to tease him. He says he likes me because I make him laugh.

'Sure it is, honey, sure it is,' he chortles. 'Of course, once I've spent it, I'll have to start leaning on you for a loan. I hear things are going pretty good.'

'Not bad,' I say, and give him a list of three modelling jobs I'm booked for, for next month – an editorial fashion shoot, a shoot for a catalogue that they may fly me to Florida for, and a swimsuit special for Neiman Marcus, a department store in Beverly Hills. Bill wants to hear all the details.

'And have you been putting your face out there? Tell me what parties you've been going to. You know that's all part of the job, don't you?'

I reel off half a dozen charity, publicity and PR events that I've got invitations to – there's one in aid of UNICEF that Angelina Jolie is meant to be coming to, an HBO fundraiser for a children's hospital, a celebrity auction in Beverly Hills that lists more A-list attendees than *People* magazine, and several launches of new Internet websites. I've stuck them all with magnets to the fridge door in our kitchen.

'But haven't you been to any yet?' he demands.

In truth I hadn't. I'd been too exhausted by the

modelling jobs – all of them had started at 5 a.m. But I don't want him to think I'm not keen on his grand plan. 'Well, I haven't exactly had my drinking buddy by my side,' I say. 'It's boring to go on my own.' Bill laughs and tells me I should be going to them anyway.

'When are you coming back?' I ask.

'February, honey. I'll be back in time for the Oscars . . .' He pauses. 'Say, there's an idea. You can come with me to the *Vanity Fair* party.'

'Is that an invitation?'

'Sure . . .' He hesitates, as if running the idea still through his own mind. 'Why not? And perhaps you'll even be brave enough to come back to my place. What do you say to that?'

'I think you'd better be ready.'

I t's hard to describe to anyone who doesn't live in Los Angeles just how big a deal the Oscars are. It's like a royal wedding, without the flags or souvenir coffee mugs. Whole streets shut down, shops close early, people take to sleeping on the pavements – and no matter if the closest your hairdresser has ever been to a star is the horoscope page of the *LA Times*, it's still impossible to get an appointment. If the city council could turn it into a national holiday, I'm sure they would. It is simply an extravaganza of DeMille-ian proportions that has to be seen to be believed.

And although there's a lot of fuss about the Oscars and who wins what, and who wears what, and who goes with whom, and who cries in their speeches, the really big deal on Oscar night is not the Oscar ceremony at all. (Too long and boring, according to Stephen, who goes every year.) The really big bazooka on Oscar night, the climax of the whole shebang, the icing on the cake, if you will, is the *Vanity Fair* party. For Los Angeles society, an invitation to the *Vanity Fair* party is the pinnacle of achievement. It means you have arrived. It means you are accepted. It means you are part of that inner circle of Hollywood's elite.

Only a thousand or so people get invited each year, by Graydon Carter, the editor of *Vanity Fair* magazine, that bible of social recognition, which means that even some A-listers have to phone up his office and beg to be let in. Sometimes they even offer bribes. It really is the most exclusive party in the world – and that means the biggest security, the most fantastical guest list and the most TV cameras parked outside.

Of course the invitation hadn't exactly arrived in my mail box personally. Bill was allowed one guest, but I was in. I was part of the in crowd. Last year Jamie and I had watched the Oscars from the telly in our living room – I'd marvelled at the frocks, he'd marvelled at the injustices of awards given to all the wrong films. Then he'd gone to bed and I'd stayed up to watch E!, the entertainment channel that had reporters standing outside all the big parties, asking ridiculous questions of the stars like 'What does it feel like to win?' Duh! And I'd thought to myself back then, I wonder if . . . I'd wondered if I ever stood a chance of making it into Hollywood nobility. I'd have done it if I'd married Stephen. I'd have been in there on the charity ball circuit, lunching with luminaries, flying high in our private jet, and only getting out of bed when I felt like it.

But as one door closes, another swings wide open. Cindy doesn't have time to dress me personally. I know my place. She's got three A-listers to dress today. But we'd spent all of yesterday going through dresses in her apartment, and chosen an oh-so-clingy, spicy-red halter-neck dress that pushes the boobs out on a shelf of silk, nips neatly in at the waist and then makes the hips a celebration of curves, tapering in at the feet. Talk about va-va-voom.

I'd actually dieted hard to achieve this look. Talk about servitude in the name of beauty. Cindy had slipped me some diet pills, told me all the stars use them. Only problem is they make me pee all the time, and fart excessively.

It takes hours to get ready. A hairdresser press-gangs my hair into an up-do à la Audrey Hepburn in *Breakfast at Tiffany's*. A manicurist sharpens the talons and paints them a matching red. Jamie loads me into the frock – I think he's more bemused than anything. But he likes to be accommodating and he's been very encouraging of my new career. A limousine collects me at 3 p.m.

'Have a great time,' he says as he waves goodbye out of the apartment window.

Jamie thinks it's the modelling agency that has got me an in to the *Vanity Fair* party, which given the exclusive nature of the event could never happen, but he doesn't seem to question it. I think he thinks I'm more of a celebrity than I actually am. I tell him I'm going to stay over at Pearl's afterwards and he tells me to have fun. It's in his nature to be supportive. He's just that kind of person. I feel bad about heading off to Bill's, but this is survival, I tell myself. And besides, he'll never know.

'Oooh baby, you look good enough to eat,' says Bill, as the limousine pulls up outside his house and I step out on to a gravel drive in heels that defy common sense, clutching my overnight bag. 'I really should put you in one of my movies.'

The Oscars start at 5 p.m. and the idea is that Bill

and I watch the proceedings on the TV at his place with a few of his friends, and then go on to the party once the ceremony is over. The house is huge. Of course. But better taste than most. It has an air of a French château about it – there are shutters at the windows, and a high grey-tiled roof with iron filigree work on the top and circular turrets. Inside it is light and airy, with a stone-floored hallway where a smell of good cooking wafts, and immediately beyond is the garden, where a line of cypress trees leads to a fountain featuring a very tasteful Neptune, complete with trident and stone fishes. Bill guides me into a living room ruled by a vast marble mantelpiece beneath which a fire has been lit, and over which a giant mirror reaches up to the tall ceiling. There's antique furniture everywhere, paintings of horses, and brightly coloured Persian carpets covering deep brown hardwood floors.

'Here, let me get a good look at you,' he says, taking a step back, and surveying my curves with a licentious grin. He's like a foodie, slathering over the prospect of a dish.

'All right, all right. Enough, now. I'm not one of your dumb actresses,' I scold him. I can't bear this sort of thing.

'Sure aren't,' he says. 'Say, don't I even get a kiss?'

He leans in and kisses me on the lips, letting his hands run over the smooth silk hugging the contours of my behind.

'Baby, you are just too much.'

I pull away. 'Don't mess the lipstick. Do you know how long it took me to get ready? Anyway, where's your suit? You're not going like that, are you?' He's still wearing jeans and a T-shirt.

'I'm running late,' he says, unable to take his eyes off

me, which is all very flattering, but even after several photo shoots I'm still not used to being leered at. 'I won't be long. Say, let me fix you a drink, you put your feet up here and I'll be changed in a second. What are you going to have?'

'How about a cuppa tea?'

'Tea? Honey, this is Oscar night. This is party city.'

'Just to start with. We've got a long night ahead of us,' I remind him.

'Sure. Sure we have.' And he disappears upstairs telling someone, presumably a maid in the kitchen, to bring me in some tea.

Against one of the walls is a giant flat-screen television. I flick it on, to see Joan Rivers on the red carpet commenting on the first Oscar arrivals. She's screeching at Keira Knightley, begging her to come over to talk to her camera, and then asks her who dressed her. Keira tells her she managed to dress herself and they both screech some more.

The maid brings me a teacup of hot water with a yellow Lipton's tea bag laid on a plate alongside, but no milk. Americans haven't a clue how to make tea. I thank her anyway, and scan the silver-framed photographs set out on a table by the window. They're mostly pictures of Bill: Bill playing golf. Bill, looking much younger, at a piano sitting next to Frank Sinatra. Bill with an arm wrapped round Sidney Poitier's shoulders. Bill pushing Elizabeth Taylor's wheelchair.

He arrives back in the room, wearing a tuxedo with a white shirt which is unbuttoned to halfway down, leaving his greying, curly tendrils of chest hair gaping over the top.

'So I've got just a couple of friends coming by,' he says, as a Bentley crunches on the drive. 'You'll like 'em.'

Malcolm Fischbein is a comedy writer and looks it. Short spiky hair, and nerdy square-framed glasses. It's the glasses that do it, I decide. His wife is a full foot taller than him, not especially beautiful, not especially thin, also square-framed glasses. So no surprise, she's his writing partner. They've written a series of teenage comedies, inspired mostly by toilet humour. And they're friendly. The Liebmans are less so. Jeffrey looks like he's swallowed a golf ball and is about to cough it up any moment. He's a banker. His wife is the closest thing I've ever seen to a human mouse in a twinset and pearls.

They're cautiously polite to me but I can see them looking me over and thinking, 'So she's Bill's latest bimbo.' They've clearly been down this road before. 'Are you an actress?' the mouse asks, looking pitifully at me. She looks even more pitiful when I tell her I'm doing some modelling work. None of them are dressed up either, which makes me feel rather overdone. Embarrassingly so. But Bill explains that they're only here to watch the show on TV. And so we settle down in front of the telly, which causes me a lot of grief what with the farting and the dress's built-in corset and the shrimps in filo pastry which I daren't touch for fear of dropping crumbs down my front.

It's a relief to leave for the party. But blimey, talk about social anxiety. The first thing that hits me (although fortunately not literally) is a thirty-foot long, ten-foot high *Vanity Fair* logo, made entirely out of a hedge. Then there's the barricade of paparazzi – the word 'roadblock' just doesn't do it justice – at one end of the driveway. At the other end is an army of television cameras, publicists, security guards and limo drivers, and beyond them is a jostling throng of fans who scream every time they see a movie star. Helicopters beat a staccato thump overhead. Searchlights swoop through the chilly night air and my heart is pounding. Bill takes my hand firmly in his and leads the way, stopping only to pose next to me for the cameras, which flash blindingly.

Inside, it's no less terrifying. Especially when you notice the crowd. They're all familiar. It's like going to an old school reunion, where you recognise everyone but somehow they've changed a bit. There's Jennifer Aniston in one corner looking like a grown-up version of the girl you used to sit next to in class and whose work you'd always copy because she always got top marks. In another is Sandra Bullock looking like the girl you used to tease because she had such an ugly nose. In another is Naomi Watts, whom no one used to like because she never joined in. And there's George Clooney looking like a much older version of the boy that all the girls wanted to go out with.

Once over the nerves, though, it's a blast. I feel like I'm at a party where I know everyone. I want to rush up to them and say, 'Hi, remember me?' A waiter serves me champagne and Bill leads me into the thick of the crowd. He introduces me to Ben Affleck. I mean, blimey, now I'm really in. Bill knows him through some movie deal or other. The star smiles politely, but it's hard to know what to say. 'Do you live nearby?' seems so lame. And everyone must say, 'Oh, I did enjoy your movie.' So for some reason I opt for 'That's a nice suit', and then feel really stupid. Of course it's a nice bloody suit. He's a movie star. Anyway, the music is so loud it's hard to hear anything. So we smile, and all round the room I notice everyone else is pretty much doing the same. And there I am beaming away, with Bill keeping an arm wrapped proprietorially round my waist, when who should I notice staring right back at me with a face like a dog's bottom but Stephen Shawe. He's sitting at a table with some suits.

There are some occasions when you can catch someone's eye ever so briefly, and get away with looking the other way and pretending you haven't seen them. But when you spot them staring at you, and they've obviously been staring at you for some time, you're sort of done for. And I'm really done for, because now he's waddling over.

'Well, well, well, if it isn't Isabella . . .' He pauses, rolling his eyes to the ceiling, as if searching for my last name. 'Shawe, isn't it?' he says caustically. He's wearing the same tuxedo he wore to the charity dinner he took me to.

'How are you doing, Stephen?' I say cautiously.

'I'm doing very well,' Stephen says ever so slowly, making sure I pick up on the note of venom in his voice. He looks me up and down like I'm a nasty stain on the carpet.

Totally failing to pick up on Stephen's tone, Bill shakes his hand cordially and beams as he always does. Please God, don't let him start on his magic tricks with him. 'And how's business, Stephen?' he asks. 'What do you think of tonight's wins?'

'Oh, much as expected, Bill. Much as expected,' he says back in an even tone. He sips on his champagne.

'Sorry to see you didn't have any of your films nominated this year.'

'Not worried about it at all, Stephen. Next year will be ours. Just wait and see. We've got some good things coming up. Good things . . .'

'Bill, darling, how are you?' An overly made-up brunette, glittering in a yellow sequined gown, interrupts him and drags his attention away.

'Got yourself a new boyfriend, have you?' Stephen asks me scathingly once Bill is out of earshot. If he'd tried to do an impression of Ebenezer Scrooge on Christmas Eve, he couldn't have done a better job.

'He's a business colleague,' I tell him flatly. 'I'm modelling now.'

'Like hell he is. Does Jamie know you're here?' he asks. Then adds after a second, 'Two-timing him too?'

'Of course he knows I'm here,' I say, feeling my own temper rising. He has no reason to speak to me like this. 'Anyway, what's it to you? Suddenly showing a paternal interest? Suddenly getting protective of the son you've shown so much love and affection to? Come on now, Stephen, it doesn't suit you.'

Stephen looks affronted that anyone should dare talk back. His Adam's apple wobbles.

'And what do you mean, two-timing him too? You think I two-timed you? Is that what you think? One date with you, and that's it? I'm yours?'

For a second Stephen looks like he's about to explode. His face reddens. He holds his breath, as if he's going to start yelling. And then he gets a grip and pours the rest of his glass of champagne down his throat.

'I never two-timed you,' I say, letting out a sigh, trying

to regain my composure. 'I didn't know you even liked me. Jesus, how was I supposed to know? Mind-read?'

There's silence between us, while around us voices are screeching and cackling, screaming and laughing. Stephen looks around the room, unsure what to say next.

'Well, I can see I saved myself a whole heap of trouble,' he says eventually. He turns to leave, but then turns back. His face is suddenly softer. 'How's Jamie?' he asks, with a note of tenderness in his voice that I've never heard before.

'He misses you,' I say.

'Tell him I said hi,' he says, but then adds with the sarcasm back in his voice again, 'should you see him, of course.' He turns to head back to his table.

By the time I've found Bill again, the shaking has stopped. We stay for a few more drinks, a few more introductions and handshakes, but by midnight Bill is keen to get down to what's really on his agenda for the evening, and tonight there's no wriggling out of it.

His chauffeur whizzes us away, past the flashing lightbulbs and into the darkened streets of Beverly Hills. Bill rests his hand on my knee in the back of the limousine.

'So do you still want to be famous, now that you've witnessed it up close?' he asks as he plants a kiss on my neck and slides the hand slowly up my thigh.

'Looks horrendous,' I tell him. And I mean it.

'You're joking, right?'

'No,' I say flatly. 'Fame looks like a bloody nightmare if you ask me. Who'd want to be famous when you've got that lot taking pictures of you every time you scratch your arse or pick your nose?'

Bill bursts out laughing. 'And you're going for modelling jobs? Well, that makes sense.' He laughs some more. 'Baby, you are a case.' We pull up at a traffic light where a panhandler is begging for change. Bill buzzes down his window and throws a fifty-dollar bill into his bucket.

His house is peaceful when we get back there. The maid has cleaned up the empty glasses and party snacks. The lights are low but the fire is still roaring in the living room. I wish I'd drunk a bit more. I've never thought twice about having sex before if it meant getting what I wanted. It had always been a tool for me, no more than that. It never caused me any grief; I never even stopped to think about it before. It's just a question of going through the motions, right? But suddenly it's not that easy. Suddenly, I realise that getting intimate with someone who isn't Jamie is about as appealing as last night's leftovers. Heck, this is no time to start getting a conscience. What's happened to me? All you have to do is close your eyes and think of the shopping you've got to get in the morning, I tell myself. We need toilet paper, onions, milk . . . Anyway, it's all in a good cause. Bill offers me a glass of brandy, and kisses me softly on the lips, grinding his groin into mine.

'Shall we go upstairs?' he asks.

'Better had,' I say. ' "The best way to hold a man is in your arms." '

Bill laughs. 'Groucho Marx?' he asks.

'Don't be daft. Mae West,' I tell him and pull off my shoes at the foot of his grand staircase. I hope to God he's not into any kinky fetish stuff. I'm not sure I can deal with anything weird. You hear about that stuff sometimes in Hollywood. People who like sex with a balaclava on their heads, or insist on wearing a dog lead or handcuffs, or want sex while holding a gun to your head . . . A shiver works its way down my spine. Oh, please God, don't let him be into weird sex.

His bedroom is big enough to land a jumbo jet in. Festoons of curtains sweep across a runway of windows. There's another fire roaring in a fireplace with a sheepskin rug laid out in front, and another enormous television set. It's like walking into a set for a James Bond movie. And there are some abstract naked forms framed on the walls. 'They're by Picasso,' says Bill as I look closely at them. It's hard to make out what the shapes are supposed to be doing, but no prizes for guessing. 'I think you should only have erotic art in the bedroom, don't you?' he says. An elaborate gilt bedhead that would be at home in Versailles ensures that the focus of the room is undeniably the bed, which is covered by a real fur throw. The thought of the skin of some dead animal making a bed coverlet makes me feel vaguely sick. But Bill is keen for me to feel how soft it is.

'Come here, my darling,' he says, patting the bed next to where he's sitting. 'Come and feel this.'

'As the actress said to the bishop,' I say uneasily and sit next to him. He brushes a hair from my forehead and strokes my cheek, then he's kissing my neck. He starts at its base and works up to my ears and then my mouth. It tickles. He leans over me, his hand expertly moving towards a nipple beneath my dress. He's a good lover, I'll give him that. This is a man who's had a lot of practice. And if it weren't that I suddenly seem to have developed more conscience than a Catholic, I'd be sinking powerless in his arms, relishing every second of this – the warmth of the fire, the tranquillity of his room, the temptation of his touches. I feel like I'm sinking into treacle but fighting desperately to stay afloat. What the hell's wrong with me? For some reason, I'm just not feeling it. There's nothing to the act of sex. All it takes is a few moments. But all I can think of is Jamie at home. He'd been so encouraging in his send-off. So innocent as he helped me into my dress. I suddenly feel miserable for lying to him.

I wrap my arms round Bill's neck. I must try. But this is so different from Jamie's touch. I'd been able to let myself go when I'd been with Jamie. I'd felt it was safe to be me. This, somehow, seems fake. For the first time in my life, sex suddenly feels very intimate. It's as if a violation is taking place. Jeepers, who would have guessed that marriage would have this effect on me? Has marriage to Jamie changed me that much?

Bill's got a hand inside my dress now, creeping slowly up my inner thigh. His hands are gentle and smooth, and he knows how to tantalise and excite. I tell myself to shut my eyes, stop staring at the ceiling and at least be responsive. Women are good at faking enjoyment, and I'm an expert. I force myself to reach for the lump beneath his trousers and wish he'd just hurry up and get it over and done with. But Bill wants more than just a takeout. He's in for the full seven-course dinner menu.

'What's the matter, honey?' he says eventually, realising he could probably have more fun with a corpse. 'Aren't I pressing the right buttons?'

'No, you are, you are. I don't know what the matter is with me,' I say, sitting up and tidying my hair. Breathe deep, I tell myself, and imagine you're someone else. 'I'm sorry. Come on, let me try this . . .'

I lean back and start unzipping his flies. But he grabs my hand and sits up.

'If I wanted sex with a disinterested mule, I'd have stayed married to my wife. I thought you were into this,' he says, with just a hint of irritation in his voice. The twang of his southern accent suddenly sounds strong now.

The fire flickers, and I notice my nail polish is peeling. I thrust my hand into his, and kiss him lightly on the cheek, not sure what to do next.

'You've been so kind to me, I don't know what to say,' I start gingerly. 'I guess I'm just not feeling myself.'

Bill pulls away and starts playing with a cuff link box which was on the table by the side of the bed. He opens and closes it, opens and closes it.

I massage his shoulders. I can feel the hair on his back beneath his shirt. 'You have every right to be angry,' I say, fully expecting him to be exactly that. 'You've bought me all these clothes, helped me with the agency, and I want to pay you back. I do. I really do. Can we give it another go?' I say, sounding, I realise, too much like a nanny chivvying the children. I stand up and start unzipping my dress.

But Bill's looking stern. 'Honey, this is not a business arrangement. I'm offended that you think it is. If I'd wanted to pay for sex, I'd have got a prostitute. She'd have been cheaper.' He snorts and gets up off the bed.

Oh, God. Now I've really offended him. I reach to touch his arm, but he moves away. His head is bowed. I've never seen him this way.

'I'm sorry. I'm really sorry.' I have a surge of emotion

swelling inside my chest. I feel awful. This would be so much easier if Bill wasn't so much of a sweetheart – if he was some arrogant, egotistical control freak who did hold a gun to your head whilst having sex. Hollywood's full of those gits. How come I got the nice guy? How come I've made the nice guy feel cheap? My brain is paralysed with confusion.

'Look, this is meant to be fun for us both, but I can see you're having doubts about it, so let's stop right here,' says Bill. He sighs and wanders into the adjoining bathroom. I hear the sound of him peeing echoing against the walls – long and loud. Then he comes back, collects his glass of brandy from the table and sits down on the chaise longue at the end of the bed. He leans back and takes a long slug of the brandy. He looks hurt. I've insulted his masculinity, I can see that. I wonder, briefly, if I can redeem the situation. I can go through with this, I tell myself. I kneel at his feet and reach up to kiss him.

'I'm sorry. I didn't mean it to be this way,' I say. 'I do really like you. But . . .'

'But?' Bill looks at me crossly.

'I'd better just go,' I say, and get up to leave.

'No. Sit down, for goodness' sake,' he says severely. The sound of a helicopter passing overhead disturbs the silence. I perch next to him on the chaise longue. 'I knew it was a mistake to fall for you.' He lets out a long sigh. 'I thought I'd stopped falling in love a long time ago. But you . . . you do something to me. You're funny. You're cute. You've got that accent thing going on. You're not afraid to tell people what you think. You're genuine . . .'

Not that genuine, I chastise myself.

He sighs again. 'I guess I'm just a foolish old man to think the love could be reciprocated.'

'You're not foolish . . .' I put my hand in his. 'You're lovely, you really are.'

'But not lovely enough . . . My money is what's lovely.'

There's a long silence. I stare at our feet for want of anything better to focus on. His are still encased in their black wool socks. They're big, wide, long – Goliath feet. They make my naked toes look tiny. This wasn't how it was meant to turn out.

'A long time ago . . .' He clears his throat. 'A very long time ago, I slept with someone because I needed to get ahead in this place we call Hollywood. It wasn't pretty and I'm not proud of it . . . but it got me where I wanted to go.' He pauses to drink some more. I say nothing, but I know he's talking about his friendship with Ely Goldstein, the gay owner of Prevalent Pictures. I'd dismissed it as just a rumour when I'd read it in his biography on Google.

'I wiped it from my memory because I disgusted myself,' Bill continues. 'But I got what I wanted . . . I got the job, the leg up the ladder, the big fat paycheque, the mansion, the car . . . I got myself set up in Hollywood. But was it worth it?' He leaves the question hanging in the air. The fire lets out a loud crackle.

'You don't need to know the details. But I don't want you to have to do that. I'm not the kind of man who forces any woman to have sex with him if she's not into it.' He laughs. 'Honey, I don't need to. But you interest me. I thought so from the minute I met you with your impressive knowledge of wine and how not to behave at Hollywood balls. You're not like the other girls. You don't want to be in one of my movies. You don't want to be famous. And, clearly, you don't want me.' He chuckles. 'So what the heck do you want?'

I study my toes some more. 'You want the truth?' I say hesitantly.

'Why not?'

'I want money,' I say flatly.

'Money? That's all?' He almost laughs.

'Easy for you to say "That's all". I always promised myself that I wouldn't let losing my parents define me. I didn't want it to always be the pretext to fall back on when I screw things up, which I seem to always do. But sometimes it's a damn good excuse to have when you don't really know how else to explain why you're sitting in a rich man's bedroom, inexplicably come over with the morals of a nun.'

I give Bill the truncated version of how I ended up in Hollywood and he listens silently to it all. 'I don't just want money,' I tell him. 'I want independence, security, a happy ever after. I want the down payment on a future – a future where there's a home I don't have to move on from every ten seconds, clothes I don't have to save for ever to buy, a lifestyle that isn't overshadowed by the threat of being sent back to Britain.' Now it's my turn to sigh, and I let out a long one.

'I'm not bad,' I find myself pleading with him. 'I'm just trying to get ahead, the same as everyone. And I thought luck was really on my side when I found Jamie. I thought he was the answer to my prayers. He told me he loved me, promised me riches. But then his dad pulled everything out from under him when he got married to me. He stopped the financing for his film.

And now Jamie's sinking into an abyss of gambling debts and depression, and it's all my fault . . . I feel so bad for him.' Tears begin to fall down my cheeks.

'I wouldn't say it's all your fault,' says Bill sympathetically. 'We are all responsible for our own providence.' He hands me a tissue.

'The truth is when you first invited me to lunch I had the idea in the back of my mind of asking you to help Jamie with his movie. I thought maybe you'd fund it . . . I mean that is what you do, isn't it? Fund movies? But then I did really enjoy being out with you. It was fun. It was nice to be with you. I forgot about Jamie and our miserable little apartment in Koreatown. I was flattered that you asked me out. I felt seduced. I just wasn't expecting to suddenly get so hung up about lying. It's never bothered me before. I thought I could go through with this . . .'

I blow my nose on the tissue. 'And the thing is, when you said you'd turn me into a model, I thought, well, why not? I could see it was achievable. I could see a way to make my own money, and I kind of got swept up in the whole thing. I wouldn't blame you if you called the modelling agency tomorrow.'

'I see.' Bill plays with his beard and considers for a while. 'The gold-digger with a conscience . . . interesting.'

'Is that what you think I am?'

'No, I think that's what *you* think you are.'

'Meaning?'

'It's perfectly obvious you're in love with your husband. Here you are turning down me and my money because you're hung up on the itty-bitty problem of a husband. Darling, gold-diggers are more callous than that. I'd say you probably married Jamie for all the right reasons, but you're too frightened to admit it to yourself.' He pauses briefly. 'You're too scared to even admit you have feelings. Too frightened to allow yourself that luxury. A shrink would have a field day with you.' He laughs. 'Anyway, what other reason can there possibly be for resisting my charms?'

I'm relieved to see his sense of humour return. 'I'm sorry I led you up the garden path.'

'Is that what you call it?' He laughs again.

I wouldn't blame Bill if he threw me out now. Wouldn't blame him if he didn't ever want to have anything to do with me again. But he'd asked for the truth, and I'd given it to him. Stupid of me. Stupid. I'd ballsed everything up all over again.

Bill stands up and walks over to the fireplace. He studies the flames awhile and then turns. 'Here's what we're going to do,' he says eventually.

I brace myself. He's going to want me to pay for all the dresses he bought.

'You're already well on course to make something of yourself. You know that, don't you?' I nod, but he's not really looking for a response. 'You've got a few years left in you as a model. There are plenty of modelling agencies here in LA; they're not as busy as the ones in New York, but the fact that you've got all these jobs lined up already says a lot. You've got an interesting face and that will get you places. But you're not stupid either. You're smarter than you give yourself credit for. Your knowledge of the movies could get you a presenting job. Have you ever thought of that? That cute little accent, your barefaced cheek, all those Mae West quotations . . .

You know, the TV is really the place for you. You're
young enough, you're cute enough and if you get
enough exposure you'll crack it.'

He yawns and smooths his hands over the top of his
head. 'With a good PR team and a manager behind you,
you'll get endorsement deals, and more money than you'll
ever know what to do with. And then you can finance
your husband's movie or do whatever the heck you want
to do. And here's the deal. I'll make sure it happens. I'll
get you the best publicist this town has to offer.'

He yawns again. 'But,' he barks suddenly, raising his
index finger and pointing it in the air, 'there'll be a price
to pay.' He looks at me seriously. Oh, shit. 'You thought
ours was a business deal, and so now we're going to
really make it one. I'll take fifteen per cent of everything
you make, after costs.'

'Ten,' I say instantly.

'Deal,' he says, offering a hand to shake. I leap up
and hug him. 'And now I need my bed. The guest
bedroom's down the landing to the right.'

Los Angeles has its most perfect days in February. The
air is deliciously clear and crisp. From Sunset Boulevard
you can even see the white snowy peaks of the San
Bernadino mountains. There's none of the heat haze of
the heavy, warmer days of summer, and usually there's a
breeze whisking the pollution away. Today is one of those
glorious days when all you can do is look at the blue of
the sky and marvel at the outrageousness of its colour.

It's a day for resolve too. If last night was a test, I'd
passed. I'd been good. I'd been loyal. Pearl would have
been proud – and I'd got myself a good business deal

into the bargain with no unnecessary strings. I felt like the weight of the Empire State Building had been lifted off my shoulders, and it left me soaring with good intentions. No need for being economical with the truth any more. No need to be economical full stop. I was going to be rich. Jamie can make his documentary, and we'll have enough money for a new apartment and a car. God, we need a car! I'm sick of taking bloody cabs everywhere. Sick of bloody Russian taxi drivers who don't stop talking, like this one Bill has called to take me home.

I'm going to be a better wife from now on too. Perhaps I haven't been the best wife I could have been. Perhaps I could have been more understanding. Perhaps I hadn't realised what I had. But all marriages have their ups and downs, right? Ours had just experienced a bit of a downhill slalom. First thing I'm going to do when I get home is tell Jamie how much I love him.

Except it's hard to be a good wife when you're greeted with not so much a blast of insults as all-out cannon fire. It kind of puts the kibosh on 'How was your evening last night, dear?' Walking into our apartment was like entering a war zone in your undies. Talk about unprepared. Jamie is on the sofa with a face that looks like he's got constipation.

'So how long has it been going on?' he snaps at me before I've even had a chance to put my overnight bag down and shut the door behind me.

'How long's what been going on?' I ask crossly. I don't like to be shouted at.

'You and Bill Makepeace. Your new rich beau,' he snarls.

'Don't be ridiculous,' I tell him.

'I saw you with him on the TV, damn it.' Jamie gets up and starts pacing up and down the room, fists clenched, looking remarkably like his father. It's like déjà vu. I've lived through this already.

Stupid, I know, but it hadn't occurred to me that he might see me on the telly. Hadn't thought I'd warrant any attention.

'I told you the modelling agency were setting me up to go the *Vanity Fair* party. He was simply my way in. He's a friend of Jean Harvey's,' I say, thinking fast, and taking some groceries I'd picked up on my way home into the kitchen. It's not exactly a lie.

'Oh yeah, and why weren't you at Pearl's last night?'

'Because the party went on late and Bill offered me his guest room,' I say evenly. 'Come on, you're being daft.'

'You expect me to believe that?' says Jamie, who's followed me into the kitchen, screaming like Meat Loaf, though without the electric guitars. 'You go back to Bill Makepeace's house – the biggest womaniser in Hollywood – and you tell me you stayed in his guest room? In that dress?'

'But I did,' I say as calmly as is possible in the face of a human typhoon. I turn to look him in the eyes, so he can see I'm not lying. 'I did.'

'And what about this?' Jamie yells, pulling a piece of paper from the back pocket of his jeans. I recognise it instantly. 'You tell me what this is,' he shouts. It's a bank statement. Mine. Showing ten thousand dollars. It had been hidden in my undies drawer. When I got paid for the first modelling job, I'd opened a new account, separate from the one that I shared with Jamie. I did it because I didn't want him gambling my money away. I wanted to save it, put it towards our future. I tell him as much, but he doesn't believe me.

'What are you, Bill Makepeace's whore? Is this how much he paid you?'

What? He thinks Bill's paying me. Jesus, I'm in trouble.

'I'm telling you, it's what I earned modelling—'

'He buys you nice clothes, slips you money, takes you to parties – and you do what for him?' Tears of frustration pour down Jamie's cheeks.

'I'm giving him ten per cent of everything I earn,' I tell him flatly, but Jamie just laughs at me.

'Like Bill Makepeace needs ten per cent of what you make. Don't make me laugh, Bella.'

There's a banging on the wall from our neighbours next door. 'Shut up in there,' someone yells at us.

'Please listen to me, Jamie. It's not what you think,' I say, but now he's in the bedroom looking in the back of the cupboard for a suitcase. I want to cry, I want to scream, I want to hold him close and make him believe me. Why is it I screw everything up?

'Please, Jamie. Please listen,' I plead again. 'Bill did buy me clothes, yes. He did take me to the *Vanity Fair* party, yes. And I know what it must look like. But he did it because we've got an arrangement—'

'I'll bet you have,' he growls, throwing socks and shirts into the suitcase now. 'I must have been mad marrying you. Must have been out of my mind.'

'Can I just explain?' I beg him, standing in the open

door frame to block his exit, which I can see coming like a train down the track. 'Won't you at least listen to me?'

'What is it with you, Bella? Can't resist a rich man?' Jamie shuts his case, turns to face me and for a second I think he's going to hit me, but instead he reaches for my *How to Marry the Rich* book which is lying on the bed. He must have unearthed it from where I'd hidden it in a drawer. 'That's why you dated my father, isn't it?' He spits as he speaks. 'Did you sleep with him too?'

'No, of course not.'

'But you knew he was rich. And that's why you married me, isn't it? You thought I was rich too. But, oh dear, what a mistake that turned out to be.' His voice is mocking me. 'So now that you've discovered I'm not, you're after some other rich bastard, aren't you? Aren't you? Go on, admit it. You're nothing but a whore, Bella. You'll fit right in there as Bill Makepeace's next trophy wife.' He pushes me out of the way.

The front door slams shut after him and I can't think to do anything but cry. I sob till my face is so swollen I could win a bit part in an alien movie. I sob until even Mr Wilberforce begs to be let out and I don't have any tears left. And even then I cry some more. I've fucked up again, haven't I? And the really big fuck-up, the biggest fuck-up of all, was I did bloody love him. I especially love him now he's gone. And that's the biggest mistake of all.

26

The annoying thing about breaking up with someone is that all the times together seem like they
were happy ones when you look back on them. The past
becomes a nostalgic black and white movie with violin
strings and soft focus. You forget the arguments and only
remember the 'love you's. I try to remind myself that
our marriage was a struggle sometimes – it certainly
wasn't all a breeze. But I'm not very successful at
convincing myself – I only seem to remember being
happy. How daft is that?

I never expected to miss Jamie as much as I do. I've
been through bereavement twice over, and I had
thought I was familiar with all the sensations. He'll
come back, I tell myself at first. Denial is the first stage
of grief, according to psychiatrists. Never let the sun go
down on an argument, my mum used to say to me, and
I'd told Jamie that. He'd said what a sound philosophy
it was. So to begin with I keep expecting him to come
home.

But then, after a week, I get angry. That's the second
stage. He'd got me wrong. I hadn't just married him for
his money. And I'd bloody stuck by him when he hadn't
any. Didn't that say anything? I'd been the one who'd

bloody supported us for the best part of a year. I feel misjudged. And that makes me sad, really sad.

The point is I miss him so much, my whole body aches for him sometimes. I've still got a box of the clothes he didn't take. So now I find I'm pulling them out and rubbing my face against his T-shirts. Weird, I know. But they smell like him still, and the smell is so evocative, I can almost feel him close to me. When we slept together, we used to lie like spoons in the bed. I would wrap my whole body round his, brushing my cheek against his back and weaving my arm under his and into his chest. I do that now with an old shirt of his and pretend he's still there. Pathetic.

The final stage of grief, according to psychiatrists, is acceptance. Have I got there yet? I don't bloody know.

It's a shock being on my own again too, when I'd only just got used to someone being there. There's no one to phone and ask, 'How do I get to La Brea from Highland because I'm totally, fucking lost?' No one to eat roast chicken with and there's no point in cooking it for one. No one to share my triumphs – no one to say 'You'll never guess what happened to me today?' to.

And as the weeks go by, there *are* triumphs. Big ones. Bill is as good as his word. Not long after that awful day, an agent from William Morris invites me to his office. Would I be interested in auditioning for a new show on MTV reviewing the latest movies? They want someone who is sassy and cute. TV experience isn't necessarily a prerequisite for the right person. More important is being prepared to interview celebrities and be honest about what I thought of their movies. I can do that, I tell him. But they're looking at five other girls and they have all got TV experience. Okay, maybe I can't do it.

'Yes, you can,' says Bill when he calls me back. I'd left a message on his mobile. 'All it takes is confidence,' he tells me. 'I'll get you a week's crash course in TV presenting. Put together a showreel and just be yourself. Anyone who can bullshit their way into Hollywood can bullshit their way on to TV, and besides, you're a natural,' he adds. 'Just throw in a few Mae West lines and you'll be fine.'

A week later, I'm at the checkpoint of a studio lot in Burbank, wearing a Marc Jacobs miniskirt, boots and a fuchsia-pink T-shirt and shaking like a leaf. The security guard at the entrance shows me where to park, and which building to go into, but I must be looking nervous. 'Just give it your best shot,' he says with a friendly smile. How does he know what I'm here for?

'Isabella Shawe?' says a tall, older woman with dark helmet hair and a red suit, walking into an office I've been told to wait in. 'I'm Evelyn, head of corporate affairs. And this is Joe Van Der Meer, the show's producer.' A short, balding guy smiles briefly and officiously at me. 'We all loved your showreel. And your model book. We wanted to meet you.'

'Thank you.'

'Now I'm sure you're aware we're looking for someone with personality,' she says slowly. Seriously. Soberly. I feel a sudden overwhelming urge to laugh. 'It's not just enough to be a pretty face. We want someone who's ballsy, sassy, a little bit cynical maybe – someone who isn't afraid to tell it like it is. I've heard that you're a movie fan.'

'Well, sure.'

'And can you be sassy?'

'Sass is my middle name.'

'Do you mind if we look you over?'

' "Far better to be looked over than overlooked." '

A smile finally spreads over her face. 'Mae West.'

'My heroine.'

She leads me through to a sound stage where a TV camera is set up in front of a couch. Behind it is the fake backdrop making it look like a living room. The lights are fearfully bright. I'm offered a bathroom to touch up my make-up. And then, after painting big lines of Max Factor Lustrous 210 across my lips and giving myself a good talking to, I take up my position in front of the camera.

'Can you tell us about a couple of your favourite films, Isabella?' Joe asks soothingly. I smile back at him. 'Just take your time, don't be nervous. Just be yourself.'

In fact he didn't need to baby me. I don't even need to think hard. It's my favourite kind of question because it's not about me and I know the answer.

'Well, there're too many to pick just a couple . . .' I begin, a little nervously at first. 'But let's start with *How to Marry a Millionaire* – it was a terrible film, but who could not love the idea of Lauren Bacall, Betty Grable and Marilyn Monroe playing fortune hunters? Released in 1953, it was nominated for an Oscar, but only for costume design. And you can see why. Boy, were those costumes fabulous.'

Joe smiles back at me from behind the camera, and suddenly I feel I'm on familiar ground. This really isn't that hard. More confident now, I pick up the pace.

'Then there's *Breakfast at Tiffany's* – in Truman Capote's novel, published in 1958, Holly Golightly actually gets pregnant, which doesn't quite fit in with a Hollywood happy ever after, so they ditched that bit when they made the film.

'And I love *Pretty Woman*. It was originally meant to be a dark drama about prostitution in Los Angeles, but they realised that wouldn't sell, so they turned it into a romantic comedy, starring Julia Roberts and Richard Gere. Although it was one of the most successful films of the nineties, it was controversial because people thought it glamorised prostitution.

'Let's see what else . . .' I pause to consider. I've almost forgotten that there's a camera pointing at me. I'm too busy thinking up favourites. '*Gone With the Wind*. It came out in 1939 and broke all kinds of records in terms of its production, but did you know that it was the only novel Margaret Mitchell had published during her lifetime?

'*Scarface* with Al Pacino. Panned by the critics, but adored by filmgoers . . .'

'Okay, okay, okay.' They stop me in my tracks. I was only just getting going. 'So you like the movies?' says Joe.

'Always have,' I tell him. 'It's what I do. I watch movies and I like to know stuff about them.'

'I can see that.'

'So do I get the job?'

Joe laughs. 'We'll see . . . But cute accent. I love the accent, don't you, Evelyn?'

She nods.

A day later the agent calls me. I got the job. It's not

prime time, and it's only a twenty-minute filler, but all I have to do is be British and blather on about movies – who could not love a job like that?

I realise then that I've always dismissed myself as being incapable of anything like this. Never had the confidence, I suppose. I never imagined that I was bright enough to pull off a career of my own. I was always too busy being a hard nut. Never even realised that all that junk I'd stored up about the movies was worth anything. But it's a nice feeling to suddenly realise you're not as dumb as you think.

And sometimes all you need is the smallest leg up and everything else fits into place. No sooner do I get the TV gig than a publicist offers to work for me – she gets a teenage magazine to run a two-page spread on my favourite teen movie choices and suddenly it seems I really am a micro-star. I even get fan mail. Then a make-up company asks me if I want to be the face of a hip new make-up line; and several months in, do I want to do a guest appearance in a celebrity quiz show? The modelling agency starts charging the earth for me too – no more catalogues, only prestigious advertising endorsements. It's like winning the lottery. Over the next months, no day goes by without some new offer or invitation.

Few days go by without some kind of beauty appointment either. I'm more polished than a car. If it's not a 'mani-pedi', as they call getting your nails done, it's eyebrows, or a facial, or a fresh appointment with a stylist. My hair gets blow-dried and straightened out every day. Every day! It's fantastically boring, but gives me a chance to read the newspapers. Yes, me.

Newspapers. I have to read them to keep up with what's going on now.

My greatest triumph, though – the one that brings me real satisfaction – is Pearl. For once in my life, I manage to do something good and something right.

I am nervous of her response when I call her to tell her that Jamie has left. But maybe it's because no one expects any marriage to last longer than a lunchtime in Hollywood, or maybe it's because she is secretly relieved not to be the only one to fail so miserably at conjugality, but she surprises me and never once says 'I told you so'. The minute I call she gets a babysitter for Thackeray and takes me out to Le Petit Four on Sunset for lunch to commiserate.

'What are you going to do, Bella?' she asks, her face all twisted with concern. It seems an odd question to ask.

'Keep going, I suppose,' I tell her. 'What else? I'll be all right.'

'But did you tell Jamie that Bill Makepeace was helping you?' she asks, convinced that something could be salvaged.

'Of course I did. But he thought the same as you. Everyone thinks you've got to shag to get ahead in Hollywood.'

'But I'm sure if you'd—'

'He didn't believe me. He was pretty angry.'

'But have you tried to speak to him?'

'Yes, of course I have. But he hung up on me . . . he hasn't answered any messages I've left. I don't even know where he's living.'

I'd tried calling Candice to ask if she knew anything,

and the guys I knew he played poker with. I'd left message after message with everyone I could think of, but every time, I'd just reached a brick wall.

Pearl looks more brokenhearted than me. 'I'll be all right, Pearl,' I tell her soothingly, as if it's she who needs the shoulder to cry on. 'I'm good at looking after myself. Always have been. Anyway, I've got a career to keep me busy now . . . and at least I'm not poor any more. You should see the cheques that are coming in.'

Pearl goes quiet for a while, as the waiter serves us iced teas and we check out the Euro-trash who always eat here on the pavement tables. 'What's really sad is that love didn't win out, did it? That's the disappointment, right there,' she says eventually. 'I know it's kinda sappy, but I'd always hoped it was possible. Some marriages make it to golden wedding anniversaries. But who are those people? What do they have to make it happen? My mum and dad couldn't make it happen. I couldn't make it happen. You couldn't make it happen. What's wrong with us?'

I think of my mum and dad. I'd always thought they'd have made a golden wedding anniversary. What is it that keeps people together? Money alone doesn't do it. It hadn't worked for Stephen Shawe. And love alone didn't do it either. I had loved Jamie and he had loved me – until I'd made such a balls-up. People fall in and out of love in a marriage a hundred times over – sometimes all in the same day. What keeps couples together is loyalty. It's keeping the faith, really, believing that your partner always has your best interests at heart. Jamie had thought I was being disloyal.

'We just made the wrong choices,' I tell Pearl, almost

feeling guilty for shattering her illusions. Romance is important to her and I think I've become just about the final nail in its coffin. 'Don't give up, Pearl. Just because I screwed everything up doesn't mean you can't make it to a golden wedding anniversary.'

'With who?' She shrugs. 'Who's going to ever want to marry me, when I come with a ready-made family?'

She looks so unhappy that I decide it's time to break a confidence. 'Well, you know there's someone in love with you already. Has been for years,' I tell her.

'Don't start on about Adam again,' she says dismissively. I've tried to plead his cause so many times before that I sound like a TV repeat, but this time I'm going to fill her in on a little bit of extra detail.

'Is it that he's not likely to break your heart?' I ask. 'Could it be you never allow yourself to fall for the safe option?'

'No, it's just he's . . . he's . . .'

'He's what? Not rich enough?'

'No, don't be silly. You know money doesn't make a difference to me.'

'Pearl, you do realise that you've got a broken picker, don't you?'

She looks confused.

'Your problem is you've always picked the guys with the attitude, the guys who don't know how to treat you. Who was your first date?'

'Jesse Wheaton.'

'And?'

'Yeah, he was the biker boy. The kid who was always on detention.'

'And did he treat you nicely?'

'No. He stank . . . but he was fun.' A wicked smile spreads across her face.

'And who came after that?'

'Sirus Wagner.'

'And?'

'He cheated on me.'

'See, you think that if a guy is nice to you, he's boring. You think Adam is boring because he's keen. You think he's part of the wallpaper because he's always around. But look at him, Pearl. If you met him at a party for the first time, what would you think of him? He's a celebrated screenwriter, he drives a BMW, he looks like Tom Cruise, for Christ's sake.'

'So?'

'So, he loves you, Pearl, and he'd be good to you. He'd treat you like a princess and I don't believe any guy you've ever dated has ever done that.' I find myself pleading with her. 'He'd make you happy. What makes you so frightened that you won't even give it a chance?'

She doesn't say anything.

'Pearl, I'm going to tell you something. Do you know who it is who's been putting money into your bank account, the money that's been keeping you and Thackeray afloat?'

'Dad,' she says, sitting up sharply in her restaurant chair. 'It says the money comes from S.A.S.H. Productions on my bank statements.'

'And is that your dad's company?'

'Well, I thought it was. It is his name.'

'Haven't you noticed it's an acronym?

'A what?'

'The little dots between the letters. It means the letters stand for something. Shall I tell you what it is?'

Pearl nods slowly.

'Salvaging Adam Sisskind's Honour.'

She doesn't move. She's gobsmacked. 'What's it mean?'

'It means he wanted to pay you back for giving him the idea for his movie.'

'I don't believe you. Why didn't he tell me?'

Adam had never wanted me to tell her. Said money always complicates friendships and he wanted Pearl's and his to be unsullied. But when he had sold his movie script, he'd wanted to pay Pearl a share because he always said it had been her idea in the first place. He knew she'd never accept anything. We'd talked about it one afternoon during one of our trips to the movies. It had been a dilemma for him knowing what was the right thing to do. He'd really agonised over it. So he'd set up monthly payments into her bank account, but never told her.

And there it was, Pearl's unwavering, undying, faithful love. Her kind of love, if only she would open her eyes to see it. The kind of love that had her best interests at heart, the kind of love that would make it to a golden wedding anniversary. Adam talked about no one but Pearl, thought about no one but Pearl. He was one of the few constants I'd found in Hollywood. For years he'd hung on, waiting for her to wake up and finally notice him.

The really funny thing was, it wasn't till I told her about the money that she did.

*

Six months into working on the TV show, I'm still living at the tiny apartment in Koreatown with Mr Wilberforce. My publicist tells me I've simply got to move to Beverly Hills. Says it doesn't do my image any good for people to know I'm living in this neighbourhood, and keeps offering me details of places to rent in Beverly Hills. It's not that I'm attached to the place, although partly I haven't moved because there's a small hope in the back of my mind that maybe Jamie might find his way back here; it's that really I've got a much bigger plan.

A while back – when the cheques started coming in – I took an investment course designed especially for women. Ninety per cent of all women leave financial investments to their husbands or fathers to do. I'd read the statistic in some magazine or other, and felt sorry for myself because I didn't have either. Then I realised what was staring me in the face. I needed to learn how to do this stuff. I needed to know what investment portfolio meant other than a yawn and a headache. I needed to know how to make myself rich. If Stephen Shawe could do it, why couldn't I? My new-found confidence knew no boundaries. I wasn't going to be stupid any more. After the course, I worked out that with the kind of money I was earning, I could blow it all on renting a fancy apartment in Beverly Hills and buying myself a Porsche, or I could invest.

So I bought a cheap car and started investing – nothing too risky at first, or I'd have been no smarter than Jamie. But now I'm on the way to being a rich woman. Not quite in the same league as Stephen Shawe, but in a few years' time I'll have some assets that will keep me comfortable for the rest of my life. And I've done it all by myself. No marriage certificate required. Am I happy? Of course I bloody am. Now, six months on, I can also afford to buy my own place. I tell the real-estate agent I'm not interested in Beverly Hills. I've never understood why, with a socking great ocean at the end of Sunset Boulevard, all the Hollywood types cling to Beverly Hills and the dirty, contaminated city. Sometimes the air is so polluted there, there's a yellow haze that is pure exhaust fumes. I want the Pacific Ocean in my backyard, I tell her. And, after a few weeks, she delivers. Three bedrooms, my own private stretch of beach, Olivia Newton-John just up the Pacific Coast Highway in one direction, and Cindy Crawford and Pamela Anderson the other way. It's a joyous day when I move in, with Mr Wilberforce yowling in his cat carrier.

The best part about living on the beach is the mornings. I don't have any curtains to my bedroom so that the first light of the day wakes me. Of course sometimes I wake up to find I'm enveloped by a thick pea-soup sea mist – they call it the Marine Layer here – and you can't see a thing. But more often the sky is absurdly pink – as pink as a Barbie doll tutu – and the ocean has a purplish hue that's quite otherworldly. My glass balcony overlooks the beach. I don't even have to get out of bed to watch the waves folding on to the sand. Sometimes I can even see dolphins, dancing their way up the coast. I like the vastness of the ocean – reminds me how small we all are on the planet. My routine is to sip tea, Mr Wilberforce purring by my side, and relish the emptiness of the beach. Every morning the sand is pristine after the tide has wiped away all the signs of yesterday. Then I get up and run. See how Californian I've become? I actually run, indulging myself in the satisfaction of being the first to make footprints that day. I like running. It makes me feel strong, potent, capable. I throw on a T-shirt and shorts, dive into the sand, and strike out barefoot. Once I've found my rhythm, I can go for miles, past Geoffrey's, the clifftop restaurant, on beyond the other beachfront homes with their divergent architectural styles, way past Paradise Cove where they used to film James Garner in *The Rockford Files*. If the tide is out I can get right up to Point Dume where the rocks force me to stop and turn back. And then I race home for freshly squeezed orange juice and toast which I eat on the table out on my terracotta-tiled patio.

Jamie would have loved this house, he really would. He used to like going to the beach. I think of him, but I'm not that lonely really. I have a housekeeper who comes in every day, and I'm always busy. There are still plenty of 5 a.m. starts. Even a year after Jamie left, there hasn't been anyone else and I've become a member of what Pearl crudely calls the Cobweb Club. 'It means so little sex, you get cobwebs up there,' she'd told me with a laugh.

She tells me it's time to move on. But I'm happy by myself. I feel content. She's coming for lunch today to play on the beach with Thackeray because it's a hot Sunday. Even though it's only May, the temperatures are already beginning to climb. And she's bringing both Adam and Ashley. She and Adam are quite the happy couple these days. Not married yet, but it's only a matter of time. I've never seen either of them look so content and it makes me feel good to know I had a hand in it.

Pearl had rushed over to the film set where Adam was working straight after our lunchtime chat and the small, but not insignificant, revelation that Adam had been paying her bills. She told me later that she'd had to bluff her way on to the set and stood around for hours waiting for a moment when he was on his own. And then, when she'd found him, he had been so bewildered at her sudden arrival with her dramatic declarations of love (something she'd doubtless picked up in one of her romance novels) that he hadn't quite known what to do at first. I imagine he'd wondered if it was a joke. It had all been rather awkward and embarrassing. No passionate embraces and disappearing into the sunset for them either. Real life's never like that. But Adam had asked her if she'd like to go out to dinner with him later, and they'd stayed up all night talking, and slowly romance had bloomed.

Ashley is also coming today because Pearl's trying to set me up with him again. I'd told her it wasn't love before and so it's unlikely to be now. But what the hell? It would be nice to see him again. They arrive laden with beach bags, sand toys, umbrellas and carriers filled with takeout food – delicious-smelling burritos, quesadillas and tacos.

'Thought we'd bring lunch,' says Pearl, breezing in, followed by Adam holding Thackeray's little hand and Ashley last of all. 'God, the parking's a nightmare along here.'

Ashley is barely recognisable. 'Someone's been working out,' I say, as he kisses me on both cheeks. I haven't seen him since Pearl's wedding in Vegas and he must have shrunk ten sizes since then. He's quite startlingly good looking. Who knew that beneath those folds of flesh there was a handsome man trying to get out?

'Lost over a hundred pounds,' he tells me proudly, as he wanders on to the patio to survey the view and my garden furniture which is neatly arranged around pots of geraniums. He's wearing a T-shirt and shorts that show newly defined muscles.

'Nice pad,' he says, leaning up against the guard rail. 'This must have cost a chunka change. How much? Two mill? Three?'

'Don't you know it's rude to ask?' I chide him from the kitchen where I'm opening beers. I have no intention of letting anyone know how much I'm worth.

'But it's beautiful. Really beautiful, Bella.'

'Yes, isn't it?' says Adam, who has followed him out. He, Pearl and Thackeray have been to stay several times for the weekend, because even though he mostly just eats the sand, Thackeray loves the beach. 'And hasn't she decorated it beautifully?'

Adam is always so reassuringly kind and polite. My decorating wasn't anything that broke the mould, but I'd enjoyed making my house into a home, choosing big comfy sofas, colourful rugs, and a carved wooden dining table that had reminded me of the one we used to have in Guildford, and finally finding a permanent wall space to hang Dad's painting of the seafront at Torquay and my parents' wedding photograph.

'You ought to be proud of yourself,' says Ashley, unwrapping the takeout food and laying it on the table as I bring out the drinks.

'Yes, shouldn't she?' Adam agrees. 'But this place is too big for one. She needs someone to share it with,' he says, altogether too obviously. Are they really going to be this conspicuous? I know Pearl means well, but this is embarrassing.

'Actually, I'm really happy here on my own,' I say and I mean it. The joy in making a permanent home for myself has been immeasurable.

Thackeray toddles out on to the patio wiping sun screen off his face and wearing an all-in-one sun protection suit that Pearl has just changed him into. 'Beach,' he announces, making good use of one of the few words he knows.

'Lunch first, then the beach,' says Pearl patiently. 'Come and sit here and eat something for Mama.' Thackeray wails in protest.

'Come on, Thackeray, come and sit on my lap,' urges Adam and the two year old races to him readily.

'Won't do anything for me. Only for Adam,' sighs Pearl wearily.

'Contrary,' says Ashley.

'Just like his father,' says Pearl, biting into a burrito.

It's a chatty lunch and good to see Ashley again. When you arrive in a town as a stranger, and then a few years down the line find that there's someone you haven't seen for a long time, it makes the place feel even more like home. It gives it history. And there's lots to catch up on. After lunch, we climb down my winding staircase to the beach, and still there seems plenty to talk about, lying on rafia mats on the sand watching Thackeray paddle in the surf.

As the afternoon light starts to fade, and the sky

swathes itself once more in its Barbie doll hues, Ashley and I take a walk up the beach. 'You know, I always regret that things didn't work out between us,' he says, leaping away from a big wave that has launched itself unexpectedly up the sand.

'It was fun while it lasted,' I say. 'Don't think I've ever been to so many restaurants before in my life.'

'I think I was an idiot to listen to Brett. I really regret that, you know,' he says earnestly.

I pick up a perfect, tiny clam shell, which I shall add to my collection in the bathroom. 'Shouldn't worry about it,' I say. 'It's history now.'

'But do you think we could ever pick up where we left off?' Ashley's confidence has grown since his figure has subsided. 'Could you ever go on a date with me again?'

I'd sort of guessed this was coming. It might be nice to find someone again, I suppose. Jamie and I had never divorced, although that was only a technical difficulty. But things were different now. I'd like to say I'd grown as a person, but that would be way too Californian, and I do try to keep a grip or next thing I'll be consulting psychics and eating wheatgrass. The truth of the matter is I'd realised that I didn't need to settle for a relationship without at least a smidgen of chemical zing, or love, or attraction, or whatever you call it. Somehow, in my arse-over-tit way of doing things, I'd managed to work out a few things. You can't just marry someone because they're rich and expect spontaneous rapture. You can marry them and expect a comfortable life. You can expect a nice car and a big fancy house and the security of money in the bank. And for some women that's enough. But passion, zing, lust, infatuation – all those things I'd felt with Jamie – they weren't always guaranteed to be part of the equation. I like Ashley, but he'd never made me go weak at the knees – except after too much alcohol, and that didn't count.

I reach up to give him a kiss on the cheek. 'If things were meant to be, we'd have been together already, don't you think?' I say gently. He looks crestfallen. 'But we'll always be mates.'

It's dark by the time they leave. Thackeray is asleep over Adam's shoulder and Pearl's agitating about missing the Sunday night traffic. My home is tranquil again and it's only while I'm taking cups, glasses and the remnants of the day's gourmandising through to the kitchen that I notice that Adam has left his copy of *Daily Variety* behind. On the front page – although only bottom left – was Jamie's name.

I'd heard on the grapevine that Jamie had eventually made his documentary. He'd found someone to stump up the cash – some producer from Mexico who wanted to highlight the problems of gang culture there. It was Bill who'd heard that Jamie was doing all right and passed on what news he'd gleaned. Jamie had got his own production company together, and was standing on his own two feet without the help of his father. He had called his film *Gangland* and I knew, just because it was Jamie at the helm, that it would be good. The piece in *Variety* confirms it. It says the film is being shown at the Cannes Film Festival and is already getting fantastic reviews: 'a genuine cinéma-vérité work', 'a breathtaking achievement', 'a mind-boggling eye-opener'. There are a few quotes from Jamie about how he made it, trailing one Hispanic gang leader all over Central America.

It makes me breathless to read it. Desperate suddenly. That aching feeling that I've tried so hard to ignore reappears violently, like a bulldozer churning up my innards. I switch on the computer in my study and Google his name to see if there's any more news of him. I've done it so many times before. There's the imdb reference listing the movies Jamie's worked on, a tiny headshot of him smiling, warmly as ever, and the mini-biography mentioning our failed and separated marriage; there are also some reviews of his other movies, and the Internet version of today's *Variety* – but nothing else.

I call Adam on his mobile. 'Why didn't you tell me Jamie was in *Variety*?' I demand, just a little curtly. I'd have thought that he would have shown me the article.

'Um ... because we were trying to pique your interest elsewhere,' he says, sounding rather unsure of himself. 'Thought it wasn't quite the occasion to bring it up. But I left it behind for you. Just in case ...'

'Is Jamie there still?'

'Where?'

Oh, for God's sake. 'In Cannes, of course.'

'I should think so; it's on until next weekend. I can't think he'd leave before it's over. Why? You're not thinking of going, are you, Bella?'

I cut him off. My mind is doing the Grand National and my heart is having trouble keeping up. Was it seeing Ashley and the stark reality of what an indifferent attachment might have been that did it? There must have been a million times before that I'd thought of trying to find Jamie, but I'd been too fearful to do anything. Now, just knowing where he is, the thought of a tangible place to be able to see him, has me in a frenzy. I'm standing in my kitchen, visibly trembling, consumed by madness and whirling sentiment – a tsunami of irrational emotion. I call my travel agent. They can get me on a flight to Cannes at midnight. I tell her to book the ticket.

Heck, now what? What about the TV show? They're going to be furious, and I'm due in at 5 a.m. tomorrow morning. I call and leave a message for the PA. I tell her I've got a personal crisis . . . no, wait . . . there's been a death in the family and I've got to get on a plane back to England straight away. That sounds good. I don't know if it will wash, but it's the best I can think of. I call the housekeeper, throw a few things in a bag, and catch a cab to the airport.

Of course it's all very well being a tsunami of irrational emotion when you're six thousand miles away in southern California. It's quite another tide pool when you're in the lobby of the Hotel Martinez on the Boulevard de La Croisette, asking the receptionist for his room number, and you're boggle-eyed because it was fourteen hours, including a plane change in Paris, of sheer sleeplessness because the only ticket available was in cattle class.

It had taken some detective work to find out where Jamie was staying – but on a hunch, I'd called the travel agent that I knew his dad used to use. Bingo. It was he who had made Jamie's arrangements. He'd given me the hotel name happily once I'd told him who I was. But on the way over I'd been too consumed with the worry that

Jamie must have found someone else to think of how I was going to play this out.

In the end, standing unprepared at the hotel reception, I resolve to just knock on his door and see what happens. What else can I do? I envision a picture of his sweet, lovely face opening the door. I promise myself that I won't apologise to him – but I'll tell him I need to set the record straight. I'll ask him to invite me in. It'll be awkward, but cordial, and I'm caught up in the reverie of how it should go when the receptionist starts blabbering at me in French. She says she can't just give me his room number. Or words to that effect. Stupid French tart. She says she has to phone the room and announce me.

'*Votre nom?*' she enquires, all officious charm and lipstick. I hesitate. Now it comes down to it, I'm not feeling quite so brave any more. Supposing he won't let me come up to his room? Supposing he won't come down to the lobby even? Supposing he comes down and then starts yelling at me in front of this crowd. Needless to say, with the festival in full flow, the lobby is more crowded than Waterloo station.

'Actually, don't worry,' I say to her.

'*Quoi?*' she says.

'Forget it.'

I need to think of a better plan. I retreat outside, and curse a grinning street musician who's playing a violin far too cheerily. This is no time for happy music. What to do? Then I notice a sign that reads CASINO. Ah ha. If there's one place he's likely to be, it's in here for sure. I pat myself on the back for being so clever. But it turns out he's not there.

Outside again, the street musician is still playing. He grins at me some more, but I'm not in the mood and ignore him. I feel the warm Mediterranean breeze on my face. It's dark now, and La Croisette, Cannes's most famous promenade, is crawling with media types – mostly American, I can hear. I'd failed my French GCSE, but managed to just about get my bearings from the taxi driver, on the way from the airport, who spoke Franglais to me. He told me that Le Palais, just along the bonlevard, is the hub of the festival. And the length of this promenade, which hugs the seashore, is where everything happens. The cafés, the boutiques, the restaurants and the strident belle époque hotels are where it's at.

So much where it's at that it's hard to find an empty table at any of the cafés, but I eventually spot one on the pavement, overlooking the port with all its sailing boats lined up neatly in rows. I order a plate of frites and a beer, because I'm starving, and contemplate the crowds gliding past in front of me. These are the beautiful masses – not a single woman is overweight or wrinkled and not a single foot is clad in anything other than designer leather. I'm massively underdressed in the jeans and T-shirt I'd thrown on before I left, and still carrying the small bag I'd packed what now seems a million light years ago. Everyone else is dressed up for the night – high heels, black clothes, cleavage. If Aspen was Beverly Hills in the snow, this was Beverly Hills on Sea.

I consider sitting here all night. Maybe I'll spot Jamie's familiar chiselled features, the square shoulders, his big mop of tousled hair, in the crowd. But after an hour, the waiter is anxious for me to either order more or move on and I need to pee. I pay with a credit card, find a loo and then join the multitude as they saunter aimlessly along beneath the palm trees.

I've never been to France before, and it's quite nice to have a break from American culture and soak up the atmosphere of somewhere new. It's almost a relief to find old buildings, to see French architecture and know that it's not chipboard. Everything seems smaller, too – more human, less sterile. After the big shopping malls and uniform chains of America, it's reassuring to see small shops, little pockets of character, individualism and colour. But I hadn't come here for the views. What to do? I weigh up phoning Jamie. But he'll hang up like before. I consider sitting in his hotel lobby all night – but then I'll only get moved on, and frankly I haven't got the energy to be a stalker.

I stifle a yawn. God, I'm tired. All this emotional stuff is exhausting. My hotel is a couple of miles away – it was the only one the agent could get me into. I hail a cab. I'll go there, take a shower, get some sleep and think of something better tomorrow. Maybe I could get into a screening of his film? I call my agent at William Morris from the back of the cab and leave a message. Pretty please, could she find out when the screenings are, and get me a ticket? I remember to warn her on no account to let the television people know where I am.

And I'm just congratulating myself on a definite plan when I spot a delicatessen-style restaurant with rows of roasted chickens turning on spits in the window. I tell the cab driver to 'arrête', shove some euros in his hand and dash for it.

'*Un poussin, s'il vouz plaît* . . . pour takeaway,' I say, failing miserably at remembering anything useful in French.

The man behind the glass counter stares at me like I'm from Mars. What is it with the French?

'*Dans un sac,*' I say triumphantly, remembering the words for in a bag. This must surely be clear.

'*Quoi?*'

'*Un poussin. Dans un sac!*' I say, louder this time.

'*Un quoi?*'

'*Un sac.*' You big gorilla. It's an unwritten law that if the French don't understand you the first time, it's always best to just yell it louder.

'Can I help you?' asks another assistant.

Thank God. I order the chicken and then add some fish soup, bread, cheeses, and a bottle of white wine from the fridge. And there's a delicious-looking tarte tatin in the display cabinet. The assistant wraps it all in various containers and places them all in a large brown paper carrier bag. *Voilà!* I'm in business now.

I march back to the Hotel Martinez. The wretched violinist is still outside, looking expectantly for change. He's playing 'I Will Always Love You'. Sod him. The last thing I need now is to get all teary.

'I have a delivery for Jamie Shawe,' I say officiously to the receptionist, after I've carefully checked that the one I'd met before wasn't on duty. I point at the bag of groceries, and waft the roast chicken smell at her. 'I need his room number?'

'Room 101,' she declares with not so much as a '*quoi*', after tip-tapping on her computer.

'Merci,' I say over my shoulder and stride out for the lift.

Of course he may not even be in. Probably gone out for the evening. Why would he be in? Idiotic idea. And then maybe he is in, but he's with someone. The girl-friend. Of course he's got a girlfriend. What to do then? What am I going to say if some blonde answers the door? Stupid bloody idea, this. Perhaps I'll put the bag down outside his door, knock and do a runner? And then what? What the heck will that have achieved? Time to be bold, I tell myself. You'll never know otherwise. Never have the chance to tell him that he misunderstood. Never have the chance to tell him that it was all an awful mistake.

I'm trembling like a schoolgirl on her first date, but something makes me knock on the door. I can hear the sound of CNN on the TV from inside. Yup, must have got the right room. And I find I'm hugging the carrier bag to my chest for reassurance, heart racing, holding my breath in anticipation. And that's my mistake right there. Because unknown to me, the soup has leaked, and all of a sudden the bottom of the bag, moistened by a fine bouillabaisse, bursts open, sending a deluge of liquid all down my jeans, belching packages everywhere and leaving a jumble of soggy paper, onion, clams, octopus, parsley and a broken wine bottle on the carpet right in front of Jamie's room.

'Bella?' he says incredulously as he opens the door. 'What are you doing?'

Actually, I'm hopping up and down, cursing the French bloody packaging, because the soup is rather hot. 'Um, room service?' I say pathetically, picking an octopus tentacle off my knee.

'Here, let me help you,' he says, brushing chopped onion and parsley off my jeans. 'What are you doing here?'

Just the sound of his voice, so familiar, so warm, so comfortable, sends a wave of possession through me. He has a strange expression on his face – pleased, I think. He smiles, the crooked smile which I'd learned meant he wasn't sure what to make of things.

'I wanted to see you,' I say. 'They wouldn't let me up, so I had to pretend to deliver groceries.'

Jamie laughs. His old self-assurance is back. I can see that straight away. 'Why didn't you phone?'

'Thought you'd hang up—' I think to say 'again', but stop myself.

He looks embarrassed. 'Yes, well . . .' He coughs uncertainly. 'You'd better come in. I'll get call the front desk and get them to clear this mess up.'

He leads me into his room – average size, bland decoration, a window opening on to the promenade below, but most noticeably lacking in blondes. He switches off the TV. We both stand there awkwardly, uncertain what to do next. Jamie gets a Diet Coke from the minibar, by way of a distraction.

'Look, I know what this must look like . . .' I begin slowly. The smell of fish is overwhelming and I can feel a pool of soup in my shoe.

'Looks like a mess,' he says, letting out a small chortle. 'Do you think you should take those jeans off?'

'I came because I wanted to say I'm sorry.'

'Never thought I'd hear that,' he says softly.

A pang of desire shoots through me. I long to throw my arms round him and kiss him and forget everything that's gone before.

'Not for being unfaithful. Because I wasn't. I wasn't, you know?' There's a plea in my voice, which I hope makes him believe me. Jamie looks away, and stares out of the open window. Someone's laughing raucously in the promenade crowd below.

'I can see why you thought that I was. And I know I screwed up. I know I did it all wrong. But the reason I married you was because I loved you.'

'That's hard to believe now,' Jamie says quietly, his back to me. His big square shoulders are hunched over. He's hurt still. I can see that.

'Look, I'm going to tell you the whole truth and you can either believe me or not. But I want you to know it anyway, because I still love you. Maybe I was interested in you at the start because you were rich. I'll admit that. I'm not using it as an excuse, but if you'd been through what I'd been through, you'd understand. And I did go out with your dad because he's loaded. It's true. But you would too if you'd never had a bean in the world and some rich guy had come along and offered you a go at the main chance. You would, you know? You'd like to think that you wouldn't . . . no one likes to think they can be bought. But everyone would want to just see what might happen, just see . . .'

'But I didn't marry your dad. I married you. And I married you because I love you. I did fall in love with you. I didn't even realise how much at the time. You made me feel like I've never felt before.'

Jamie doesn't say anything. Doesn't even move. The hubbub from the streets below seems unbearably jolly by comparison to the anguish up here. I don't even know if Jamie's listening. I wonder if it's even worth going on.

'And I'll tell you the truth about Bill. I wanted his help. He came into Barney's one day, and invited me to lunch. I went. I went because I thought he could help us. You were a miserable old grouch, we needed money, and one of us had to do something.

'He did want to sleep with me. You're right about that. And at first I thought I could go through with it, just to get us some cash. I was stupid. I thought I could detach myself for a few minutes, get it over with, pretend to be someone else, just to get us on the right road. But in the end I couldn't go through with it. I kept thinking of you. And that's the truth.'

Jamie sniffs, and I realise he's crying. His back is still turned to me. Obviously, he doesn't believe me. It was a mistake coming here. A pain surges inside me. 'I'm going to go,' I say eventually, and walk towards the door, one shoe still squelching with the soup.

But then he turns, wiping away the tears. 'Is that really the truth, Bella? You don't know how much I want it to be.'

'But look at me.' I face him head on. 'How could it be anything else? Why else would I be here?'

'You don't know how much I've missed you. You can't possibly know. All this time, I think of you every minute.'

'But it is the truth.' I touch his arm gently, and look up into his eyes. There's light in them. 'Really, really, it's the truth. And do you know how much I've missed you? Every day I miss you. I even sleep with your old clothes.'

His face softens. 'Really? No one else?'

'Cross my heart and hope to die.'

'I was a difficult man to live with. I know I was. The gambling, the depression . . . I know I wasn't what you signed up for.'

'Not half. You were a bloody moody bastard.'

'I didn't blame you for finding someone else. I was angry with myself as much as with you for letting it happen. I let you down.'

'But I didn't find anyone else. I really didn't. I was foolish about many things, and I know I got it all wrong, but I didn't find anyone else.'

A smile breaks – that familiar, penetrating, gorgeous smile that brings out goosebumps every time. I feel weak with longing, and remember what it's like to feel secure, settled, loved, wanted. To look at someone and know they love you back for all the right reasons.

'What a fuck-up! What a fuck-up we've made.' Jamie almost laughs. The reality of our lives sinks in. 'To think of all the time we've wasted when we could have been together.'

He takes both my hands. They're so much smaller than his. He squeezes them. 'I'm sorry to have doubted you,' he says quietly. 'Can you forgive me?'

'Of course I can.'

'I've given up gambling, you know,' he adds.

'It's okay, you don't have to sell yourself to me. I'm already a fan.'

'But it's true, I have given it up. I realised I was gambling with our marriage. You'll notice I'm not down in the casino.'

'I noticed.'

'And I realised when I left how much you'd taught me, Bella. You didn't realise it, but you did. You taught me to stand up on my own without Dad. I was always in his shadow before. I had to get away from Dad in order to do it. And it was you who taught me about persistence and optimisim, and not giving up. You're an amazing woman, you know, because you never give up.'

'Don't be daft,' I tell him.

'Hopeless at taking compliments, but an amazing woman none the less.'

I laugh.

'So? Do you think we could try again? Would it be possible, do you think?' he asks.

'I was so hoping you might say that. I mean, we could try, couldn't we?' I lean forward to kiss him. I soak up his smell, his strength, his whole being. God, it feels good. So familiar. So right. I don't want to ever let go. And Mr Wilberforce will be so pleased to see you. He has been asking where you've gone,' I say, eventually, when our long embrace subsides.

'You've still got him?'

'Well, of course. Where was he supposed to go?' Jamie hugs me again. Below us the crowds on the promenade are getting thicker and the hubbub louder. 'You know, if we were in a movie, there'd be violins playing right now,' I tell Jamie. 'Happy ever afters and all that. I like happy ever afters.'

'But this is real life, Bella. I'm afraid real life isn't nearly so glossy.'

But then I remember the violinist on the street outside. 'Actually, it is,' I tell him with a wry smile. 'Optimism, remember?'

I lean out of the window. 'Oi,' I yell down to the violinist. '*Où est la musique?*' He looks up at me and rattles his tin. I race to find my handbag, still sitting in a pool of soup at the door. But there are only credit cards in it. I feel in the pocket of my jacket for some change, but find only gum. Then I remember a roll of euros in the back pocket of my jeans. Aha. I throw it down, and the violinist waves his bow at me gratefully as he catches them and strikes up again.

'Optimism . . . and persistence,' says Jamie.